Praise for The Wrongfu[...]

"Caspersen Beach keeps your interest all the way through. The story Janet weaves is universal–this could happen anywhere to anyone. You won't be able to put the book down until you know the truth."

-**Susan Reichert**, Editor-in-Chief,
Southern Writers Magazine

"In Caspersen Beach, Heijens reunites Cate Stokes and Lalo Sanchez, the investigative duo from Snook Wallow. Heijens' cast of characters and well-paced story take the reader on a wild ride to a satisfying resolution with hope for future books in the Wrongful Conviction Series."

-**Teresa Michael**, author of the
Mariposa Café Mystery Series.

"One of the most horrific crimes that screams for justice is the kidnap and murder of a toddler but when an innocent man is convicted and the guilty go free, Cate Stokes along with Lalo Sanchez set out to right the wrong. Caspersen Beach is beautifully written and keeps a reader eagerly turning the pages while being whisked away to the Florida gulf coast. A wonderful mystery/thriller and highly recommended."

-**Susan Klaus**, author of the award-winning *Flight of the Golden Harpy* trilogy and *Christian Roberts* thrillers.

"Heijens delivers another tightly woven thriller with Caspersen Beach. Retired lawyer Cate Stokes sets out with Detective Lalo Sanchez to find the real killer of a murder committed 20 years before. Heijens takes the reader back and forth in time to string together the elusive details of the crime. I recommend you dive into Caspersen Beach for a satisfying adventure."

-**Sheila Reed**, Sarasota Literary Guild

KENDALL
ROAD

A Wrongful Conviction Mystery

JANET HEIJENS

Canterbury House
an Imprint of Dudley Court Press

Canterbury House
An imprint of Dudley Court Press
www.CanterburyHousePublishing.com
www.DudleyCourtPress.com

Author's Note:
This is a work of fiction. Names, characters, places and incidents are either
the product of the author's imagination or are used fictitiously, and any resemblance to actual persons living or dead, business establishments, events,
or locales is entirely coincidental.

Names: Heijens, Janet, author.
Title: Kendall Road : a wrongful conviction mystery / Janet Heijens.
Description: [Sonoita, Arizona] : Canterbury House, [2021] | Series: Heijens,
Janet. Wrongful conviction mystery ; 3.
Identifiers: ISBN: 978-1-940013-88-6 (paper) | 978-1-940013-89-3 (ebook) |
LCCN: 2021935346
Subjects: LCSH: Judicial error--Fiction. | Cold cases (Criminal inves-
tigation)--Fiction. | Murder-- Investigation--Fiction. | African Ameri-
cans--Crimes against--Fiction. | Race discrimination-- Fiction. | Police
misconduct--Fiction. | Discrimination in law enforcement--Fiction. | Legal
stories. | GSAFD: Mystery fiction. | LCGFT: Detective and mystery fiction.
| Legal fiction (Literature) | BISAC: FICTION / Mystery & Detective /
Private Investigators. | FICTION / Mystery & Detective / Women Sleuths. |
FICTION / African American / Mystery & Detective.
Classification: LCC: PS3608.E3655 K46 2021 | DDC: 813/.6--dc23

For Jeffrey

Prologue

Marley Booker twisted her shoulder to get a better look at the bruise. Her eyes welled up as she prodded the plum-colored skin with a manicured nail. With an angry shake of her head, she cursed Leland knowing it would be days before the telltale sign of his temper vanished from her pale arm. Reaching into her closet for a long-sleeved blouse, she paused for a moment to consider showing up at the country club in a sleeveless shirt. That would teach him, shocking all the old biddies with a glimpse into the darker side of their charming golf instructor. But pride took hold and her common sense prevailed. All her well-crafted efforts to create the illusion of a perfect family would be gone in a heartbeat if the members saw what Leland had done to her.

Before heading downstairs, Marley peered into the guest bedroom and saw the unmade bed. A few hours earlier she pretended not to hear when Leland slipped into their room for a fresh change of clothes. She picked up his wrinkled shirt from the floor and pressed it to her face, drawing in the musky smell of her husband's cologne. Despite all that passed between them since, she could still remember the thrilling sensation that ran down her spine when they first met. She smiled to think of the rednecks hanging out at that bar, staring at them. Small wonder a fight didn't break out, her slow dancing with a Black man like that. Hugging his shirt to her breast, she now imagined Leland coming home at the end of the day with flowers, telling her

1

he was sorry for losing his temper. They would put the girls to bed early and have make-up sex that would light up every nerve in her body. After that, on the surface at least, everything would return to normal.

Catching a glance of reality in the mirror, her smile faded. Marley stared at her image, pondering her present situation. At eight weeks she was not yet showing. She felt trapped between getting rid of her unborn baby or losing her husband. Leland was not perfect, but she tallied up all he provided and weighed that against the distant voice of her Sunday Bible School teachers threatening damnation if she terminated the pregnancy.

"Mama, will you fix my hair?"

Marley turned to see Lissa, fully dressed and holding a hairbrush in her outstretched hands.

"Sure, darlin'." Marley took the brush and pulled Lissa close.

She watched as Lissa's eyes scanned the guest room, taking in the unmade bed and Leland's dirty clothes. She wondered, not for the first time, how much the child knew. Scraping back Lissa's wild hair, she caught the mass in a rubber band. Lissa turned to face her and Marley stroked her first-born's cheek, white fingers against amber skin.

"In a few years you'll be fighting the boys off with a stick," she said.

Lissa squirmed away from Marley's touch. "I don't like boys."

"Where's your sister?"

"She's still in her pajamas."

"Do Mama a favor and help her get dressed while I fix breakfast, okay?"

Lissa nodded and padded back to the girls' room.

Marley took one look at the bed, decided to leave the covers as they were, and headed downstairs.

Standing before the open refrigerator, Marley frowned in annoyance. She'd specifically asked the babysitter to pick up some groceries at Gordon's, but the teenager apparently forgot. After grabbing the carton of orange juice, Marley filled three glasses and placed them on the table. She set the cereal boxes out, lit her first cigarette of the day, and leaned against the counter while she waited for the coffee to brew.

The night had done nothing to relieve the heat wave. Marley cranked the knob on the air conditioner to full blast and turned on the radio. The forecast was for another hazy, hot and humid day, temperatures into the 90s.

As Marley sat down with her coffee, her two children appeared, arguing as usual. Robin stuck her tongue out at Lissa and took hold of her glass with both hands. After one mouthful she dribbled the juice back.

"This tastes yucky. Don't we have any apple juice?"

Marley drew in a deep breath. "Orange is all we've got. Cate forgot to go to the store. After breakfast we'll go shopping. Now mind your manners. Ladies don't spit." Marley watched as both girls drank, then raised her own glass and took a sip.

She forced it down with a grimace. "Damn, it's spoiled. Leave the rest. Now run and play while I clean up."

The first wave of cramps hit as she loaded the dishwasher. Doubling over, she held onto the countertop. Lissa's high-pitched voice rose above the sound of Robin retching in the other room.

"Mama, Robin's sick!"

At the sight of Robin curled on the floor, her rosy cheek lying in a pool of vomit, Marley dropped to her knees. Fear gripped her chest as Robin's skin turned blue. Lissa stood several paces back, eyes wide in panic, both hands covering her mouth as her rib cage contracted and heaved.

Marley tried to keep her voice calm, but the sound that came out rang with urgency. "Lissa, run and get a wet towel for your sister." Fighting her own nausea, she stroked her younger daughter's hair, murmuring, "I'm right here, sugar." As Marley reached for the towel that Lissa offered, another wave of convulsive cramps hit. She closed her eyes, thinking about the baby.

Robin whimpered and Marley glanced down to see a thin stream of white foam seeping between the little girl's closed lips. She gathered the child in her arms, willing her unsteady legs to hold. After she placed the unconscious Robin in the car, Marley returned to the house where she found Lissa bent over the toilet. A moan of protest escaped Lissa's lips as Marley grabbed her arm and pulled her to her feet. She wiped the sweat from the child's brow, bent down, and whispered, "Please don't make me carry you."

Lissa nodded, fresh beads of sweat blooming on her face as she clasped her mother's hand.

Fifteen minutes later, Marley brought the car to a screeching halt inches away from the double doors of the hospital's emergency room. A nurse at the reception desk looked up as Marley staggered in with Robin cradled in her arms.

The words tumbled out of Marley's mouth. "My other daughter . . . Lissa . . . in the car."

The nurse jumped forward, too late to catch Marley as she slumped to the floor.

Chapter 1

Marley Booker and her children were dead and there was nothing I could do about it. That's what I told Adam Bennett, the University of New Hampshire law student who called to ask me about the three murders that happened forty-four years ago.

"I don't see how I can help you." I reached for my cigarettes. "I was only the family babysitter. Now please don't bother me again."

As I was about to hang up, I heard Adam say, "Leland Booker is an innocent man. He has spent more than half his life in prison for a crime he didn't commit. I think this is important, Mrs. Stokes."

I brought the receiver back to my ear. A few moments of silence hung between us as I considered his words. Adam had explained that he picked the Booker murders for a class assignment, something called a Criminal Defender Clinic. As part of his research he wanted to talk about my time with the family. In the end I decided Adam was on a fool's mission, and though I agreed with him that Leland wasn't a murderer, there was no use getting involved. After a few beats, I sharply denied Adam's request and slammed down the phone.

I slept badly that night, waking to a sense of guilt, my sheets damp with sweat. Rising, I stepped into the shower, hoping to wash the residue of my dream away. After toweling off I paused to study my reflection in the mirror. Dark circles under my eyes gave me a haunted look. Pressing my palms against both sides of my neck, I lifted the loose skin. A younger self stared back at me and I thought—not for the first time—about making an appointment with a plastic surgeon. I was wise enough to know that nothing could restore my youth, but at that moment I would have given anything to turn back the hands of time and prevent the murders of Marley Booker and those precious girls.

When the phone rang, I checked the caller ID. Lacking the energy to debate the issue with Adam again, I decided to let the machine answer his call.

"Mrs. Stokes . . . Cate, are you there? I know it's early but I wanted to catch you before you leave for work. I'm going to be in Keene next weekend, and I'd like to meet over a cup of coffee. I've got some new information about the case that I think might interest you. Call me, okay?"

It was a nice try, but Adam would have to do better than that.

For the past eighteen months, ever since my husband, Arnie passed away, I have made it a point to bury myself with work. I'm not saying taking on an insane case load is a totally effective—or healthy—way to deal with grief but focusing on my client's problems does help me to forget my own. I run a family law firm. Divorces and trusts mostly. Saturday morning, car keys in hand, I was about to leave for the office when the doorbell rang. Standing before me was a young man in a suit that looked too pricy for one of those guys canvassing to save my soul. A leather messenger bag with his initials, AKB, was slung over his shoulder. Adam gave me a vaguely familiar grin, letting me know that in our little dance he had just gained the upper hand. I frowned at him.

"I told you to leave me alone."

"Mr. Booker promised me that you would help."

It surprised me to hear that Leland sent Adam. After all, we both had secrets that were best kept in the shadows of the past. A gray squirrel dashed across my lawn, scurrying up a black oak where he stopped and looked around. His tail twitched some kind of warning before he bounded up the trunk and disappeared in the branches. The distraction gave me time to think.

"I didn't know the Bookers very well," I lied. "And I can't add to what I told the detectives at the time. Unfortunately, you caught me as I was on my way out so if you don't mind . . ."

"I'll wait." Adam's grin was infectious. I couldn't help but smile back at him.

I won't return until noon."

"Leland Booker spent half his life in prison for a crime he didn't commit. What are a few hours of my time compared to that?"

Something shifted inside and I felt my resolve slipping. I found myself nodding at him.

"I'll give you fifteen minutes."

Stepping aside, I pointed the way to the kitchen. Adam sat in the breakfast nook while I brewed the coffee. The way he scanned the room, taking in everything, reminded me of Lissa.

"Cream and sugar?" I asked.

"Black, thanks."

The sun streamed through the window, warming the bowl of tomatoes on the table. I considered setting out a plate of cookies, but decided against making Adam feel too welcome.

"Tell me exactly what you hope to accomplish," I said. "And give me one good reason why I should speak with you."

"Well, as I explained on the phone, I'm participating in a clinic at school. The idea is to investigate old murder trials toward the end of legally challenging a conviction. It's a really big part of my grade this year."

"Why did you choose the Booker case?"

Adam's eyes flickered, a small movement, a telltale sign that he wasn't being totally honest with me.

"Based on the circumstantial nature of the prosecution's case, and the inconsistencies of the evidence put forward, I believe there's a good chance he was wrongfully convicted. I intend to help right a wrong."

His varnished answer clearly glossed over a deeper truth. My curiosity got the better of me. I decided to play along.

"Surely there are other cases that meet your criteria. What I want to know is what drew you to this one?"

"This case appealed to me because of the racial over-tones. A Black man living in a white community, a mixed mar-riage with children, an all-white jury . . . you get the picture. I think race might have played a significant part in the convic-tion. It's an angle that deserves exploration." Adam locked eyes with me. "You're a lawyer. What do you think?"

"It doesn't matter what I think." I checked my watch. "Your fifteen minutes are up."

"But I have questions—"

"Listen, Adam. I don't know anything about criminal law. This is a waste of time." I stood, making it clear that I wanted him to leave.

A desperate tone crept into his voice. "When you spoke to the investigating detective, you stated that you didn't be-lieve Mr. Booker killed his wife and children."

"Obviously the jury came to a different conclusion." I called over my shoulder as I walked toward the door. "At the time I did everything I could to help Leland. It didn't do any good then, and I don't know what difference I can make now. I really don't want to talk about this any further."

I heard the scrape of wood on tile as Adam pushed his chair under the table. Turning, I caught him staring at me.

"One sip of that juice was all it took," he said. "If you went to work that day you would have been poisoned with the rest of them."

He sounded churlish. Law student transformed into sulky child. I pulled open the door, placed my hand on my hip, and glared at him.

"That's highly unlikely. Now if you don't mind . . ."

"The prosecution made their case based on the theory that Mr. Booker killed the whole family to collect the insurance. I have an alternate theory. Maybe it's a long shot, but I think Mrs. Booker was the killer's main target. The kids were innocent victims."

I felt the cold hand of the past brush the back of my neck.

"How would that make any difference now?"

"Well, for one thing, if I could prove someone else had a motive for killing the wife, it could lead to establishing reasonable doubt. The police never investigated any other suspects. There was someone . . . wait, let me check my notes." Adam pulled out his phone and started tapping the glass. "Here it is. Marley Booker had a stalker."

"Henry." I didn't realize I had spoken out loud until I noticed Adam nod in agreement.

"Henry Rusak. Worked as a handyman for the owner of the house that the Bookers rented. A few weeks before she died, Mrs. Booker complained to the landlord. Said she didn't want Rusak to come anywhere near her or the children."

"Henry loved those girls," I said. "He would never have harmed them."

"Maybe not, but all things considered, I find it strange that the detective never interviewed him. You were part of the household in August of '72. Practically one of the family. I need your help to find out what really happened."

Against my better judgment I decided to get involved. After all, Adam needed more than a theory to work his way through this case. And I saw this for what it was; a chance to make up for a mistake I made all those years ago.

I sighed. "You caught me on the way to the office. If you come back next Saturday I'll make time for you then."

Adam nodded, a slow grin spreading across his face.

I gave him a stern look. "Don't get your hopes up. I honestly don't know what good it will do but I will tell you what I can remember about the family. And for god's sake, when you come back leave that suit back in Durham. I want to keep this whole thing informal."

He was in the car with the engine running before I remembered something. As I flagged him from my open door, he rolled down his car window.

I cupped my hands around my mouth and shouted. "You said on the phone that you had some new information about the case."

"Oh, that. I don't have anything yet. I thought if I caught your interest, hooked you, so to speak, that you would . . ."

Laughter rose in my chest, erupting through my nose. I saw a gleam in Adam's eyes as he waved and drove off.

I should have been annoyed, but there was something about Adam Bennett that was undeniably charming. Despite my resolve to keep my distance, I was starting to like the kid.

The following Saturday, before the pink faded from the morning sky, I slipped into my jeans and pulled out a client's file from my briefcase. After thirty years of practice, I still looked forward to tackling a case with the zeal of a rookie lawyer. Reviewing the case, I saw the opposing counsel was Jack

Burquest. Jack and I dated once, many years ago. The son of Keene's chief of police, he was in and out of trouble all through high school. That he ended up as a lawyer was remarkable. That he turned out to be a particularly bad one was no surprise. He had a reputation for showing up to court half-drunk and unprepared. As I considered a strategy for approaching Jack with the end game of settling out of court, the doorbell rang. I gathered my papers and placed them in my brief case before letting Adam in.

"I brought muffins." He held up the pink and orange bag from the donut shop on Main Street. They coated the bags with wax so the grease wouldn't leach through. Six thousand calories per serving.

"Let me take those," I said. "Make yourself comfortable in the front room. I'll join you in a minute." I went into the kitchen, put the muffins on a plate and grabbed a handful of napkins. By the time I joined Adam in the living room, his laptop was open on my glass coffee table. Ring binders and copies of news clippings spilled all over the floor. Adam appeared to have made himself at home.

He took a healthy gulp of the coffee I set before him. "Great, thanks. I'm no good in the morning until I've had my third cup."

To be polite I broke off a small piece of a muffin and put it in my mouth. Artificial apple, cinnamon flavor. Adam pulled out his cell phone, tapped the glass, and scrolled down the page. He looked up and grinned.

"I promise not to take up too much of your time. Would it be all right if I start by telling you what I have learned about the case?"

"Of course."

He looked down at his phone. "This is what I got from the original police report. On August 9, 1972, Leland Booker, an African American, age thirty-eight, was arrested and charged with murdering his wife and children. He was read his rights and signed a waiver stating that he freely agreed to answer questions regarding the murders. He was then held in the Cheshire County jail without bond due to the nature of the charge."

He shoved the last of his muffin into his mouth, washing it down with a slug of coffee.

"I downloaded a copy of the medical examiner's toxicology results. They found traces of an insecticide called Aldi . . . Aldicar . . ."

"Aldicarb."

"Right. Aldicarb was discovered in the blood of all three victims." Adam paused to take a look at the remains of my muffin. "I googled it. The effects on their bodies would have been immediate resulting in—"

"Stop." I closed my eyes and held up a hand. Shaking my head, I fought to clear the images in my head. "I know how they died. It was horrible."

The corners of Adam's mouth twitched. He nodded before continuing. "Sorry about that. I know you were close to Marley and the girls. Is there anything you can tell me about Leland Booker that will help prove he didn't poison his family?"

"Help yourself to the rest of my muffin while I get more coffee. This is going to take a while." As I walked to the kitchen, I added, "And put something under that computer before it scratches my coffee table."

Chapter 2

During that afternoon, I told Adam how I came to know the Booker family. The first time I heard Leland's name was in the spring of my final year at high school. There were only three of us home at the time, my mother, father and me. My sister Nancy who was in her second year of community college was out somewhere with her boyfriend, Tim. Mom chatted about her day at work while I sat at the kitchen table with my father. Mom loved her job waiting tables at the country club. It gave her access to a social tier that she wouldn't otherwise reach. One of her greatest pleasures was picking up bits of local news and sharing them with Dad and me. She was like the National Enquirer of Keene's social scene. Some of the stories she repeated were real, some completely fabricated. And none of her gossip interested me in the least.

"I met the new club pro and his wife today." Mom winked at me. "I must say, he seems very nice. Quite the gentleman. And his wife, Marley, well she positively oozes southern charm. I can only imagine what her family must think about her marrying a Black man."

"Um-hmm." Dad turned the page of the evening newspaper.

"They come from somewhere near Atlanta. I love their accent." My mother drew out the word "love," ending the sentence with a question in her voice as if to mimic a southern drawl. I shook my head but she continued without giving me any notice. "Leo Bishop introduced Leland to everyone in the restaurant, proud as a new father. I heard that he's paying Leland much less than the old pro. And listen to this, Leo is renting one of his properties on Kendall Road to the Bookers for twenty percent more than the last tenants. That old fox is taking advantage of the situation. More than he normally does, if you ask me."

"No one is asking, Mom. How do you even know that?"

"Believe me, it's true. You'd be surprised what I hear. Club members don't pay any attention to the waitresses while they're chatting over their coffee and crème brulée, but we listen to everything. Now, where was I?"

"Mr. Bishop is charging inflated rent for his house on Kendall Road."

"You shouldn't be surprised, knowing Leo."

Leo Bishop was the president and majority shareholder of the Keene Country Club, or as everyone called it, KCC. He was perhaps the richest man in town, which meant my mother admired and scorned him in equal parts. I never met the man, but he appeared regularly in the society section of our local newspaper. From what little I knew of Leo—most of it through the lens of my mother's gossip—I didn't like him much.

My father glanced up from his paper. "Why did the guy take the job?"

I looked at him in surprise. He didn't often comment on my mother's rambling gossip.

"Well, I heard that he and his wife wanted to leave Georgia." Mom lowered her voice as if to keep what she was about to say between us. "The whole interracial marriage thing is a big problem down there, you know."

"And it won't be in Keene?" Dad asked.

Mom leaned back and crossed her arms. "I'd like to think we're much more open minded around here."

Against my best intentions I was drawn into the conversation. "Aside from being charming, what's Mrs. Booker like?"

"Marlene? She's drop-dead gorgeous. Blond hair, blue eyes . . . it's a pity the children favor Leland."

"You pretend you're not prejudiced like those people in Atlanta," I snapped. "But you're just as bad as they are."

Dad cleared his throat. "That's not true. Your mother didn't mean—"

"What I meant is, it's all well and good when people fall in love and get married, no matter what their backgrounds. But the sad facts remain. Society does not accept children from mixed marriages. Those poor little girls will never belong anywhere."

I felt the heat rise to my face. "That's a terrible thing to say."

"Calm down, Cate," my father said. "Your mother did say she likes the Bookers. Didn't you, Sandra?"

"That's right," Mom said. "I do. But Marlene has been looking for someone to watch her two girls while she works in the pro shop and she can't find anybody to take the job. Of course, no one would dare to say this out loud, but I think the problem is the fact that the children are mixed race . . . that's the polite way of putting it, right?"

"I just call them kids, Mom. But you're wrong to say no one would want that job. I would love to work for Mrs. Booker."

My mother looked at me, her mouth hanging open.

"Are you sure? You've never even met these people."

I shrugged. "I need the money for school."

For years, my parents had scrimped and saved to build my college fund, but despite their sacrifice, the money they put aside barely covered the cost of my first year's tuition. The

15

last time I checked, my own savings account had a balance of $72.45. There was no avoiding it. I needed a job for the summer.

My mother caught Dad's eye. He frowned.

"Why don't you get a summer job at the plant like your sister? You can make more money there. I'm sure Tim would put in a good word for you."

Tim had been working in the local factory since he and Nancy graduated high school. They planned to get married at the end of the summer. I could picture them working in that place for the rest of their lives.

"I'd prefer to work for Mrs. Booker if she will hire me."

"I'll ask if she's still looking for someone," Mom said.

I smiled, feeling that somehow, I'd proved something to my mother. Not to mention that as summer jobs went, this one sounded like it was going to be a piece of cake.

I spotted Marlene Booker before she noticed me standing in the doorway of the KCC clubhouse. If anything, my mother's description of the woman fell short. She flashed a smile at the smaller of her two children, revealing two deep dimples in her pale skin. As the little girl wiggled in her seat, the older child, who I judged to be about seven, concentrated on eating her soup without spilling a drop. Both girls had skin the color of amber. Tight ringlets framed their faces. If not for the age difference they could have been twins. Maybe Mrs. Booker thought so too because she dressed them in identical outfits. Smoothing her linen napkin on her lap, Mrs. Booker turned her head in my direction and caught my eye.

"Here she is now," I heard my mother say as I approached the table. "Mrs. Booker, I'd like you to meet my daughter, Cate."

"Marley. Everyone calls me Marley."

I glanced in my mother's direction, noting the look of

disapproval on her face. She had a strict rule that I was to call adults by their last names.

I extended my hand. "Pleased to meet you, Marley."

"Won't you join us?"

She waved me to the only empty seat at the table. I'd never seen such perfect fingernails, almond-shaped with a clear polish. Her diamond ring caught the light in the room, throwing a prism of color around the table when she lifted her wine glass and took a sip. As she set the glass on the table, a simple gold bracelet slid down her arm, colliding with what looked like an expensive watch. She shook her arm loosely, a casual gesture to settle it back in place. Platinum blond hair, a turned-up nose, and the straightest, whitest teeth I'd ever seen.

Both girls stared at me, the light in their inquisitive eyes suggesting they were as curious about me as I was about them. Turning to the younger one I asked, "What's your name?"

"Robin Booker."

"Hello Robin, I'm Cate." When she put her hand in mine, I intentionally shook it hard enough to make her head bob up and down. Robin started to giggle, and out of the corner of my eye I could see her older sister's face break into a timid smile.

"And you are?"

"I'm Lissa."

"Pleased to meet you, Lissa."

My mother, standing with pad in hand, asked, "What do you want to drink, Cate?"

"Whatever the girls are having."

Robin sang out. "I'm having apple juice because orange juice makes me gag."

I saw the edge of the tablecloth ripple as Lissa kicked her sister.

"Ow! Cut that out!" Robin cried.

"Now children, mind your manners. We don't want to give Cate a bad impression."

While Marley and I chatted, the girls slurped their juice through straws. Over lunch, Marley and I came to an agreement about my wages and the schedule. We agreed I could work weekends until the end of the school year, then go full time for the summer. I liked Marley. Everything about her was graceful in the way I always imagined a southern lady would be. She settled the bill by signing the check and charging the meal to her membership account. It was the normal custom at the club, but I'd never eaten with anyone who could do that before.

————————————————

I started work the following Saturday. Biking across town, I noticed how the forsythia bushes bent under the burden of their yellow blossoms. Daffodils grew wild beneath the oaks that lined the side of the road. The day begged to be spent outdoors, but I soon learned Marley had something else in mind.

"Good, you're early." With her soft accent, the words rolled off her tongue in gentle waves. "Come in and I'll show you where to find everything."

She took me on a quick tour of the house starting with the family room where the girls sat comatose watching TV. From there we breezed through the kitchen, the dining room, and the girls' bedroom. Back downstairs she waved a hand as we passed a closed door, indicating the exit to the backyard. Marley then told me not to let the girls outside alone as she was afraid they might fall into the pool.

"Give them peanut butter and jelly for lunch." She threw a sweater over her shoulders, tying the sleeves in front. "No cookies, no matter how hard they beg. They like to watch cartoons on Saturday so you should have an easy morning."

She reached for her pocketbook. At that moment a daddy longlegs spider chose to feel his way across the counter. Marley shrieked, jerking her hand back like she'd been stung by a wasp. Without hesitation, I reached out and picked the spider up by one of his jointed legs. As he struggled to free himself, I opened a window and tossed him outside. Turning to Marley, I caught her looking at me in wide-eyed horror.

"How could you touch that thing?"

"They don't bite." I shrugged. "Actually, they kind of tickle."

"I cannot tolerate spiders. I'll tell Leo to send someone over to spray."

She opened her pocketbook, peeking inside as if she were afraid there were spiders lurking in the dark. After fumbling around for a while, she extracted her wallet and pulled out a few bills.

"Do me a favor, won't you?" She pressed the money into the palm of my hand. "I promised the girls you would help them dye eggs for Easter. I believe you'll find everything you need at that little convenience store around the corner."

"Sure, sounds like fun."

"Leland's business card is on the counter in case you need to reach me at the club. I should be home around six." Marley checked her makeup in the compact from her bag. She lifted her chin and sang into the other room, "Bye darlings. Be good for Cate while Mama's at work."

Then she was gone, leaving a trace of Chanel in the air.

Before prying the children from the TV, I took another tour around the house. Kendall Road was an upscale neighborhood, far above my parent's low-rent section of town. Located within a few miles of the country club, the houses were spaced far apart with lush front lawns and carefully tended flower beds. Taking a peek through the kitchen window, beyond the in-ground pool that Marley mentioned I saw the large back yard stretch all the way to the edge of the woods. The place felt private, protected from view by the hemlocks, birch and sugar maple trees.

I returned to the family room to find the girls essentially in the same positions when I left them. Lissa was curled up on the brown leather couch while Robin lay on the floor, propping her head up with her hands, her knees bent, her feet crossed at the ankles.

"It's too nice outside for you to watch TV all day."

They turned to me, eyes wide, noticing me for the first time that morning.

"We're watching Mister Wizard."

"I have a better idea. Let's dye Easter eggs."

Robin's mouth turned down in a pretty pout. "Mama forgot to buy eggs."

I held up the money that Marley gave me. "You have bikes, don't you?"

A nod of the head.

"Then let's go."

I led them the long way to Gordon's Market, keeping to quiet back streets. In time we emerged at the parking lot behind the store. Jack, a guy from my class at school, nodded in greeting from behind the cash register as we entered. Showing no interest in us, he immediately went back to reading the latest issue of the Keene Sentinel. I glanced around, unfamiliar with the layout of the store.

"What are you looking for?" Jack kept his eyes on the paper. I noticed it was turned to the sports section where a photo of him in his football uniform filled a third of the page.

"We're going to color Easter eggs."

At the sound of Robin's squeaky voice Jack looked up

and gave her a smile. "That sounds like fun. We keep the eggs in the refrigerator against the back wall."

"What about the dye?" I asked.

"On the shelf at the end of aisle one."

I thanked him and made my way to the back of the cluttered shop. While I showed Robin how to check for broken eggs, Lissa stood on her toes to reach for a box of dye. When we returned to the checkout, my eye caught a rack of children's books next to the register. I selected my personal favorite from when I was a kid and set them on the counter.

Robin tugged on my shirt. I bent down and she put her mouth right next to my ear. "Make sure there's lots of purple dye."

Jack grinned, picked up the box of dye, and showed her the six pellets in the package. "Gotcha covered," he said.

"But they're different colors. I'm want to make all of my eggs purple."

"Can you guess what will happen if Cate mixes the red and blue together?"

"She makes more purple?"

"Exactly." Jack pushed back a lock of his hair from his forehead and winked at me.

My breath caught in surprise. I couldn't remember ever speaking with Jack before. As far as I was aware, he didn't know I existed, let alone my name. The sound of a motorcycle roaring into the parking lot distracted Jack, saving me from the embarrassment of having him see me blush. I turned to watch the rider dismount and recognized him immediately.

I hadn't seen Billy Reynolds at school in months. Rumor had it he was failing too many subjects to graduate. He simply stopped coming to class, determined to enjoy his freedom to the fullest. That freedom would be short lived as he recently decided to join the Marines. Billy was Jack's best friend, and probably the main reason Jack signed up too.

"Give me a pack of my regulars." Oily strands of hair were tucked behind his ears, reaching down to his shoulders. With a creepy grin he looked down at Robin. She moved closer to me and pressed her face against my jeans. I wrapped a protective arm around her shoulder.

"Wait a sec," Jack said. He took his time counting out my change before placing the coins in my open palm.

"Look what we have here." Billy jerked his head sideways in Robin's direction. "This neighborhood is really going downhill."

Jack fixed him with a cold stare. "Cut it out, Bill," he said.

"Who are you tryin' to impress?" Billy gave me a leering grin that sent a shiver down my spine. "Just gimme me my smokes so I can get out of here."

Jack picked up a pack from under the counter and tossed it to Billy. It was obvious that he wasn't going to ring the sale up on the register. Taking Robin by the hand, I turned to go. Jack reached out and touched the sleeve of my blouse.

"Wait," he said. "I want to ask you something."

Billy laughed and gave the counter a swift kick with his black boot. I felt Robin flinch. The bells above the door clanged as it slammed behind him. He peeled out of the parking lot in a spray of gravel. After he was gone I realized my hand, still clutching the change, was shaking.

"Don't let him get to you," Jack said. "He didn't mean anything by all that."

"What did you want to ask me?"

"I'm having a party at my house after graduation. My folks are going to be out, so there'll be booze and stuff. You can come if you want."

"I've got other plans."

Jack grinned at me and shrugged his shoulders.
"Suit yourself." He turned to Lissa. "Hey kid, do you like
purple too?"

Lissa nodded.

"On the house." He reached into a jar stuffed with candy. A label was stuck to the outside that said five cents each.
Jack grinned at Robin as he passed two purple lollipops across
the counter.

"I'll pay for those," I snapped.

"Forget it. Can't you see I'm trying to be nice here?
What's the matter with you, anyway?"

Plucking a dime from the change and slapping it on the
counter, I grabbed the bag and turned to leave. Lollipop sticks
protruding from their mouths, the girls followed.

———————————————

Adam's cell phone rang, breaking into the story of how
I first came to know the Bookers. I glanced at my watch, surprised to see how much time had passed since we started.
Adam looked at the screen to see who was calling before begging my forgiveness with a raised eyebrow.

"Hi Dad," he said. "I'm running late . . . I don't know. I'll
call you when I leave . . . Okay, see you soon."

"You have to go?" I asked.

"My dad is expecting me for dinner."

"Do your parents live near here?"

Adam shook his head. "My mom lives across the state in
Durham, near where I go to school. But my dad lives right here
in Keene. Rather than drive back to my mom's, I'll probably
stay at his place tonight. Would it be possible for me to come
back tomorrow so we can continue talking?"

"I'm afraid I'm busy tomorrow."

"How about next week then? Same time, same place?"

"I think I can manage that."

As I watched him drive away, I frowned. I don't know why I lied to him about being busy the next day. After giving Adam such a hard time in the beginning, I found it hard to admit I enjoyed his company. Though there was no doubt in my mind that Leland Booker was an innocent man, I couldn't see how all this talk could help. Still, Adam's unexpected intrusion into my life lit a spark of hope that justice would be done.

Chapter 3

The following Saturday Adam arrived with another bag from the donut shop pinned between his teeth. He stood like the scales of justice, balancing his computer case in one hand and his overstuffed messenger bag in the other. I waved him into the living room where I set out cups and plates. This time I was better prepared, placing a plastic mat on the table to protect it from his laptop.

"Good morning." He spoke through clenched teeth. I took the bag from his mouth and peered inside. Two sticky muffins and a sesame seed bagel.

"I noticed you don't go for the sweet stuff," he said. "I thought you might like a bagel instead."

"Thanks." I removed the contents of the bag and put them on a plate.

"How are things at work?" he asked.

"Not bad." I poured coffee from the carafe and sat down on the couch. "I've been thinking of cutting back on my case load a bit. Now that the weather is getting warmer, I'd like to spend some time in my garden. How about you?"

"I'm busy. In addition to the Defender Clinic, I've got three other classes. I can barely keep up with the workload. The saying goes that in the first year of law school they scare you to death, in the second year they work you to death, and in the third year they bore you to death. Even though this is my last year, I seem to be stuck in the 'work to death' phase."

"Then I imagine you have better things to do than spend

your weekends going over all this." I waved my hand in the direction of his files. "You must have a girlfriend or significant other . . ."

"Nope." Adam smiled, that charming smile. "I don't have the time or the money for a girlfriend right now. Unfortunately, that's going to have to wait until after I graduate."

"Well, you're obviously under a lot of pressure at school. Are you sure you want to spend your time listening to me talk about the Bookers?"

He waited a beat before answering. I felt a twinge of anxiety, expecting him to tell me this would be our last session. The realization that I wanted to share stories from the past with Adam surprised me.

"What you've told me has already been a great help," he said. "I did some research and chased down answers to the questions you raised last week."

"Questions? What questions?"

"You got me thinking. I never gave any consideration as to why Leland moved to Keene in the first place. While it might not have anything to do with the murders, I thought it would be a good idea to look into it. You never know where a lead will take me. Anyway, you said the Bookers left Atlanta because they experienced some racial problems?"

"That's what my mother told me. Something about their mixed marriage and not being accepted down south."

"You'll be glad to hear that your mother was way off base. Leland joined KCC for a completely different reason."

"You spoke to Leland?"

"Sure. Who else? Turns out he took the job for the same reason most people decide to pull up stakes and move. Leo Bishop offered Leland more money than what he earned in Atlanta."

Adam cracked his knuckles and looked down, studying the pattern in the carpet.

"What's the matter?" I asked. "Don't you believe him?"

"I sensed there was more to it. Like there was something about leaving Atlanta that he didn't want to talk about."

I nibbled at the edge of my bagel, thinking about what Adam said. A thought was moving around in my brain, the germ of an idea or a piece of the puzzle that I still couldn't put in place. I decided not to say anything about it until I worked it all out.

Adam's voice broke into my thoughts. "I tried to track down Billy Reynolds too."

"You did what?"

"Yeah, I'd be interested in speaking with anyone here who remembers the Bookers."

"If you'd asked me I could have saved you the time. Billy joined the Marines and left for Parris Island in September of that year. From there he was shipped out to Vietnam. His name is etched into the wall in Washington."

He nodded his head slowly. "I figured that out. He didn't make it back from the war. I'd like to speak with Jack too, but you never mentioned his last name."

"Burquest." I closed my eyes and took a deep breath. "Jack Burquest. He's still around, but I doubt he can tell you anything useful. He didn't know the family very well."

"I can't afford to assume anything at this point. Because the case is so old, I don't have much to go on. Like I said, I have to follow every possible lead. I'm just pulling at straws, hoping to find something I can use to illustrate wrongful conviction in this case."

While Adam booted up his computer I rose from the couch to refill our coffee cups. Watching him out of the corner of my eye, I tried to figure out how I could keep Adam from

contacting Jack. Not that Jack would be stupid enough to confess his role in what happened to the Bookers. Still, I wanted
to change the subject in the hope that Adam would forget all
about contacting Jack Burquest.

"Tell me how this works," I said. "What do you hope to
accomplish with this project of yours?"

"Well, to get credit for the Defender Clinic I have to produce a paper, a thesis that proves I've approached the case with
a critical eye, uncovering any legal missteps in Leland's case."

"That's all?"

"What do you mean? That's what the course is
all about."

"Perhaps I misunderstood. You led me to believe there's
more to it than that. When we first met, you told me you wanted to learn what really happened to Marley and the children.
Why am I wasting my time if you're not going to get Leland
out of jail?"

Adam sat back, squinting slightly as he measured his
reply. While the seconds ticked by, I grew annoyed. This young
law student barged into my life with the promise to help
Leland and now it seemed the whole exercise was purely academic. As I pondered the situation, I realized I'd been drawn
into something that was better left alone.

Adam rubbed the back of his neck. "I didn't mean to
mislead you. The chances of overturning a conviction are so
miniscule that, well it almost never happens. But I can promise you this: I'm going to do everything I can to help Leland.
Best-case scenario, we can compile enough evidence to bring
the case to a federal judge for review. It's a long shot, but if I
can prove that the prosecution screwed up, then maybe . . ."
He shrugged.

"Are you saying you're not out to find the real
murderer?"

"Not necessarily. There are several reasons why a judge would give a case a second look. None of them require proof that someone else killed Marley and the girls."

"Name a few."

"The big one these days is DNA evidence. I don't hold a lot of hope for that in this case since it happened so long ago and most of the evidence has been destroyed. But there's always the possibility that there was suppressed or mishandled evidence. Or we can try to prove government misconduct on the basis of racial prejudice. There's a long list of legal precedence that I need to research before I can determine exactly what path to take."

"And then?"

"Then I convince my professor to bring the case to one of his colleagues from the Defender Project. He doesn't do that often; he's not one to risk his reputation on a lost cause. But he says when a student presents a good case, he does what he can to open doors."

"What is the Defender Project?"

"A nonprofit organization that works to free prisoners who were wrongfully convicted. It's a long process, but ultimately, the charges against Leland could be dismissed and he'll be a free man."

"Is that possible?" I was beginning to see the whole picture, to better appreciate the long journey ahead.

"It happens. I should have told you this up front, but at least now you know what I'm looking for. Anything you recall that exposes a prosecutorial misstep will help."

"Last week you mentioned Henry Rusak, the handyman," I said. "I can't see how anything of this relates to . . . what did you call it? A prosecutorial misstep? But it was true that Marley had some problems with Henry and wanted him to stay away. I don't know what those problems were exactly, but I can explain Henry's relationship to the children."

Adam seemed so eager, doggedly determined. He was attempting to unravel the prosecutor's case with whatever scattered bits of information I could provide. Now I knew he didn't care about tracking down the real killer. He simply wanted to concentrate on finding a legal loophole to free Leland. I just had to be careful to keep this law student from straying too far from that goal. Before I began, I took a moment to think back to the day when I first met Henry.

Chapter 4

I opened my mother's refrigerator, drank some milk out of the carton, and slipped the strap of my pocketbook over my shoulder. My father raised an eyebrow as he watched me over the rim of his coffee cup.

"Where are you off to in such a hurry?" he asked. "Aren't you going to eat breakfast?"

"Today is Lissa's birthday. I have to stop at Gordon's Market and pick up a few things before I go to work.

"You'll be home in time for dinner, right?"

I nodded and Dad gave me a smile. The skin around his eyes folded into a thousand creases, his cheeks growing rounder.

"Marley is planning to take the girls to the club for supper. I'll be home in plenty of time to help Mom with the potatoes."

"We don't see much of you since you started watching those kids."

"The more hours I work, the more I earn. Isn't that the whole point of a summer job?"

"Well, don't spend all your hard-earned money on presents for those kids. College can be expensive."

He watched from the kitchen window as I mounted my bike and coasted down the driveway. Stepping into Gordon's, I stole a glance at the counter and saw Jack was not working. Old Mr. Gordon nodded to me in greeting, and I quickly paid for my purchases and left. When I got to the Bookers' house

I checked my watch and realized the family would still be in church. Heading straight to the backyard I stood by the pool and took in the view. Last month's daffodils lay wilted in the flowerbeds. Most of the dandelions in the grass had already transformed into white moons and in the center of the lawn, a crab apple tree was in full bloom. As I stood there, a deer with a spotted fawn by her side emerged from the woods. She froze for a moment, then darted away. Both of them vanished among the hemlocks.

I tore open the package from Gordon's—a bag of fifty lollipops, the kind with loops for handles to make my job easier—and set to work. By the time the bag was empty, the crab apple tree was covered with candy hanging by curls of ribbon.

Satisfied with the results of my handiwork, I let myself in with a key Marley gave me. I settled down in the living room and picked up a copy of *Vogue* magazine to read while I waited. Marley's choice in magazines was typical for her style. A black leather sofa with a matching lounge chair were arranged around a glass coffee table. A silver box filled with cigarettes rested on the table next to a crystal ash tray. Signed Wyeth prints hung on the wall. The clean, modern feel of the place contrasted dramatically with my mother's cluttered, kitschy style. This was the kind of house I wanted for myself someday. I could easily imagine what it would be like to live there.

I heard the creak of the front door and turned in time to catch the surprised look on Marley's face. Setting down the magazine, I stood to greet the family. Robin ran straight to me, grabbing me in a welcoming hug. I kissed the top of her head and looked up to see Lissa staring out the bay window.

"Happy birthday, Lissa," I said.

She held her father's hand, a half-smile playing at her lips.

"You must be Cate," Leland said. "The girls talk

about you nonstop. You've made a pretty good impression around here."

I felt my face go red, the blush spreading down my neck. Leland held me in his gaze, a look of amusement on his face. The first thing I noticed about him was the color of his skin. How much darker he was than his children. His eyes were a deep, rich brown. A smattering of freckles ran across the bridge of his nose, giving him an open, friendly look. I'd never met anyone like him before, and without meaning anything by it, I found myself staring. He smiled, a million-dollar smile.

"What is that?" Lissa asked. She dropped her father's hand and walked to the window overlooking the backyard. Robin ran to her side.

"Cool," Robin said. "Lollipops!"

"That's a birthday tree," I said.

Robin pressed her nose against the glass while Lissa turned to look at me, a broad smile on her face.

"There's no such thing."

"No, really. I've heard they grow around here," I insisted.

"Well, that is a surprise," Marley said. "And all along I thought that was just a common old crab apple."

"Lissa, let's go see."

Robin raced out of the house. Lissa, with a backward glance, followed.

"That was nice of you, Cate." Marley picked up her pocketbook and looked at her husband expectantly. "We really should get going or we'll be late."

Leland nodded, pulled the car keys out of his pocket, and flashed that amazing smile in my direction. Marley looked over her shoulder, her eyes passing over her husband's face before meeting mine.

"I believe I already told you we will be celebrating

Lissa's birthday at the club tonight. Be sure the girls are ready when I get home. After their bath, dress them in their matching strawberry print dresses. I believe you know where to find everything."

She turned, leaving me to watch her walk to the car, her hand resting on Leland's arm and her pocketbook swinging from the crook of her elbow.

I sent Lissa and Robin outside to spread an old blanket on the lawn for a picnic lunch. In the kitchen, I cut our sandwiches into quarters, arranging them on paper plates with a handful of potato chips in the center of each. Loading everything onto a tray, I was about to join the girls when Robin reappeared, her lower lip jutting out, her eyebrows pulled into a frown.

"Why aren't you outside with your sister?" I asked.

"Lissa is talking to that weird man."

"What man?"

"The creepy guy from the club. I don't like him."

I stepped into the living room and peered out the back window. A man I never saw before was standing next to Lissa. His mouth opened in a lopsided grin as he reached out to touch her hair. Something about his eyes didn't look quite right.

"Stay here," I instructed Robin. "I'll be right back."

"Hey, what are you doing?" I shouted as I stepped out the door.

The man took one step back. Lissa cocked her head, giving me a questioning look. She turned back to the stranger, said something I couldn't hear, and shrugged her shoulders. Quickly crossing the lawn, I grabbed the sleeve of Lissa's blouse and pulled her to me. My heart pounding, I looked up at the tallest person I'd ever seen. A drop of saliva dripped from his bottom lip.

"Henry asked if he could touch my hair," Lissa said. "He just wanted to know what it feels like."

I'd heard my mother mention Henry before. He was the KCC handyman. Though Mom claimed he was harmless, I tended to agree with Robin. He gave me the creeps.

"You don't belong here." I said. "Go back to the club."

"Leo said I have to clean the pool."

He spoke like his tongue was swollen, unable to pronounce his words correctly. *Hafta keen da poo.* The muscles in his face worked overtime, contorting his features.

I held Lissa against me, my arms crossed against her chest. She tipped her head back and smiled up at Henry.

"Come back inside, Lissa. Lunch is ready."

She gave me a dark stare. "But you said we could have a picnic."

"I changed my mind."

Her mouth turned down in a pretty pout. "I have to go now, Henry. See 'ya later."

"Okie dokie." Henry lifted his chin and gave Lissa that same, open-mouthed smile I saw from the living room window. "See 'ya later."

———————————

At five o'clock I sent Adam away with a loaf of my homemade zucchini bread and the promise to meet again the following week. After he left, I sat down at my desk and pulled a stack of paperwork from my satchel. After reading a few pages, I pushed everything aside. Reaching into the bottom drawer, I retrieved my old scrapbook. I hadn't looked at it in ages, but many years ago I'd clipped an article from the local paper and pasted it in the book. The headline read, "New Golf Pro joins KCC." The story provided a glowing review of Leland's golf achievements, together with a few lines about the Booker family. It featured a picture of Leland, Marley, and the children at a table in the club restaurant. Lissa and Robin wore their strawberry print dresses. When I looked closely, I could see the remains of a birthday cake on the plates. Lissa stared at the photographer with a straight face while Robin smiled for the camera. Leland had one arm wrapped around Marley, and with his free hand he raised a glass of wine, toasting the occasion. Marley sparkled. She looked like a model, not a blond hair out of place, her diamond earrings a starburst in the camera's flash.

I closed the book and glanced back at the stack of papers. With a shake of my head, I shut the door on the past, and concentrated on the work before me.

Chapter 5

Adam gave me a mischievous grin and tossed the bag with my bagel to me. He arrived dressed in blue jeans and a polo shirt. I noticed he left his briefcase behind.

"Where's your paperwork?"

"I loaded everything onto my laptop. I've been too busy to scan everything myself so last week my dad did the job for me. Newspaper articles, court transcripts, even the Keene police reports, are in here now."

He patted his laptop like it was some kind of pet. I glanced over his shoulder and watched him click an icon titled Booker Arrest Chronology. The file opened, filling the screen before me.

"What you're looking at is a synopsis that I'm putting together," Adam explained. "An outline of events starting with the murders and going right up to the last day of the trial. My dad suggested incorporating links so I can jump from each bullet point directly to any supporting documents."

He passed me the laptop and I scrolled through the ten-page summary. I clicked on an underlined name I recognized and a file titled Transcript: Mildred Bishop Interview jumped to the front of the screen.

"I'm impressed. How does your dad know so much about computers?"

Adam took the laptop back from me. "He works in IT. I was hoping we could go through this today."

"Sure. But before we begin, I've been thinking about

something you said last week. Something about racial prejudice being a factor in wrongful convictions. I remember an
incident that happened while I was working for Leland that
you should know about."

He studied me for a few beats. With a slight nod he
turned his attention back to the laptop.

"You can tell me about that later. First I want you to
check this out and let me know if I've missed anything."

I hesitated, remembering what he said about loading everything related to the case onto his computer. When Leland's
trial began, the *Keene Sentinel* printed a photo released by the
State Attorney's Office. In my mind I could still see that picture
of a smiling Marley, holding hands with Lissa and Robin at the
clubhouse. A few weeks later, though the paper refrained from
printing autopsy photos offered into evidence by the prosecution, they reported that those exhibits raised a gasp from every
member of the jury. When I read that, it was clear to me that
Leland's fate was sealed.

"Do you have the medical examiner's report in there? I
don't think I can stand to see those photos."

"No, not yet. I'm still working on getting the county
reports." Adam clicked again and we were back to the beginning of his summary. "Let's start with the day of the murder.
The 9th of August was a Wednesday. Marley and the children
had cereal and orange juice for breakfast. It's a small detail,
but I thought you said the girls hated orange juice, so why
would they—?"

"We ran out of apple juice the day before." My throat
tightened. I took a deep breath, steadying my nerves so Adam
couldn't see the emotion I fought to control. "Marley asked me
to pick up more but I forgot."

"Okay, that answers that question. Leland told me he left

for the club early, before Marley and the kids got up. He said he let Marley sleep in because she had the day off."

"She stayed home with the kids on Wednesdays which gave me the day off too. That was the slowest day of the week, so Leland worked in the shop and used the time to catch up on paperwork. If he had to give a golf lesson or was invited by a member to lunch, he would just turn the sign to CLOSED and lock up."

"He gave the club president's wife, Mildred a lesson that morning. Have a look at what she told the police."

I leaned forward to get a good look at the screen. Mildred Bishop's transcript confirmed that she was at the driving range with Leland from ten to eleven that day. After the lesson, she invited Leland to an early lunch. Mrs. Bishop stated that over his plate of grilled chicken, Leland mentioned he was starving because he skipped breakfast that morning.

"She makes it sound like Leland knew what was going to happen."

"Exactly. That's why the defense chose not to put Mrs. Bishop on the stand. They thought his comment could be used against him. You know, while his wife and kids were dying, the murdering husband flirted with the boss' wife over a martini lunch."

"Anyone who knew Leland would realize just how crazy that is. He loved his family. Not to mention that he didn't care for Mrs. Bishop. She was . . . well, she was not his type."

"I spoke with her last week."

"You were lucky to catch her. Leo is semi-retired now. They spend a lot of time in Florida."

"We had a good conversation. Leland may not have cared for her but apparently, she liked him very much. Said that she offered to testify as a character witness, but Leland's lawyer didn't want to take the chance of opening her up to cross examination by the prosecution in light of her statement. In retrospect, I think the defense missed an opportunity to use her. At the very least she could have testified as to Leland's state of mind that morning. I might argue that his lawyer made a mistake. There's something on the list . . ."

Adam clicked through several files. A document popped to the front of the screen titled "Reasons for Wrongful Conviction." Adam scanned the list quickly. "Here it is. One of the reasons for wrongful conviction is incompetent legal representation. I'll keep that in mind as we move forward. For now, let's keep going."

He closed the document and the screen jumped back to the summary. The next entry was for 10:28 a.m., when hospital records indicated Marley pulled up to the door of the emergency room, leaving her car running in the loading zone. The nurse on the desk reported that Marley was hysterical, bursting through the doors with Robin in her arms. Robin was seized by violent spasms, her mouth foaming. Marley screamed something about another daughter who was still in the car. An orderly caught the child as Marley collapsed. The nurse went outside to discover Lissa already dead in the back seat. The other two were rushed into examination bays and a team of doctors went to work on them. I scanned the coroner's summary. Lissa was declared DOA. Marley and Robin were pronounced dead two hours later.

Adam pointed to the screen. "The reason there's a gap in the timeline here is that the hospital had no way of identifying her. Marley left the house without her pocketbook. The hospital authorities had to call the police and ask them to track down Leland through the car registration. That took some time."

Adam's next entry indicated a Keene police officer by the name of Keith Sterling found Leland at the pro shop at 1:45 p.m. Another link brought me to Sterling's official report. He said he told Leland there had been an accident and offered to drive him to the hospital. In transit, Leland repeatedly asked what had happened. The officer denied any knowledge of the details. When they arrived at the hospital, a uniformed patrolman, James McKeon, met them in the lobby and informed Leland that his wife and children were dead.

"Sterling and McKeon were locals," Adam explained. "And local cops have to turn over all homicides to the Major Crime Unit in the Cheshire County sheriff's department. Officially, they could have waited for the cause of death to be declared by the coroner, but based on what the doctor told them, it was a foregone conclusion that they were looking at either a suicide/murder or a triple murder. While Sterling went to pick up Leland, McKeon made the call to the sheriff's office, and by the time Leland arrived at the hospital, someone from the county was already processing the paperwork to transfer the case."

"I remember one of the county detectives," I said. "The woman was a dragon. Her name was Marianne Weede. She interviewed me at my house."

"From what people tell me, Weede was a good cop," Adam said. "She's retired, but I hope to speak with her and her partner, Lou Bragg, soon. I also want to see all the records of their investigation. It may take some time, but I've got someone working on that for me."

"Let's keep going."

Adam pointed to the next entry. "There's no official record of the conversation Leland had with McKeon while he was kept waiting to see the bodies so I had to make a reasonable guesstimate as to when that occurred. Leland admits his memory is sketchy, and understandably so since he was probably in shock. But he does remember McKeon brought him a cup of coffee and stayed to keep him company. McKeon was very sympathetic, encouraging Leland to talk about Marley and the kids. Leland confessed to fighting with Marley the previous evening. He said that in the morning he was still mad at her, and that they weren't speaking to each other. In McKeon's report he quoted Leland as saying, 'I will have to live with knowing that the last words I said to my wife were spoken in anger.'"

I pinched my lips together. "They fought all the time. All married couples do. But with them it was never serious. Leland's comment was hardly grounds for bringing murder charges against him."

"Think about it from the cops' point of view. The lab results weren't in yet, but it was clear that they were looking at a case of poisoning. In addition to that, there were bruises on Marley's arms. Obviously, they had to consider the possibility of murder. Keep reading."

I turned my attention back to the summary. By 4:00 p.m., the blood tests were back from the lab. Aldicarb was detected in all three bodies. McKeon wrote in his report that he asked Leland to help with the investigation down at the station. The notes emphasized that McKeon made it clear Leland wasn't being charged with anything at that point, and Leland wanted to cooperate. McKeon was talking like it was a case of accidental poisoning, not once inferring that he suspected anything different. After spending an hour in the station interview room, Leland saw where the questioning was going and declined to answer any more questions. McKeon read him his rights.

"I had to make another guess about time here." Adam pointed to the place he was talking about. "While the Keene police waited for the county detectives to arrive, they put Leland in a cell with a guy who was picked up for DUI. If you want to read the drunk's testimony you can go to the link."

I shook my head, already knowing what was said at the

trial. "He claimed that Leland confessed to the murder while they were in jail together."

"That's right. But Leland claims that was a lie."

"You believe him, don't you?"

"Sure, but it was his word against the other guy. Meanwhile, as Leland was allegedly confessing to a total stranger, Officer Sterling went to the house and blocked off all access with crime scene tape. At 5:30 the county detectives arrived. Detective Bragg went to take control of the scene while his partner, Detective Weede, stayed at the Keene police station where Leland was being held."

The summary showed that at six thirty Leland called an attorney. The next public defender on the list was Scott Turner. Turner said he would get to the station within the hour. Before the lawyer arrived, Weede took Leland into her custody. One short notation spelled the beginning of a process that would ultimately take away his freedom.

19:00 Leland Booker remanded into the custody of Detective Marianne Weede, Major Crimes Unit of the Cheshire County Prosecutor's Office. Charged with three counts of murder. Marley A. Booker, Melissa A. Booker, and Robin M. Booker.

While Weede transported Leland to the county jail, her partner, Detective Bragg, searched the house with Officer Sterling. The last entry of the day was marked just before midnight. I clicked on the link and read the search-warrant return, the document filed with the court that listed the items seized. The police removed all the food from the kitchen, bank statements and invoices from Leland's desk, and some letters found in Marley's dresser drawer. They also took several containers of fertilizer and insecticide from the garage. Among them was a partially empty box of Aldicarb.

With a sigh, I pinched the bridge of my nose.

"Do you need to take a break?" he asked.

I looked at him and nodded.

"Take your time. I know how you must feel."

His words rubbed me the wrong way. How could he possibly know how I felt? By getting me involved, Adam had stirred all the anger and guilt that I worked hard to suppress for over forty years. Controlling my impulse to snap at the young man, I forced a smile that I didn't feel and said, "I think I'll step outside for some air."

A cool, autumn breeze brushed my face. Unexpectedly, the craving for a cigarette hit me hard. Eighteen months earlier, after my husband, Arnie died of lung cancer, I decided to quit cold turkey. That lasted for a while but the urge to light up still kicks in when I am stressed. And honestly, dredging up memories of the day Marley and her girls died was hard for me to handle. I took a deep breath and stared out at my garden. It was time to bring in the last of the butternut squash. The soil was ready to be turned over and put to rest for the winter. The thought of thrusting my hands into the rich earth soothed me and I pushed the thought of my cigarettes to the back of my mind.

Back in the house, Adam was refilling our coffee cups.

"You looked like you were going to faint or something," Adam said.

I took a sip and smiled at him over the rim.

"The fresh air helped. I feel better now."

"What went through your head the day after the murders when you showed up at the Bookers' house and saw the police cars out front?"

"I don't know. I suppose I thought it was about the break-in."

"What break-in?"

"The day before someone broke a window and entered the house while Marley and I were out with the kids. Marley left work early and wanted to treat us all to an ice cream. We were shocked to see what they did to her bedroom."

"I don't remember seeing anything in the police reports." Adam frowned. His fingers danced over the keyboard, paging through his files, looking for something that wasn't there.

"Marley was shaken by the whole thing. She checked her jewelry box but nothing seemed to be missing. Then she remembered to look for the gold bracelet that she kept in her dressing table drawer. Sure enough, it was gone. The bedroom was trashed. Drawers emptied, all her clothes in the closet dumped on the floor. Worse of all, the thief wrote something awful in lipstick on her bathroom mirror. Marley didn't want to upset Leland so she asked me not to say anything. I helped her clean up while the children watched TV. After we finished I went straight home."

"Why didn't she want to tell Leland what happened?"

"You will understand when I get to that part of my story."

I set my coffee down on the table and stared at him. I didn't want to say any more about the break-in. At least not now.

"This could be important. Who else would know about this?"

"Leo Bishop, for one. And Henry of course. Marley called Leo right away and asked if he could send Henry over to repair the broken glass before Leland got home."

Adam folded his hands behind his head and looked up to the ceiling. "What if the person who broke into the house poisoned the juice? If the murderer knew the family well enough to realize the girls didn't like orange juice, then my initial suspicion could be correct." He looked at me, eyes wide open. "Marley *was* the target."

I closed my eyes. Hearing him express the truth of what I already knew wrenched my heart. I could feel Adam looking at me.

"I'm sorry, I forgot how much they meant to you."

He must have thought I was reflecting on the loss of the children. But what I felt at the moment was much worse than sorrow. I was pierced by guilt.

Chapter 6

With the whole country on a campaign to quit cigarettes, I decided to make my office a no-smoking zone. When Jack Burquest came looking for me at lunchtime that Friday, he knew he would find me out back, lighting up.

"Got a minute?" he asked.

I jumped at the sound of his voice, nearly dropping my pack of Marlboros.

"I wish you wouldn't sneak up on me like that, Jack."

"I thought you quit after Arnie died."

"I did. I've had a tough week."

"Got one for me?"

I offered him the pack. Jack accepted one and leaned in when I took out my lighter. The stench of vodka, sour as a Russian potato field, rose from his skin. Taking a deep drag, he blew out a stream of smoke and winked at me.

I frowned my disapproval, rolling my eyes when he reached to scratch under his frayed collar. A new crop of dandruff rained down. He followed my stare to his shoulder, saw nothing wrong, and turned his attention back to me.

"What are you doing here?" I allowed a note of annoyance to creep into my voice.

"Your client is suing my client for divorce."

"Yes, I noticed that. Are you here to discuss a settlement?"

A puff of smoke escaped from his nose. "You've got to

be kidding. I want to keep this battle going until my client runs out of money."

"Is that really in anyone's best interest? My client is prepared to be reasonable. The house is heavily mortgaged so there is no equity to divide. All she wants is to remain in the home, work out a joint custody agreement and keep the investments she inherited from her father."

"Yeah, well that could be a problem. My client wants half of that inheritance."

"You should be honest with your client. No judge would ever agree to that. Her father died after they separated so that money was never part of their marital assets."

"I'm going to tell him to keep fighting."

"That would not be in your client's best interest. All a protracted fight would achieve is increased legal cost."

He shrugged. "Would that be such a bad thing?"

I looked at Jack in disbelief. "What you're suggesting is immoral. When all is said and done he could file a complaint with the Bar Association. You may lose your job."

"Hey, that might happen anyway."

"What are you talking about?"

"A few months ago I deposited a client's check in my personal account instead of handing it over to the firm."

"Jack!"

"I had every intention of paying it back but one of the partners found out before I had the chance."

I tapped the ash off the end of my cigarette. "Was that the first time you did that?"

"No, but it was the first time I was caught before returning the money."

"How in the world did you get into this mess?"

"I was in a cash crunch. Listen, I need to work for at least another five years. I can't afford to retire sooner."

"You must have some savings put away."

"My first ex-wife stripped me clean and now with this second divorce, Cindy's picking the bones. Do you have any idea of what it cost me to send the boys to college? I barely get by."

"Can I give you some advice?"

Jack heaved an exaggerated sigh. He held out his hands, palms upraised as if he was waiting for me to hand him something. A thin stream of cigarette smoke rose between his right fingers. "Nothing I'd say would stop you, so give it to me."

"Clean up your act. Explain exactly why you did it and maybe you'll get away with a stern warning. Better yet, admit you have a drinking problem. Tell your partners that you want to check into a rehab center to get yourself cleaned up. They may cut you a break this time if you do."

"It's a little late for that, don't you think?"

"Never too late."

"Yeah, well listen. The main reason I stopped by was to ask if you were going to the Keene High homecoming game tomorrow."

"What are we, back in high school? Are you asking me on a date?"

"No, I just wondered . . . that is, if you were going anyway I thought we could sit together."

"I have other plans."

"For real?"

"I promised to help a UNH law student with a project."

"What student?"

"No one you would know. Listen, go to the game. Have a good time. Think about what I told you. Maybe this is your chance to make a new start in life."

Shaking his head, Jack flicked his cigarette to the ground. "See you in court, counselor."

The next morning Adam sat in my living room cracking his knuckles. I knew him well enough by now to know that something was bothering him.

"You keep that up and you'll be sorry. When you're my age your fingers will be full of arthritis."

"My mom says that all the time," Adam said with a grin. "Hey, listen, did you know Henry Rusak is still alive?"

"Of course. I see him every week."

"Why didn't you tell me?"

"You didn't ask."

"I went to visit him yesterday."

"Did you learn anything useful?"

I looked at Adam, knowing what his answer was going to be. Henry was so fearful of strangers that he never opened his door unless he knew the person on the other side.

Adam cracked another knuckle. "He wouldn't talk to me."

"You probably frightened him. Henry is afraid of most people. I've often thought it has something to do with his disability."

"What exactly is wrong with him?"

"Army surgeons put a plate in his head after he picked up some shrapnel in Korea. When he returned to Keene with a medal and no other prospects, Leo Bishop gave him a job as a handyman. Of course, Leo took advantage of him, paid him next to nothing. But at least he was loyal enough to let Henry work until he got into Social Security. I think Leo even pays him a small pension."

"Would you ask Henry to meet with me?

"I can do better than that. I'll bring you over sometime and introduce you."

"That would be great, thanks." Adam flipped open his laptop. "Shall we pick up where we left off?"

"Remind me, where were we?"

"When I explained that racial bias was a reason for wrongful conviction, you said there was something you remembered. What was it?"

"After my first few weeks with the family things settled into a smooth routine. I worked weekends until mid-May and then went full time after graduation. I knew of course that some people had a problem with the Bookers moving into town—the incident with Billy at Gordon's Market, for example—but then something worse happened. It was also around that time I started to notice problems between Marley and Leland."

Adam raised one eyebrow in expectation. His fingers lightly drummed the keyboard. He opened a blank document, ready for me to resume. I leaned back on the couch, closed my eyes, and stepped back in time.

Chapter 7

Marley and Leland attended my graduation. I had no idea they were there until they found me in the crowd after the ceremony. When the Bookers approached, my mother straightened her back and flashed a smile. My father stood next to me, studying my diploma like it was an Olympic gold medal.

"How nice of you to come and see our Cate graduate," my mother said.

"We wouldn't miss it for the world." Marley put her arm around my shoulders. "Cate is like family to us. Why, the girls just adore her."

It may have been my imagination, but Marley's southern accent seemed stronger than usual. Dad stared at her, an expression of lust on his face. I wanted to disown him on the spot.

"We haven't met yet." Leland flashed a dazzling smile in my father's direction. I'm Leland."

Dad hesitated a beat before he reached out to take Leland's outstretched hand. The corners of his mouth turned up, but it looked more like a grimace than anything else.

"Pleased to meet you. Cate loves your kids. They're all she talks about."

Glancing down at the girls, my father let loose with his full-blown smile. They stared back at him. Lissa studied him carefully with her deep brown eyes. Robin smiled right back.

"We brought a little something for you." Marley pass me a box wrapped in silver paper. The paper was embossed with the KCC logo.

"You didn't have to get me anything," I said.

"Nonsense. You don't graduate from high school every day. And with honors too. Your parents must be very proud."

"Won't you come back to the house and join us for coffee and cake?" Mom said.

"Perhaps another time." Marley patted me on the arm. "See you tomorrow, Cate."

Secretly, I was glad she turned down the invitation. I didn't want Marley to see our small house, our shabby furniture, my mother's tacky knickknacks. Taking their leave, the Bookers turned and walked back to their car. Dad stared as Marley sashayed away.

My mother babbled incessantly all the way home. She commented about the principal's speech, the clothes people wore, and of course, about Marley and Leland. Resting my forehead against the window, I ignored her chatter. I searched for the deer that sometimes grazed along the roadside after the sun went down. They thrived in the suburbs, wild things venturing out of the woods to feed on carefully manicured lawns. All the while I wondered about my father's cold reaction when he met Leland. I remained quiet until Dad turned onto our street.

"Why don't you like Leland?" I asked.

"I never said that," he replied.

"You didn't have to. I could tell."

"Nonsense," Mom said. "Why wouldn't your father like Mr. Booker?"

The Buick's headlamps hit our garage door with a glaring light. My mother was struck silent by the glossy black words sprayed on the white background. My father pounded the steering wheel with his fist and swore.

"Goddamn it, I knew no good would come of you working for those people."

I just stared, numb with anger. Clapping my hands over my ears, I tried to silence the voice that I imagined in my head; the voice of Billy Reynolds repeating over and over the words that I saw before me. N----- LOVER.

"What made you think it was Billy who wrote that?" Adam asked when I paused to refill our coffee cups.

"I just know."

"I don't see how that story helps our case. We can't link an isolated case of graffiti to the possibility of racism affecting the trial. I would need something more specific. Something that proves the police or jury was influenced by racial prejudice."

My brain raced as I strived to come up with an answer. Adam waited patiently in the silent void.

"It takes time . . ." I stopped, gathered my thoughts, and began again. "Shifting culture takes generations. The ugly truth is, most people in Keene don't consider themselves racists, but deep down inside that is exactly what they are. They conceal their bias; you only have to scratch the surface to expose their true feelings. This whole town was polite to his face, but most people didn't want Leland here. Not only that, he lived an expensive neighborhood in Keene. That struck everyone as wrong somehow. You said racial prejudice is one reason for a judge to overturn a conviction. What would it take to prove that happened in this case?"

"Statistics," Adam replied. "We would have to check and see if the number of arrests and convictions made in the Cheshire County court were disproportionately based on skin color. The fact that the judge seated an all-white jury will work in Leland's favor. I don't know where to begin looking for the data we need. I do know someone who can point me in the right direction, but the problem is I don't have the time to plow through it all."

I nodded. What he said made sense. Unfortunately, the task ahead seemed daunting. My disappointment must have shown on my face.

"Don't give up so easily," Adam said. "What you've told me confirms the belief I held from the start. If Leland Booker were white, everything would have been different. Maybe I should move this issue to the front burner."

"Hang on. If we can prove racial bias existed within the legal system, and that helps Leland, it will be great. But despite the fact that racism runs deep in Keene, I find it hard to believe the crime was racially motivated."

"Maybe it wasn't." Adam tipped his head and looked at me strangely. "But I do believe Leland's skin color had something to do with his conviction.'

"Get me that data and I'll see if there is evidence of racial bias."

One corner of Adam's mouth turned up. "I don't doubt that for a minute. We just have to prove it."

Chapter 8

Adam and I headed out pick up a copy of Marianne Weede's files on the Booker murders. After that, we planned to stop at a restaurant for a bite to eat. As I turned onto Court Street, a river of cars poured out of the parking lot, employees speeding away to catch a quick lunch. The exodus enabled me to find a spot in the first row.

Forty years earlier, I attended the opening statements of Leland's trial here. The Courthouse pulsed with history. Built out of red brick, the building stood two stories high. Arch windows were set in each of the four bays on the ground floor with three on the second. The entrance was located front and center with square columns framing each side. On top of the roof a weather vane perched on a distinctive belfry. The place was impressive.

Adam pointing to the corner stone etched with the year it was built, 1849. "They didn't even have electricity or plumbing back then. Can you imagine going through a New Hampshire winter without central heating?"

"Lots of buildings in this part of town are like that. My own house was built before indoor plumbing became common. My husband and I poured money into renovations but it's still a bear to heat. With him gone the place feels empty. My sister tells me I should sell it and move into something smaller but I . . ."

I paused, staring straight ahead. Gripping the steering wheel, I tried to shake off the wave of grief that hit me out of the blue. That happened from time to time. Knocking around in my big house alone, I sometimes felt like Arnie's ghost lurked around every door. And with Adam's arrival, my memories of the Booker family haunted me once again. Adam's voice brought me back to the present.

"We're going to have company for lunch," Adam said. "You'll never guess who."

"Who?"

"Marianne Weede, the detective who put together the file we're here to collect. I also contacted her partner, Lou Bragg, and asked him to join us, but he declined. He actually said he didn't want to talk about the case. That surprised me but I don't think we need him. Weede did most of the work on the case. Apparently, she kept pretty good records. I'm hoping there's something in them that will help."

"She must be retired by now."

"She stopped working years ago," Adam replied. "But I tracked her down and she seemed happy enough to meet with us."

"If she's retired, how did you arrange to get a copy of her files?"

"The case is closed, so all related documents are available to the public. Having said that, the cops are sometimes slow to turn things over, so I had to pull a few strings to cut through the red tape."

Entering the building, we passed through a security process that rivaled anything I'd been through at the airport. One of the agents, a man I often saw when coming to court with a client, stopped talking with his co-worker long enough to point his stubby finger at a plastic tray into which I stuffed my purse, coat, and shoes. I slid the gray bin onto the rolling conveyor and watched it disappear into the x-ray machine. At the end of the conveyor another uniformed man I knew rooted through my pocketbook. He pulled out my cell phone and turned it over once before dropping it back. When I peeked inside, I found the phone lying on top of all my other possessions in disarray.

"Good morning, Mrs. Stokes. I didn't see your name on the roster this morning."

"We're here to see Detective Erika Tripp."

Both of his eyebrows shot up. "The detective's offices is at the end of the hall on the second floor."

Inside the elevator, Adam punched the button for the second floor. I noticed holes in the wall and a grungy outline where a poster or notice once hung. A tile was missing from the ceiling, exposing the chains and cables that lifted us. The elevator stopped and the doors slid open. I expected to see people waiting to get on, but the hallway was empty. A plaque on the opposite wall indicated that Family Court where I often conducted my own business was to the right. Angry voices from that direction reached us as we stepped into the lobby where another bank of x-ray machines and conveyor belts blocked our way.

After passing through the second security check, we were told to wait while the agent called ahead. A short while later we made our way down a long corridor where we found Erika Tripp waiting. She waved us into a conference room where a weak October sun filtered through a dust-streaked window. A pigeon perched outside on the ledge. Erika hit the wall switch and a fluorescent bulb blinked on. The room was cramped. There was barely enough space for me to pull the chair back from the round table before I took a seat.

"Thanks for taking the time to meet with us today." Adam extended his hand across the table. "I'm Adam Bennett."

I judged the detective to be in her mid-to-late forties, solidly built but not what I'd call overweight. Her bleached hair was pulled back and wrapped in a knot at the base of her neck. Five diamond studs crept up one earlobe. A single gold ring pierced the other ear. She wore heavy eye makeup, but I detected no trace of perfume, only soap. I could picture her working out at the gym without breaking a sweat. Giving me a cursory sweep with icy green eyes, Tripp turned her full attention to Adam.

"I want you to know that I went to a lot of trouble to dig this stuff out for you. When Marianne called to say you were looking for some of her old files, I said yeah, sure. When I got around to it. Then she explained who your old man is, and I figured, what the hell. He's helped me out on more than one occasion. I owed him. But don't be getting any ideas. I know you're working on this project for school and all, but I've got better things to do than spend time on a case that was closed before I even joined the force."

"I appreciate your help." Adam flashed her one of his contagious smiles. "Since I'm probably taking time from your lunch break . . ." With a flourish Adam slipped his hand into the pocket of his overcoat and produced a bag from the deli. The detective smiled as she pulled a foil-wrapped sandwich from the bag. A strong smell of onions filled the room.

"You play dirty." She returned his smile. "Philly cheese steak. Your dad must have told you they're one of my guilty pleasures."

Adam's natural charm worked. In a heartbeat he had transformed Erika from hard-assed cop to blushing girl.

"Who are you?" Tripp looked straight at me, giving me a second sweep with her heavily made-up eyes.

"Cate Stokes. I'm helping Adam with his research."

"The babysitter." Tripp's eyes widened as she studied me. Nodding, she turned back to Adam. Putting her hand on a blue three-ring binder that rested on the table in front of her, she slid it across to him. "Hard copy only. We haven't

got around to scanning the files from back then. I told one
of the temps to dig the original out of the archives. Not a lot
of room in this building. Most of our files are stored off-site.
It's a friggin' mess over there. Took the kid the better part
of a day to find Marianne's murder book. I had him make a
copy for you."

"How did you know Cate was the Booker's babysitter?"
Adam asked.

"I thumbed through the murder book. Curiosity got the
better of me, wondering why you're digging this one up."

"Did anything jump out at you when you read the file?"

"Sure, but not the kind of thing you're hoping for. What
hit me was that detectives Bragg and Weede did a helluva job.
No surprise there. Marianne was the best. I partnered with her
for a while before she retired. In fact, she's the one who showed
me the ropes when I first made detective. Back in the day,
when she worked this case she was the only female in the unit.
Couldn't have been easy for her, surrounded by all those cow-
boys. But Marianne could hold her own. She certainly nailed
that son-of-a-bitch Booker. Put him right where he belongs."

I flinched, not so much from what she said, but from the
callous tone in her voice when she said it.

"Nothing unusual about this case caught your eye?"
Adam asked.

"I know where you're going. Your father told me he
thinks there was something hinkey about those murders. And
what the hell, maybe he's right. Cops aren't trained to look
for holes in a case. That's why defense lawyers get paid the
big bucks. Marianne followed procedure right down the line."
Tripp tapped the cover of the binder with an acrylic fingernail.
"All her reports are in here together with everything else the
prosecution used to put that bastard away."

Adam picked up the binder and pushed back his chair

until it hit the wall. Erika was all smiles as we took our leave. It occurred to me that despite her tough talk, she would probably do Adam another favor if he asked for one down the road.

I waited until we reached my car before I turned to Adam and spit out the question that had been nagging me for the past thirty minutes.

"How does that woman know your father?"

"He works here."

"He's a cop? You told me he works in IT."

"Well, he does. He heads up the County's Computer Crimes Investigations Unit."

"What do that mean, computer crimes? As in Internet pornography?"

"Among other things. Most of his work goes to support criminal investigations. You know, I'm sure you've seen the cop shows on television. His guys conduct forensic examinations of computers, cell phones, that kind of thing. They're the geeks in the Division. When it comes right down to it, jurors trust electronic evidence. The detectives rely pretty heavily on Dad and his team for what they need to make their case."

"And you didn't think to mention this to me before?"

"Look, all my life I've lived in my father's shadow. I intend to work this case on my own."

His eyes darted away as he spoke, that same telltale sign I saw before that suggested he wasn't being altogether honest with me. Whatever it was, I figured he wanted to keep to himself. After all, we both had our secrets. As I thrust my hand into my pocketbook, I remembered what a mess the security agent made of everything. The car keys weren't in the side pouch where they belonged. Finding them at the bottom of the bag, I knew I would have to dump the entire contents and reorganize everything after I got home.

Adam made our lunch reservation at The Stage, one of my favorite restaurants in Keene. The place was something of an institution where I often took my clients for a bite to eat after their day in court. Though the restaurant was located within walking distance from the Courthouse, I decided to move the car and park right in front. As usual for that time of day, the place was packed when we entered. The maître d', a girl who I knew only as Gillian, looked up with a confused look on her face. She glanced down at the reservation book and ran her finger down the list of names.

"Someone forgot to write in your reservation for today, Cate. Give me a minute and I'll get a table prepped for you."

"I think you'll find us under Adam's name. Adam Bennett."

"Oh, right. Your third part is here already. I put you in a booth at the back."

Gillian stared at Adam. She looked to be about his age, tall, thin and pretty. She batted her long, fake eyelashes at him. "Right this way."

Marianne Weede looked up as we approached. We met once before, forty-four years earlier when she interviewed me in the presence of my father. At that interview, the detective pressed me to tell her what I knew about Leland and his relationship with Marley. As soon as she realized I wasn't going to give her anything to use against him, she snapped her notebook shut and left our house.

If we met on the street I wouldn't have recognized her. I figured she had ten years on me, but she wore it like twenty. Marianne had aged badly, her arms marked with ulcers, her gray hair so thin I could see her pink scalp underneath. She was morbidly obese, filling most of her side of the bench while her stomach pressed against the edge of the table.

Weede set her menu down on the greasy table. "Hey

Adam, look at you. You're all grown up. I haven't seen you
since you were just a little kid, tagging along behind your dad.
What's all this I hear about you becoming a lawyer?"

"I'm in my last year at school. I won't officially be a lawyer until I pass the Bar this summer."

"Let me guess. Your dad will pull a few strings to get
you a job in the prosecutor's office."

"I'm more interested in defense."

"Why the hell would you want to join the dark side?"
Weede looked around for the waitress who took our drinks
order earlier. Failing to spot her, the retired detective shouted at
the busboy wiping down the table next to us.

"Hey, you. We're waiting here. Can someone bring us
something to drink before we die of thirst already?"

The Hispanic busboy looked up at her, grabbed his tray
with dirty dishes, and made for the kitchen without saying a
word. I wasn't sure if he went to find our waitress or if he was
heading for the border. Weede was scary, even in her old age.
I remembered what she was like in her prime when she sat in
my parents' living room and pummeled me for information.

"This place used to be good," she said. "Gone to hell like
most places around here. Damned illegals, that's the problem.
Lazy bastards. Someone oughta round 'em all up and ship 'em
back where they came from."

The waitress reappeared to take our order. Adam and I
requested iced tea. Weede ordered a Budweiser. Within minutes the waitress reappeared to set our drinks on the table.
Before I finished squeezing the lemon wedge into my glass,
Marianne downed half the contents of her beer. The waitress
pulled out her pad.

"Separate checks or all on one?" she asked.

"One check, please," Adam replied.

Our orders placed, the waitress put the pad back in her

pocket and turned to go. Weede reached out a hand and spun her around.

"Get me another Bud when you bring our sandwiches out." After releasing the waitress, Weede turned back to Adam, picking up the conversation without missing a beat. "You want to free the innocent, do you? I got news for you, kid. They're all guilty. By the time a guy goes through the system and finds himself standing before a judge, it's pretty certain that he's guilty as hell. Especially that bastard, Booker. Jesus, I don't get why you're so hot to help him. He killed his whole family for Christ sake."

When we first connected with Detective Weede, Adam introduced me as "my friend, Cate." Now she looked to me as if wondering for the first time what I was doing there.

"Don't I know you from somewhere?" she asked.

"You probably don't remember," Adam said. "You spoke to Cate as part of your investigation. She's helping me with the project."

"Oh yeah, shit. The babysitter." Weede held me in her hard stare. "You wouldn't talk to me then, but after all this time you're a goddamned expert on the subject of what happened in that house?"

"I told you . . ." I took a deep breath to steady my voice and started again. "I told you at the time that I didn't believe Leland killed his family. I still believe that."

"We had that guy cold. Our case was solid. I've never lost any sleep from putting his black ass behind bars."

"But the evidence was all circumstantial," Adam said. "Isn't it possible that you missed something?"

"Listen, kid. I know you're working on this project for school and all, but you're barking up the wrong tree here."

"Humor me. Walk me through your investigation. What was it that convinced you Leland killed his family?"

"It's always the husband, kid. But aside from that simple fact of life, there was plenty of evidence. For starters, we had a witness swearing Booker confessed to the murders. And then there was the insurance. Six weeks before the murders, your guy took out a policy on his wife and kids that would keep him in Cadillacs for life. But for some mysterious reason, he didn't bother insuring himself. If something happened to him, his wife got zilch, nada, nothing. But when she and the kids died, he hit pay dirt big time. That alone raised a big, fucking red flag."

Adam shook his head. "He claims the insurance company made a mistake. There was a problem with the application. When the policy arrived in the mail, Leland just assumed he was covered with the rest of the family."

"Yeah, right. And you believe him? Come on, kid. He's a murderer. And I've got news for you, killers lie. But to make you feel better, I can tell you we checked that insurance thing out. Booker said his physician never sent the results of his physical to the insurance company. I checked with the doctor myself. Come to find out, Booker never even had a physical, so I was left with Booker's word against the doc's. I ask you, who was I supposed to believe?"

Weede was warming to the subject. She leaned back in her chair and took a bite out of her sandwich. Reaching for her second beer, she paused. "Then there were his fingerprints. They were all over the insecticide and the carton of juice, which, by the way, had enough poison in it to kill a herd of moose."

"It was his own house," said Adam. "His fingerprints would be everywhere. That doesn't prove a thing."

"Okay, kid. You tell me, what makes you sure this guy is innocent?"

"Everyone who was close to the family said Leland

Booker could never have killed his wife, let alone his kids. Now that I know him, I agree. You were a good cop, Marianne, but you moved too fast on this one. You never gave so much as a cursory look at any other suspects. The insurance just doesn't stack up as enough motive to convince me."

Weede pointed her sausage-like finger at Adam. "I'll give you one thing. Maybe, just maybe Booker didn't mean to kill those kids. Something about that didn't sit right with me at the time. But I'm telling you, we got the right guy. You're pissing in the wind here. Your dad filled your head with some story about his childhood and you think you're out to right a wrong. But step back and see this case for what it is. Black man murdered his white wife. Kids ended up dead. End of story. Our justice system works."

"Our justice system?" Adam's laugh cleared the tension that swirled in the air around us. "If Leland had F. Lee Bailey as a lawyer instead of that sorry excuse of a public defender, he would never have been convicted."

"O.J.'s lawyer? Really? Bad example, kid." Weede smiled back at Adam, looking like she won a match point. "Tell you what. Do your homework, and let me know if you turn up anything from my old files. I'm not saying I didn't screw up a case now and then, but this one? I don't think so."

Chapter 9

We were back to our normal schedule. Saturday morning, drinking coffee in my living room. In addition to his computer, Adam brought along the blue binder that we picked up from the County offices. The thick file sat on the floor by his feet.

Adam took a bite of his first muffin. "Tell me about their relationship."

"What do you mean? You have to be more specific than that."

"Last night I was looking through the files and saw the photos . . . the ones with the bruises on Marley's arms." Adam paused, taking a moment to gauge my reaction.

I was glad he didn't reach for the binder to show me.

"Are you talking about the autopsy photos?"

"Are you okay talking about this?"

"You're asking me if I ever saw Leland hit his wife."

"If he did, it's better that I know about it up front. What can you tell me?"

I crossed my arms. "I never saw him hit her. Not once."

"You're ducking the question."

"They had some problems, but all couples do from time to time, right?"

Adam stood up and paced the room. Ever since we met with Marianne Weede, he seemed to be arguing the case for the prosecution.

"Every man's wife doesn't end up murdered."

I glared at Adam, angry that he doubted Leland's innocence.

"Sit down. There's something that I want you to hear."

———————————

On the morning of the big KCC golf tournament, my mother found me sitting on our front step, waiting for Leland to pick me up. I moved over, pushing my packed bag to one side to make room for her.

"You forgot this." She draped my new scarf around my neck

I kept my eyes turned down the street, watching for Leland's white Cadillac.

"It's beautiful, real silk." Mom ran a finger across the material after she tied the knot. "I saw it in the pro shop a few weeks ago and thought how the color would suit you, but it was very expensive and I—"

"Thanks." I untied the knot and draped the scarf over one shoulder like Marley wore hers.

"I still don't understand why you have to sleep over there."

"Because Marley asked me to. The club foxhunt tournament starts tomorrow."

"I know that. Leo put me on double shifts. By the end of the weekend I'll have the corns to prove it. But at least I'll be sleeping in my own bed each night."

I took a deep breath and let it out slowly. We'd been over this before. For some reason my mother didn't want me to stay with the Bookers. I was afraid that if she had more time to think about it, she might pull rank and keep me home. Glancing down the road again, I was glad to see Leland's car heading our way.

"Listen, Mom. You know what these tournaments are like. The Bookers will be up early every morning and out late every night. There's no point in my coming home just to catch a few hours of sleep before going right back. I'll be better off there."

As Leland pulled into the driveway I stood and grabbed my bag. "I've got to go."

She reached up and held my arm. "Your father's worried about you. He thinks you're working too hard."

The morning after graduation, my father had covered the graffiti on our garage door with three coats of white paint. He never spoke about it but I knew the vandalism and the meaning behind it gnawed at his mind. Without telling me directly, he was using my mother to send the message that he wanted me to quit my job. And that was something I would never do.

"I'll be fine. Tell Dad we will watch the Red Sox game together on Monday when I'm back."

Giving her no chance to respond, I ran to the car and slid into the passenger seat next to Leland. Leaning back, I drew a deep breath. The air in the car smelled of Leland's cologne, a musky scent, warm and earthy. As Leland backed the car out of the driveway, my eyes searched the garage door for any trace of the painted words that put my father on edge. After three coats, nothing of the graffiti remained. I had asked my mother not to say anything about the incident to the Bookers and as far as I knew, she had honored my request. I glanced at Leland and caught him looking at me, his eyes moving quickly from my face to the scarf around my neck.

"Is that the scarf Marley gave you for graduation?"

"I love it. She has great taste."

"Um-hmm. She sure does."

He threw the car in gear and we rode in silence for a few minutes. It wasn't like Leland to be so quiet, and I began to wonder if my mother had mentioned the graffiti to him after all. Finally, when I couldn't stand it any longer, I spoke.

"Is something wrong?"

"What?" Leland turned his attention back to me. "No, of course not. My mind was on something else, that's all."

"The tournament?"

"I suppose I should get my head in the game. There's going to be some pressure on me from the crowd."

"I don't really know much about golf," I confessed. "Why is it called a foxhunt?"

"The club pro leads the pack, setting the pace of the game. Everyone else is measured by how well they score in comparison. This is my first foxhunt at KCC. People will be watching closely."

"I'm sure you'll do well," I murmured.

"You're going to be there, right?"

"Marley asked me to bring the children so they can watch you."

Leland looked out the window at the cloudless sky. "Well, Leo Bishop must have connections with the weather gods to produce such a perfect day. Make sure you get a good seat. You know, I'm surprised to hear you don't play. I think you'd like it."

I didn't respond. He wouldn't understand how tight my finances were. Golf lessons were pretty low on my list of priorities. Not to mention there was no way my father could afford a club membership. Though the lifestyle that accompanied the sport certainly appealed to me.

Leland dropped me at the shop where Marley waited for me to pick up the children. We sat in beach chairs by the first tee, waiting for the event to begin. The sun occupied a cloudless sky, the temperature was an ideal seventy-two degrees. A light sea breeze chased the mosquitos away from the course. Before long, Leland appeared with the other men in his foursome. He stood with his legs apart, head down, hands wrapped around his club, preparing to drive his ball down the fairway. The other golfers stood respectfully to one side while Leland shifted his weight. Robin and Lissa, well versed in golf etiquette, sat stone still.

When his club finally struck the ball, the children and I exhaled as one. Based on the reaction around me, I assumed Leland hit straight and far. Leo Bishop grunted his approval.

Leland glanced in our direction, briefly locking eyes with me before turning to Leo with a nod. Robin tugged on my shirt and I looked down at her smiling face.

"Daddy saw me. Did you see? He winked right at me."

I was pretty sure the wink was meant for me, but I stroked her hair, allowing Robin her moment of joy. Lissa shushed her sister as Leo stepped up to the tee and studied his ball. We remained in our chairs until the other golfers in Leland's group got into their cart and drove off. The crowd dissipated slowly as some followed while others waited for the next foursome to step up to the tee.

"I'm bored," Robin said. "How long do we have to stay here?"

"Your mother only said she wanted you to watch your dad hit the first ball. But now that he's moved on I think we can leave. We just have to drop the chairs at the house, and then we can go to Gordon's for an ice cream."

"But how are we going to get there?" Lissa asked.

I pulled the keys to Marley's Mustang out of my pocket and dangled them in front of her. "After the tournament is over, your parents are going to stay here for the banquet. They won't be coming home until late. Your mom gave me her car for the day."

I drove carefully, awed by the power of the engine under

my control. When we got to the house, we grabbed the chairs and carried them into the garage. After she set hers against the wall, Lissa turned around to leave. I sensed her freeze and looked up to follow her gaze. Robin's scream pierced the air when she saw the boy.

Cowering behind a pile of cartons crouched the grungiest child I had ever seen. From his bare feet to the fringe of his cut-off shorts he was covered with slime. His arms were brown with muck and his shaggy hair fell over his eyes. He cradled something in the front of his T-shirt that he gripped with a tight fist.

"Close the door," he yelled. "Quick!"

Having determined that there was nothing to fear from this small creature, I pulled Robin to me and covered her mouth with my hand to stop the screaming. "What are you doing here?"

"What do you think? I'm hiding from that retard. Are you going to close the fuckin' door or not?"

"There's nobody out there."

"Ha! I knew it. That dumb bastard couldn't catch crabs in a whorehouse."

"Hey, watch your mouth in front of the girls." I let go of Robin, who stepped behind me.

Throwing me a challenging look, the boy bent down and released the contents of his dirty shirt into an empty bucket. He picked up the pail and thrust out his chest. Robin's fascination for this wild creature overcame her fright and she peered around to watch.

"Who are you?" I asked.

"Kenny Mazza." Lissa, quiet until now answered before the boy had a chance. "He goes to my school."

I wasn't particularly surprised to hear he was a Mazza, but I was shocked to learn that Kenny was young enough to be in Lissa's school. Looking into his eyes I saw an edge that comes with more experience than any ten-year-old should have. Though he was a scrawny kid, I would have judged him to be at least twelve.

"Okay, Kenny. What's in the bucket?"

"What do you think? Golf balls. The lady in the shop gives me ten cents each. Cash money."

Despite my desire to give the boy a hard time, I couldn't help smiling. He wiped his runny nose with his free hand and stood with his feet spread slightly apart, defiantly glaring at me. I was surprised to hear how much Marley paid for the recovered balls, but I now understood why someone had been chasing him. With the tournament in full swing, Leo wouldn't want anyone, especially a swamp rat like this kid, out on the course. Henry must have spotted Kenny hanging around the ponds and chased him away.

"Don't worry, I'm not going to touch those disgusting balls of yours," I said.

He snickered in a dirty sort of way. "I'd like to see you try."

"Was it Henry who chased you?" I asked.

"Yeah, the fuckin' retard."

"I'm not going to warn you again about your language."

"What? Since when is 'retard' a swear word?"

He shook his head like I was an idiot, then shifted the bucket into his other hand and walked past us, out the door and onto the driveway.

"Hey, where do you think you're going with our bucket?" Lissa said.

"I'll bring your crappy old pail back later."

He listed to one side as he walked off with his treasure, and I wondered how far he had to go.

Lissa turned to me, the expression on her face clear. She expected me to stop him from running off.

I called out to him. "Hey, Kenny!"

He stopped dead in his tracks.

"We are going to Gordon's for ice cream. If you clean yourself off and get back with the Booker's bucket before we leave, you can come with us."

When he glanced over his shoulder, I caught a childish glimmer of greed in his eyes.

"Who's buyin'?"

"I am."

"Fuckin' A! Wait for me."

Before I could correct him again, he was gone.

Lissa sighed and gave me a disappointing frown. "We'll never see our bucket again."

"Sometimes you have to take a flier and give people a chance to do the right thing," I replied. "Maybe Kenny will surprise us. Let's wait and see what happens."

I didn't expect Lissa or Robin to understand. The Mazza family was infamous in Keene. Everyone knew they were responsible for most of the petty crimes in the neighborhood, even if they were too crafty to ever be caught. My mother called the Mazzas white trash. Rumor had it that there was more than a touch of incest in the clan, and they dominated the town's welfare roles. From the look of things, Kenny was well on his way to fitting the mold. But I thought I saw something redeemable beneath his crusty exterior. He reminded me of a stray mutt in desperate need of a new home.

Robin tugged on my shirt. "How long do we have to wait?"

"We'll give him an hour," I said. "If he's not back by then, we'll go without him."

I ended up driving the girls to the market without

Kenny. When we arrived at Gordon's, we found the boy sitting on a bench outside. He looked like he had hosed himself off. His hair was slicked down to his scalp and his T-shirt and shorts clung to his skinny body. His face and arms were clean, revealing some nasty bruises obscured by the mud that covered him earlier.

"About time you showed up." He held the bucket out to Robin. "I'm sorry if I scared you."

She accepted the pail along with the apology, but when she looked down and discovered the handle was broken, she glared at him. Taking the bucket from her, I threw it into the back of the car then led the way to the store. Lissa and Robin passed through the door while I held it open. Kenny hung back, peering up at me from under his shaggy, wet bangs.

"Do you want some ice cream or don't you?" I asked.

"I'll wait here. Get me a chocolate cone. Double dip with sprinkles."

"Suit yourself." The bell on the door sounded as I let it close behind me.

"Haven't seen you for a while," Jack said. "You missed a great party. I was hoping to see you there."

"I told you I was busy."

"Doing what?"

"Working."

Jack nodded like he saw my excuse for what it was. With a little shrug that told me he didn't care one way or the other, he turned to Robin. "What can I get for you, princess?"

"Ice cream! And one for Kenny too, please."

I pointed through the glass door. "That's Kenny outside."

The boy stood back a few paces from the building. He was partially hidden by Marley's car.

"I know who he is. He's that Mazza kid. I'd watch myself around him if I were you."

"He's just a boy," I snapped. "I explained to the girls
that Kenny may surprise them if they give him the benefit of
the doubt."

"Yeah, well, he's not going to get the benefit of the doubt
around here. Old man Gordon caught the kid stealing a bag of
potato chips a while back. Put the fear of God into him before
he banned him from coming into the store again."

That explained why Kenny was waiting outside.
Wondering if I'd made a mistake by allowing the girls to asso-
ciate with the little criminal, I paid for the ice cream, thanked
Jack, and left.

We sat outside at the picnic table in front of the store.
Robin finished hers first, taking big bites and popping the last
bit into her mouth. Lissa kept her eyes on Kenny while she
lapped her ice cream like a kitten. Kenny took his time, lick-
ing the sprinkles first and then twirling the cone, catching the
drips with his tongue as the ice cream melted. By the time he
was finished, his chin and arms were covered in chocolate.
Thinking of the Mustang's leather seats, I didn't offer the boy a
ride home. I loaded the girls into the car and we parted ways.
Kenny walked toward home, kicking a stone in the road with
the toe of his torn sneakers. He looked up and smiled, waving
to the three of us as I drove away.

Chapter 10

The New Hampshire sun sets early in November. I reached over to turn on the lamp next to my living room couch. Adam took my lead and hit the switch of its mate on his side.

"I seem to have lost all track of time," I apologized. "You should have stopped me before I drifted away from the main thread of the story. I don't know how I got off on a tangent about Kenny Mazza. He had nothing to do with Leland and Marley. Now the day is over and I never got around to telling you about their fight."

Throughout the afternoon Adam paid close attention as I told him about that day Kenny appeared at the Bookers' house. Perhaps I was encouraged by his interest. Or maybe I couldn't talk about that summer without bringing Kenny into the story. Either way, the afternoon slipped by and I still hadn't answered Adam's question about Leland and Marley. The funny thing was, Adam didn't seem to mind.

"It sounds to me like you had a special interest in that kid."

"Yes, I suppose I did. There was something about Kenny . . ."

"I've got plenty of time if you want to talk some more."

The prospect lifted my spirits. I didn't get much company, and the opportunity to share a meal with someone appealed to me.

"Only if you stay for supper. I wasn't planning anything fancy, but there's plenty for both of us."

Adam accepted my invitation. While he called to let his father know he was staying for dinner at my place, I put the water on to boil. As the linguini cooked, I sliced a pint of fresh mushrooms, threw them into a sauté pan and added a pat of butter together with a heavy dash of red wine. When the excess fluid cooked away, I stirred in a can of my homemade marinara sauce. Grabbing a cold Chardonnay from the fridge, I pointed to the drawer where I kept the corkscrew. Passing the bottle to Adam, I asked him to pour us each a glass. Fifteen minutes later we faced each other across plates piled high with pasta.

"This is delicious."

There was a dab of tomato sauce on Adam's chin. I passed him a napkin and indicated where he should wipe.

"A toast." Adam raise his glass of wine. "Here's to our legal system. You've got to admit, it can be a thing of beauty."

I hesitated a beat before I touched my glass to his. The cold wine slipped down my throat. It did nothing to warm the chill in my bones.

"I've been meaning to ask you about Leland," I said. "How is he?"

Adam gave me a searching glance and turned back to his dinner. "Not even his relatives come to visit. You probably wouldn't recognize him. He's aged beyond his years. But what else would you expect, right? He's been in in the NH State Prison in Concord a long time. His hair is completely gray and he has a persistent cough."

Nodding, I tried to picture an older version of Leland. I decided not to think about it. I set the glass of wine down and wound some linguini around my fork.

"Smoker's cough. He smoked Marlboros."

"You remember his brand?"

"Marley's too. One night after the girls went to bed I pinched a cigarette from the box on their coffee table. My first."

The memory came back to me. My heart pounding, my hands shaking as I removed a Marlboro from the silver box. Fumbling with the lighter, I took a deep drag and nearly died choking. After that I merely sipped and puffed, concentrating on how to hold the cigarette between my fingers. In no time I mastered the look I was after. Ring finger and pinky bent slightly down, not quite touching my thumb in the Boy Scout salute. The way Marley smoked.

"What are you smiling about?" Adam asked.

"Just remembering that first cigarette. I loved smoking, really loved it. But after my husband died of lung cancer . . . I've been trying to quit ever since. And for the most part I stay away from them. Problem is, there isn't a day goes by I don't crave one. Just talking about it now makes me want to run out and buy a pack."

Adam laughed and shook his head. "No way. I'm not letting you leave now. Dinner was great, but you promised to tell me about the problems between Leland and Marley. Something happened between them the weekend of the tournament, didn't it?"

I nodded, accepting his invitation to continue the story.

"I had trouble falling asleep at their house. It was the first time I remember sleeping anywhere other than in my own bed. Have you ever noticed the sounds a house makes at night? You never pay attention until the lights are off and everyone is asleep. Anyway, I was still awake when Leland and Marley come home from the club. It was late, I'm guessing around 2:00 a.m. The guest room was down the hall from theirs, but they were loud—more than a little drunk. I had no trouble hearing when they came upstairs.

"Leland was yelling at Marley, saying that he received another call from a bill collector that day. Their credit cards were maxed out, and he had no idea what Marley spent all that money on. Then, much to my chagrin, he brought up that expensive scarf she gave me for graduation. He warned her that they were overextended, and that he didn't know where the next month's rent was going to come from. Everything he said came as a surprise to me. I had no idea. In fact, I was under the impression that they were rich. He was really yelling, telling her that moving to Keene was their chance to start over and she was going to ruin everything for them. He warned her that he wouldn't stand for it anymore. Then Marley said something that I didn't quite get. Something about getting more money from Leo. Leland only shouted louder and then I guess he grabbed her because Marley started to whine, begging him to let her go. I didn't know what to do. I thought if I called out, pretended that I just woke up, whatever was going on in there would stop. Then I heard a crash, something fell, and Marley started to giggle. Pretty soon it was obvious what they were doing. I buried my head under my pillow and eventually, long after they stopped making love, I fell asleep."

Adam looked at me with his lips pressed tightly together. "They had money problems?"

"Big time. Marley was out of control. And apparently the same thing happened when they lived in Atlanta. Leland was furious. They were buried in debt and he couldn't figure out how to get out from under. Why are you looking at me like that?"

"I'm thinking about the insurance money. Was the problem serious enough for him to—"

"I don't know. But this is exactly why I never told anyone. They would jump to the same conclusion you just did. Not to mention that the following day I saw bruises on Marley's arms. I feared if anyone learned Leland was angry enough to hurt her that night, it would count against him at the trial."

I watched Adam, gauging his reaction. He nodded

knowingly, like he agreed with my decision to keep things to myself. I wondered if Adam would verify the incident with Leland. If he did, I knew Leland would either confirm what I said, or he would confess that he was too drunk that night to remember anything. Either way, Leland would tell Adam that the part about their money troubles was true. I was happy to know Adam's trust in me was growing, and I suspected that whatever I told him in the future, he wouldn't challenge my version of events.

A loud bang interrupted our conversation. I lifted my head, but before I could guess who would come knocking at this time of night, a familiar voice reached me from the other side of the door.

"Cate! Open up. It's friggin' cold out here."

The slur of his words gave him away. I found Jack slouched against the door frame. His face flushed, eyes half-closed. Despite the bitter wind his coat was open. When he saw Adam standing behind me, Jack pushed back from the wall and straightened up in an attempt to mask his condition.

"Oh, you have company." He blinked twice, trying to focus on Adam's astonished face.

I grabbed Jack by the sleeve of his coat and pulled him into the foyer. "Come in before you freeze to death."

He draped an arm around my shoulder and grinned at Adam.

"You must be Cate's mystery student. Something about you looks familiar. Have we met before?"

I spoke before Adam had a chance to answer. "Doubtful. Adam, I'd like to introduce you to my friend, Jack. He works for another law firm in town."

Jack leaned against me. He squinted at Adam, trying to focus. My mind raced, thinking of ways to get rid of him as quickly as possible.

"I know I've seen you before. Never forget a face. Oh well, it will come to me eventually. So tell me Adam, what are you doing here?"

"Cate's helping me with a project for law school. I'm looking into a murder trial that took place here a long time ago."

"Ha! I knew she was up to something. This is about those Bookers, right?" He stole a quick glance at me over the top of his glasses, looking for confirmation. I leaned away from the stench of his breath.

Turning back to Adam, Jack said, "I'll bet Cate told you all about them. How cute those kids were. And the wife, man what a knockout! Damned shame that bastard went and killed them."

"Did you know the family?" Adam asked.

"Oh, I knew them all right."

I looked at Adam and shook my head as I gave Jack a not-too-gentle push in the direction of the living room. "Wait in there while I get my keys. I'm going to take you home so you can sleep this off. You're in no condition to drive."

Jack dropped onto the couch and began snoring within minutes.

Adam stood staring at him for a few moments. "This is the same Jack Burquest who was your high school football star? What happened to him?"

"Life, I guess. This isn't the first time he's turned up at my house too drunk to know where he is and I dare say it won't be the last. I don't know why I put up with him. I try to be understanding. On top of some trouble at work, he's going through a nasty divorce. But really, there's no excuse."

"I thought you said he didn't know the Bookers."

"He didn't. Not well, anyway. Jack worked at the corner store where I sometimes took the kids for ice cream. It would be a waste of time speaking with him. I'm just sorry he ruined our evening like this."

"No problem. We were pretty much finished for the day anyway."

"Will you be coming by next week?"

"Definitely. There's a lot more to cover."

After Adam left I considered leaving Jack on my living room couch for the night. I stood and watched him for a few minutes—the stained clothes, the unshaven face. Adam's words repeated in my head. "What happened to him?" Indeed, what happened to the two of us, I thought. Deciding to let Jack stay, I covered him with a blanket and went upstairs. I lay awake in my own bed, listening to the silence. I reflected on Jack's statement about Leland killing his family, and wondered at how easily he could lie. There was a limit to how much more of Jack's behavior I could take. True, our shared history counted for something, but my loyalty was wearing thin. I knew that sooner or later I was going to have to do something about him.

Chapter 11

Henry sat riveted in front of his television while I prepared Thanksgiving dinner. Much to my annoyance, he kept the volume cranked up high to cover the noise from his squawking parakeet. Between peeling the sweet potatoes and stuffing the turkey I peered into the living room to see Henry, dressed in his flannel shirt, enjoying the Macy's parade. His mouth slightly ajar, he watched as Snoopy flew above the buildings on 34th Street. I felt a pang of tenderness for the old man, and wished life could be as simple as Henry believed it to be. No wonder Lissa loved him. He was little more than a child himself.

Later, over dinner Henry rattled on about Santa Claus riding into town on the float at the end of the parade. I envied him his happiness. More and more I felt weighed down by dark thoughts of Leland Booker, wasting away in prison. I wondered what the past forty-four Thanksgivings had been like for Leland. Did he think of his family every day or only on the holidays? Did he ever think of me? I had a sudden urge to talk with Henry about Lissa and Robin, but something held me back. In all the years since the murders, Henry never once mentioned the Bookers. Maybe it made him sad to think about them. Thinking of them caused me pain too. If only I could put them out my head.

Jack told me I was a saint, cooking for Henry this Thanksgiving. He gave me too much credit. My sister, Nancy invited me to join her family for the day. While I would have loved to see my nephew, Ben, I didn't relish the thought of spending all that time with her husband and in-laws. On the other hand, since Arnie died, the holidays were the most difficult time for me. Cooking dinner for Henry seemed like the perfect solution. Going to his house instead of inviting him to mine allowed me to take my leave after the leftovers were put away and the dishes were loaded in the dishwasher.

After dinner, Henry thanked me in his child-like way as I wrapped my old silk scarf around my neck and tugged on my gloves. "Tank you Cate. Everything was dee-licious."

On my way home, snow flurries danced in the air while wisps of snow scuttled across the road. I couldn't miss seeing the three-ring binder on the front porch, the blue cover standing out against the white drifts of snow. Taped to the cover was an envelope with my name written in Adam's tight scrawl. Bringing the binder into the house, I removed the single sheet of paper from the envelope and read the note.

Sorry I missed u. At Dad's 4 turkey day. Will stop by tomorrow. Slammed with work @ school. Here is Weede's file. Look 4 prosecutorial missteps. Thx. Adam

PS - suggest u skip coroner's report!

His handwriting was barely legible. I reflected a moment on his generation and how computers crippled their penmanship not to mention the shorthand that crept into their writing. After rereading the last line, I folded the paper and stuffed it back into the envelope. Picking up the binder, I turned back the cover. Catching a loose sheet of paper before it hit the ground, I saw it was a list titled "Reasons for Wrongful Conviction."

Marianne Weede's binder was four inches thick. Flipping through the pages I noticed Weede filed everything in chronological order of her investigation. The first section dealt with Leland's arrest by the Keene police officers, followed by his transfer to the county sheriff's department. Weede added additional fuel for the prosecution's fire as she went. There were witness interview reports including my meager contribution, copies of insurance policies, and the damning statement from the drunk who heard Leland "confess" when they shared a cell in the Keene city jail. A large section of the file was allocated to physical evidence and Forensics results. Taking Adam's advice, I skipped the coroner's report.

Weede was certainly organized, but because of her filing method I found it impossible to think about the evidence in terms of Adam's criteria. My mind started to turn over a more useful system. I snapped the book closed and carried everything into my office.

I stared at the binder for a while, unsure if I was in the right frame of mind to begin sorting through the material. With a deep sigh, I went to the kitchen and poured myself a generous glass of Chablis. Thus fortified, I returned to the office and snapped on the desk lamp. The light spread across the blue binder, giving it an ominous aura. I turned back the cover and removed the loose sheet of paper that Adam had inserted. Fortunately, it was printed from his computer so I didn't have to decipher his handwriting. Taking a sip of wine, I studied the list.

Eyewitness error

Government misconduct—police and/or prosecution

Mishandled or suppressed evidence

Snitch testimony exchanged for a reduction in sentence

Racial prejudice

Community or political pressure to solve a case

Inadequate legal representation

As I spent my entire career practicing family law, I hadn't seen these legal terms since law school. Adam made it clear that legally challenging the conviction was the way to go. I understood exactly what he was looking for. Using a marker and sticky notes, I wrote EYEWITNESS, GOVERNMENT

MISCONDUCT, EVIDENCE, and so on until I had one yellow slip for every reason on Adam's list.

Next, I removed the coroner's report and turned it face down on the desk. Along with it I set aside an envelope with the words, "Autopsy Photos" written in black ink. It took some time for me to decide how to categorize some of the documents, but two hours later, the papers were organized to my satisfaction. There was a short stack that didn't seem to fall into any of the seven classifications. I wrote OTHER on an eighth sticky note and slapped it on the pile of misfits. Happy with the work I'd done, I picked up the first report from the EVIDENCE pile and began to read.

It was midnight before I fell into bed.

As promised, the next day Adam arrived at my house early in the morning. He looked every inch the city lawyer, cashmere scarf draped over his black overcoat, leather driving gloves on his hands. I noticed the political pin on his lapel and that, together with his two-day beard, struck just the right balance between trendy and scruffy.

"Come in out of the cold. I just put on a fresh pot of coffee."

He stomped his feet and brushed the snow off his coat. "I can't stay long. My mother wants me back home for *her* Thanksgiving dinner. It's crazy, but since my parents' divorce that's the way they plan all the holidays. Double-dipping, they call it. And if that wasn't bad enough, Mom's invited a friend with a daughter who just happens to be a first-year law student at Columbia." Adam raised his left eyebrow. "My mother's idea of a blind date."

"I promise not to be offended if you don't eat any of my leftover cranberry bread. Give me your coat and come into the kitchen. There's something I want to show you."

After hanging his coat in the closet, I motioned for him to follow me into the kitchen. Adam took a seat and looked at the stacks of papers on the kitchen table. I pushed them to one side and set two mugs of coffee and a plate of cranberry bread before him.

"What is all this?" Adam cracked his knuckles and frowned at the piles. "It looks like you rearranged the whole file."

"You said it's more important to prove prosecutorial error than to find the real killer. What better way to start than organizing everything from the perspective of a wrongful conviction?"

Adam gave me an approving nod. "Okay, I get it. Tell me what I'm looking at here."

I picked up a forensic report from one of the stacks. Waving it in front of Adam, I said, "Suppressed evidence."

"Suppressed evidence?" Adam looked at me like I was crazy. "Let me see that." He took a moment to scan the first page of a report I spent hours reading the night before. "This is the Forensics report. The prosecuting attorney, Jed Williams, used it to prove Leland's fingerprints were on the Aldicarb and the juice carton. Not exactly suppressed evidence. In fact, Williams hammered Leland with this evidence. The jury bought it hook, line, and sinker."

"But take a look." I took the report from Adam and flipped through the pages stamped County Evidence Control Unit. The first half went into great detail about the items dusted for prints, the method employed, the location of prints on the evidence, and the techniques used to verify the number of points that matched Leland's fingerprints.

"Read this." I pointed to a section on page twenty-five. "In addition to Leland's prints, they lifted several others from both the Aldicarb and the juice carton. Every one of them had at least eleven points but they were marked as unidentified. I looked it up last night. Eleven points is enough for a positive match. If Weede had bothered to run those prints through the FBI's database, she might have found a hit. As far as I can tell, she made no effort to find out who they belonged to. Doesn't that mean she suppressed evidence?"

Adam took back the report and rifled through the pages, forward and backward, until he was satisfied. One corner of his mouth turned up.

"Good work. I didn't catch that stuff about the un-identified prints before. But I hate to disappointment you. Suppressed evidence is defined as something the prosecution had knowledge of but didn't share with the defense. Since Williams used this report in court, then I'm pretty sure it was included with the discovery documents that he sent to the pub-lic defender's office. As you know, that means Leland's lawyer received a copy of this entire report before going to trial. I'll check it out to be sure, but I don't think what you found meets the criteria of suppressed evidence."

"In that case, Leland's lawyer should have raised the issue of the unidentified prints." I snatched the report out of his hands and slapped one of my unused sticky notes on it. "That's inadequate legal representation!" I tipped my head and dared him to challenge me.

Adam smiled. Pulling his cell phone out of his pocket, he opened an app and began typing. "I'll check it out tomorrow." After closing the app, he began reading something else on the screen. I waited impatiently for him to return to our discussion.

"Is that important?" I allowed my irritation to show in my voice. I wasn't about to be put on hold while Adam checked his messages.

"What? Oh no, sorry." He gave his phone a final tap be-fore returning it to his pocket. Where were we? Oh yeah, I was thinking . . . Marianne Weede was supposed to be one of the best detectives in the department. It wasn't her style to ignore evidence like those unidentified fingerprints."

I nodded agreement. After poring through every piece of paper in Weede's murder book, I gained an appreciation for her investigative skills. I'd gone through everything in the files twice. The first read-through earned me nothing more than a familiarization with the various forms and acronyms used by the police. It was on the second pass when I concentrated on the evidence section that I picked up the unidentified prints. But throughout, an overriding sense of Weede's attention to detail came through. Given her normal standard of work, I had a passing thought that perhaps she ignored the mysterious fingerprints on purpose. If so, I could also categorize the report as government misconduct. Reining in my excitement, I decided that was stepping into the realm of guesswork and decided to move on.

Lifting the next group of papers from the evidence pile, I recognized the Burquest Insurance Company letterhead. Upon Marley's death, if Leland hadn't been convicted of her murder, he would have been a rich man. I stared at the policy resting on my knees, knowing there was nothing there that met the definition of suppressed evidence.

"What's that?" Adam asked.

"The insurance policy. I can't put my finger on it, but something bothers me about this."

"I read that document several times." Adam took a sip of his coffee. "It's ninety-nine percent legal jargon. I believe Leland when he says he didn't read the fine print before signing. He insists that he intended to insure the whole family, but in fact he was left off the policy. I checked Leland's bank records and matched the cancelled check to the amount of the company's invoice. The policy was put in place six weeks before the murders, a little too close for anyone to think the timing was a coincidence. Like Marianne Weede said, the prosecution had him cold."

"Okay. . ." I'd come to the same conclusion, but in the back of my mind I couldn't shake the feeling that something was wrong.

"You know," Adam shook his head. "I appreciate how you are approaching this but I have a feeling we won't find what we need in these piles of paper. It's the evidence that's not in there that could give us cause for dismissal."

"What do you mean?"

"These files were used by the prosecution. I'm pretty sure nothing here was suppressed. What you need to find is evidence Marianne Weede knew about, but that she kept out of the official file."

"You're telling me to find a needle in the haystack, except we're not even sure there's a needle to be found."

"Exactly. I never said this was going to be easy. But if Leland isn't guilty, then there has to be a flaw in the prosecutor's case."

Since sitting down, Adam had been eyeing the cranberry bread in the center of the table. I passed the plate to him and he accepted a slice. Washing the first bite down with a slug of coffee, he shoved the rest into his mouth.

"This bread is great."

"A Thanksgiving tradition of mine. I baked extra. You're welcome to take a loaf home to your mother."

"What time is it?" He pulled out his phone and touched the glass. "I've got to run or I'll never hear the end of it from my mother."

"Where are you on getting the racial bias data for me to analyze?"

"Still working on that. Listen, thanks for the cranberry bread. I'll call you later."

He jammed his arm into the sleeve of his coat as he dashed out. Too late, as his car peeled away from the curb I discovered his gloves on the kitchen counter. Ten minutes after he was gone someone knocked on my door. Thinking it was Adam, I grabbed the gloves and opened the door.

Chapter 12

Jack Burquest stood in my doorway smiling. In that smile I recognized the teenager I'd known long ago. It took me a minute for me to notice his eyes were free of the bloodshot that became a permanent feature over time. His coat was unbuttoned and underneath I could see his shirt was clean and wrinkle free. In short, he looked better than I'd seen him in years.

"Jack? What are you doing here?"

"Is this a good time? If not, I can come back later."

"Yes. I mean, come in. I just made a fresh pot of coffee."

In the narrow foyer we brushed arms, and as he passed I caught a whiff of dandruff shampoo. There was only a faint smell of alcohol on his breath.

"How was your Thanksgiving?" I busied myself getting a clean mug from the cabinet and pouring his coffee. Cutting a few more slices of cranberry bread, I started to set everything down when I realized the papers from the notebook were still spread out on the table.

"Shitty. Worst Thanksgiving of my life." He stared at the insurance policy. I could read the recognition in his eyes.

"I thought you were with the boys."

"At the last minute my first ex called to tell me the kids decided to join her at a ski resort in Vermont. I ask you, how am I supposed to compete with that? I try to be nice, but that woman is such a bitch. We ended up in a shouting match and in the end, I slammed down the phone. Still, I gotta tell you that after I cooled down, I thought about what she said. It was all true."

He tipped back his mug, draining the last drop of coffee. Sticking a cigarette in his mouth he fished around in his pocket for a lighter. Catching my disapproving frown, he hesitated.

"What? You smoke too."

"Never in the house. Besides that, you know I'm trying to quit."

"Seriously? You're going to make me stand outside in this weather? It's like ten degrees out there."

"Just one." I refilled his mug, pausing to open a window before rejoining him at the table. His hand shook as he raised the lighter. I took it from him and held the flame to the tip of the cigarette while he drew the smoke into his lungs. I breathed deeply, savoring the secondhand smoke. Shaking my head, I returned the lighter to Jack's trembling hand and sat down.

"Why didn't you call when you learned the boys were going skiing? You could have joined me for dinner at Henry's."

"Yeah, Henry." Jack watched the smoke rise from his cigarette. "He gives me the creeps. I don't get why you bother with him."

I shrugged. "He was always good with the Booker children at a time when most people weren't. Except for you, of course. The way you treated the girls counts for something in my book."

A thin smile touched his lips.

"They were cute, sure, but being nice to those kids was just something I did to worm my way into your heart."

"I don't believe that for one minute."

He kept speaking as if he didn't hear me.

"And your friend Henry, well, he was only interested in those girls because he's a sick bastard. Even their mother knew that."

Despite all the innuendo I'd heard regarding Henry's fondness for children, I never saw any evidence to support the ugly rumors. I followed Jack's gaze to the table and made a move to gather the insurance papers together.

"This stuff is for that Bennett kid's project, isn't it?"

"That Bennett kid's name is Adam."

"Why are you looking at the insurance policy from my old man's agency?"

"Case evidence. It was in the file."

I finished putting everything back into the blue binder and set it on the counter. Jack grew quiet. He stared into space while the smoke from his cigarette wavered in the breeze from the window.

"What did you end up doing for dinner yesterday?"

"I drank straight from the bottle until I passed out."

"Oh, Jack . . ." I looked at him, torn between pity and disgust for what he was doing with his life.

Jack's eyes opened wide. I got the feeling he read my thoughts. "Don't pity me. I can stand a lot, but not that. Not from you. Over the years we've had our ups and downs, you and I. But you've always been straight with me. That's more than I can say for my two ex-wives. They hate my guts, you know. Funny thing is, I still love them in a way. They would never believe that, but I swear I do."

"I don't doubt it. The problem is . . ." I paused, realizing too late that I didn't want to hurt him with more of the truth.

He went ahead and finished my sentence. "The problem is I love booze more than them. That's it in a nutshell."

"No one can change that but you."

"Yeah, that's what everybody says. And I try. I swear I do. Still, as soon as I got my head out of the toilet yesterday, I decided to drive to Gordon's Market to buy another bottle. Half way there I had an epiphany. I passed this crazy-ass church, you know the kind you see in strip malls where they put crap on a board outside like Jesus loves you. Anyway, the sign yesterday said "AA Meeting Come Join Us." So I did. Just like that, I pulled into the parking lot and walked right in."

"How was it?"

"Weird, but you know, good. Yeah, it was good to hear that other people go through the same shit I do. I went back this morning, and when the meeting was over I didn't feel like going home. Well . . . to be honest I was afraid to go home. Afraid I couldn't get through the day without a drink. When I tried to think of someplace else to go, I realized you're the only person I know who wouldn't turn me away." Jack shrugged.

After all these years, I knew Jack well. We'd been here before. Whenever Jack hit bottom, he came running to me. That said something, but I wasn't anxious to dwell on what it was.

"I'm flattered that you know you can trust me that way."

"Who else?" He reached across the table and placed his hand on mine. It took every ounce of my control to keep from jerking it away.

"Well, I'm glad you think of me as a friend."

"Uh-oh, you said the 'F' word." He drew his hand back and slurped more coffee. "We're back to that, are we?"

"Look, Jack. There's no point in rehashing the past."

"Like you're doing with this Bennett kid? What is it with you and that Booker family? It's not healthy, you obsessing about those people. You gotta let it go."

"I can't. You know as well as I do that Leland didn't kill his family."

"Do I?" Jack gave me a sideways glance. He drew a final drag on his cigarette, crushed it on his plate, and slowly released the smoke through his nose. "I hardly knew the guy. I once overheard my father talking business with that son-of-a-bitch at the club. That's it."

My thoughts had been trained on something else entirely, but like the strike of a match, Jack's words ignited a flash of memory. The evidence Adam was looking for was within my grasp. Closing my eyes, the fireworks at the club returned to me, as clear as if they lit the sky yesterday and not more than forty years before.

Chapter 13

With Kenny added to the mix, I found myself caring for three children that summer. On most days the kids splashed in the pool while I sat on a lounge chair and read a book. Kenny either didn't own a bathing suit or couldn't be bothered, but that didn't stop him from getting wet. He showed up barefoot, wearing the same cut-off jeans every day. The only variation in his wardrobe was the dirty T-shirt he stripped off before plunging into the water. Lissa and Robin were much better swimmers than Kenny, but he made up for the difference with a fool's courage. The first time he dove into the deep end of the pool I had to leap in and drag him to safety. After that I changed tactics. Whenever he swallowed too much water, I simply threw him an inner tube. He drank buckets of chlorine that summer, but he never stopped jumping in over his head.

We lunched on sandwiches and Tastykakes while the children guzzled gallons of apple juice. Kenny ate more than both girls combined, but if Marley noticed the increased consumption of food, she never said a word. The boy was careful to time his arrival each morning after Marley's departure, and he was gone before she came home at night. Though she never saw him, Marley must have been aware of the company her children were keeping. The girls spoke about Kenny incessantly. He was like nobody else they knew, and his outrageous behavior entertained us all. I continued to chastise Kenny for his dirty mouth, but Robin's giggles only encouraged him. In time I realized I couldn't change him any more than I could stop the summer from melting away. There was a gentle rhythm to my days, and sometimes I could almost forget I wasn't the mother of these three children, but only the hired help.

As for Kenny's mother, I knew very little. The picture I formed in my mind was hazy. When I asked about her, Kenny evaded my questions with a shrug of his shoulders or a shake of his head. I gathered there was no father, or at least no father that Kenny knew. And if his mother cared where her son spent his days, she certainly didn't show any interest. Kenny frequently appeared with bruises on his arms or legs. He once arrived with a black eye. That day Kenny swore he fell off his bike. Having witnessed his recklessness, I could almost believe him. Almost, but not quite.

On the days I had Marley's car, I brought the kids to Swanzey Lake for a swim in the crystal clear water. There the mountain air filled with the aroma of pine trees worked its magic. A cordon of nylon rope buoyed with Styrofoam floats restricted the children to water no deeper than their waists. The four of us ate our bag lunches on a blanket spread under one of the giant hemlock trees at the edge of the black sand. I gave each of the children a quarter to spend in the snack bar as they desired. Kenny always went for chocolate bars that he shared with the girls. Robin bought trinkets, cheap things that rarely survived the day. Lissa pocketed her coins and put them in her piggy bank after we returned home.

A few weeks into our summer vacation, on the Fourth of July, Billy and Jack found us at the lake. I sat under the trees, hands shielding my eyes from the glare of the sun as I watched the children play in the water. A shadow stretched the length of the blanket as a pair of hairy legs blocked my view.

Looking up, I saw Jack planted in the sand in front of me. "You're in my way. Would you please move?"

"Mind if I join you?" he asked.

I couldn't help but notice his toned body. He was shirtless, exposing a newly minted tattoo on his tanned forearm. Semper Fi. Billy appeared by his side and raked me with a leering smile.

"Man," Billy whistled softly. "Who would have guessed you were hiding those under your school clothes."

Pulling my T-shirt over my bathing suit, I rolled my eyes in what I hoped he interpreted as pure disgust before I turned to Jack.

"Actually, I do mind. Can't you see I'm working?" I kept my eyes fixed on the children, hoping Jack would get the message and leave me alone.

"Working?" Jack stepped aside and glanced over his shoulder. Behind him I saw the children emerge from the lake. Kenny was in the lead as the three trudged through the soft sand.

"No way," Billy said. "You still work for those Bookers?"

Out of the corner of my eye I saw Robin tag Kenny, then charge past him on her way toward me. Kenny picked up the pace, doing his best to catch up, but Robin reached my blanket before he did. Breathless with laughter, she threw herself down next to me.

Billy shook his head. "Let's go, man. I don't want to swim in this water after they've been in it."

"Give it a rest, Bill," Jack said.

Kenny arrived moments behind Robin. He bent over, bracing his hands against his bent knees while he caught his breath. Both Billy and Jack turned to look at him.

"Shit, she's picked up a Mazza too," Billy said with a sneer.

Kenny glanced up from under his dripping hair. There was an edge to his stare that made me more than a little nervous.

"What's it to you?" Kenny said.

"Nothing, kid. In fact, I was thinking of dropping by your place to visit your mother tonight. Let me see . . ." He shoved his hand into the pocket of his shorts and pulled out a few coins. "This should be enough for a quickie, right?"

Kenny stood rigid, his fists clenched, his cheeks flushed red in anger. Lissa, last to arrive, stood next to me with a look of confusion on her face.

I looked up at Billy, a warning note in my voice when I said, "What kind of a thing is that to say? Apologize to Kenny or I'll—"

Before I could finish my sentence, Kenny tore into Billy like a barracuda. The impact of the small boy was barely enough to push Billy back a few paces, but the grin was momentarily wiped from his face. Grabbing Kenny by the hair, Billy held him at arms' length. Kenny's arms swung wildly, slicing through the air, his whole body twisting in an attempt to break free. Billy laughed so hard he could barely get the words out.

"Will you look at this?" he called to Jack. "This little shit thinks he can—"

Billy's laughter was cut short by a horrible moan that escaped from the back of his throat. A contorted grimace of pain transformed his face as he clutched his groin with both hands and dropped to his knees. Kenny took one step back and looked down, gloating.

"What did you do to him?" Jack asked.

"I kicked him in the balls, what do 'ya think?" Pride leaked out of every pore of Kenny's body.

I never thought to correct his language. I was trying too hard not to laugh.

———————————————

Back at the house, Robin climbed on my lap, leaning

her head against my breast before closing her eyes. Lissa slid closer on the couch to snuggle. Baby shampoo and Noxzema. I wrapped an arm around Lissa's shoulder and gave her a squeeze. Her skin radiated the warmth of the sun. Looking up, I caught Leland standing in the doorway. I wondered how long he had been holding me in his gaze.

"How was your day?" He was dressed for the barbecue at the club in a navy blazer and dress pants. His pastel blue shirt was open at the neck, no tie. I was about to answer his question when Robin piped up.

"We went to the lake," she said. "And Cate helped us build a sand castle."

"You're their hero," Leland teased me. Or maybe he was being serious. I couldn't tell which.

"Wait until you hear what Kenny did, Daddy." Robin sat up straight, infused with renewed energy. "He got in a fight with Billy."

Leland grinned. "Who won?"

Robin exploded into giggles. "Billy was winning at first but then Kenny kicked him in the balls. You should have heard Billy scream."

"Cate," Marley's voice carried from the kitchen.

I heard a definite something in her tone. A trace of tungsten steel that wiped the smiles from all our faces. When she stepped into the living room, there was a crease between her carefully plucked eyebrows.

"Come upstairs. We need to find you something to wear this evening. You can't very well show up at the club dressed in those jeans."

I glanced down at my best Levi's and realized I should have chosen something a bit dressier for the occasion. Sliding Robin off my lap, I stood. The child crossed the room and climbed next to her father. Lissa lay down, curled on the warm leather where I had been sitting. I followed Marley up the stairs to her bedroom.

"I heard Robin talking about Kenny," Marley said as she pulled clothes from her closet. "If I'm not mistaken, he's the child who hunts for lost balls on the course. But the other boy . . . is that the same Billy you ran into at Gordon's a few weeks back?"

Marley pulled a blue skirt and a white blouse from a hanger and held them up together. With a shake of her head she tossed them on the bed, returning to the closet as she searched for something different.

"His name is Billy Reynolds."

"Shameful, a young man picking on a small boy like that. What did he say exactly to cause Kenny to kick . . . um, to hurt him?"

"Billy was talking about Kenny's mother and—"

"I don't need to hear the details." After dismissing a number of outfits, she settled on a pair of white slacks and a navy-blue halter-top. She held the outfit against me. "Here, let's see how these fit. What size shoes do you wear?"

"Eight."

"Hmm, I've got a pair of white sandals that might work."

While she sorted through her collection of shoes, I slipped into the bathroom. When I finished getting dressed, I stood before the full-length mirror on the back of the door. I couldn't believe my own image. Everything fit perfectly.

"That'll work just fine." Marley nodded approval. "Now sit here and let's see what we can do with your hair."

I took the seat she indicated in front of her dressing table. While she released my hair from the rubber band at the back of my neck, she resumed the conversation. "I've heard mention of Kenny's family. You know, we southerners judge a person by their family's reputation."

Bracing myself, I waited for the inevitable. If Marley knew about the Mazzas, she certainly wouldn't want her girls to have anything to do with Kenny. She had brushed my hair to a silky shine and pulled it into a French twist. Freeing a few strands of hair from the pins, she coiled them around her finger and let them fall free around my face. The effect was amazing. She bent over my shoulder and looked at my reflection in the mirror.

"It's a pity. I have some sympathy for his situation at home." Marley paused, seemingly lost in her own thoughts as she stared vacantly into space. She frowned, as if recalling an unpleasant memory, but a second later her eyes met mine and her expression hardened. The trace of steel in her voice returned. I inhaled, waiting for the hammer to fall. "God knows that boy needs a break. And I know the girls are very attached to Kenny but I will not tolerate my children speaking like trailer trash. If you can't stress the importance of that to the child, then he won't be welcome here. Do you understand?"

Nodding, I broke eye contact. Marley placed her hands on my shoulders. "You are a beautiful young lady. That tan brings out the gold flecks in your eyes. A little lip gloss and the boys won't be able to take their eyes off of you."

"I will speak to Kenny. I promise."

Marley's southern drawl rolled off her tongue, soft as cream. "That's a good girl. Now, stand up and let me look at you."

Feeling self-conscious, I pushed back the chair and stood for inspection. Her eyes appraised me, running up and down. A slight frown, disapproval of some imperfection she found in me, touched her lips. "Take off that cheap watch. You need a nice piece of jewelry."

"I don't own any."

"I have just the thing for you."

She slid open the drawer of her dressing table and extracted a red box. When she opened the lid, I couldn't resist reaching out to touch the tennis bracelet nestled on a bed of satin. The gold was silky smooth, almost oily to the touch. The diamond-encrusted chain sparkled in the lamplight. I'd never seen her wear this particular piece before and it struck me as strange that she kept her most beautiful bracelet tucked away. I extended my arm and she deftly worked the clasp. Standing back, Marley paused for a moment to admire how it fit. Returning her smile, I followed her downstairs where Leland whistled as we made our entrance.

The crowd at KCC reminded me of the Ascot scene in *My Fair Lady*. Beautiful people dressed beautifully. Everyone posing, making sure they smiled just so, saying all the right things to all the right people. The atmosphere was surreal. I felt the members staring at me as I followed Marley and Leland into the room. Eliza Doolittle in the flesh. Even my own mother, dressed in her waitress uniform, didn't recognize me at first. She carried a tray of champagne flutes, offering me one before she realized who I was.

"Cate, what are you wearing?" She retrieved the champagne from my hand and placed it back on the tray.

"Marley loaned me some clothes. Can't I have a drink? I don't want to stand out."

She looked around, seeing everyone else holding a glass before nodding assent. "Just one, but make it last all night. Wait here and I'll get some apple juice for the girls." Mom leaned close and whispered in my ear, "Have a good time." She turned and disappeared into the crowd.

I took a sip, the bubbles tickling my nose. Looking

around, I saw Marley and Leland had moved to the patio.
They were engaged in conversation with people I didn't know.
Heading in their direction, I towed Robin and Lissa behind
me. The crickets that hid in the woods sang their final evening
song. Out on the golf course, a team of Leo's workers stood
ready to launch fireworks once the rays of the setting sun
disappeared beyond the horizon. The sound of chamber music and the smell of grilled steak reached me, a reminder that
I wasn't at one of my father's barbecues. On those occasions,
Dad passed around hot dogs and beans while the radio blasted
Country Western into the back yard. This was better. Much,
much better.

Marley spoke as I approached. "Ah, Cate, there you are.
Look who's here, Tom and Milly's son, Jack. I believe you know
each other from school."

Looking at the faces of the people before me, I realized
these were Jack's parents. Smiling, I nodded. I was about to
reply when Jack wrapped his arm around my bare shoulder.

"Of course we know each other. Mother, Dad, I'd like to
introduce you to my friend Cate Stokes."

"Friend" was not exactly how I would have put it, but
I wasn't about to correct him in front of everyone. Jack, who
had changed out of his beach clothes, was dressed like all the
other men at the club—open-necked shirt, navy blazer, white
trousers. He looked better than I'd ever seen him, and he
smelled nice too. His eyes took me in, and I could tell he liked
what he saw. He slid his arm down to my elbow and pulled me
to his side.

Milly Burquest nodded absently in my direction before
turning to Marley. "Our Jack has signed up with the Marines.
We're so proud."

Marley returned the comment with a stiff smile, but I
don't think anyone noticed but me. She took the children by

the hand and excused herself, saying Mrs. Bishop would never forgive her if she didn't bring the girls by to say hello before the fireworks began. Mr. Burquest engaged Leland in some business about insurance. While their attention was diverted, I squirmed free of Jack's grip.

Dr. Keating, our family doctor walked up and joined us.

"Well, speak of the devil," Tom Burquest said. "I was just telling Leland here that I'm waiting on your report so I can put his insurance policy into effect."

A frown line creased Dr. Keating's brow. "You should have received that already. Doris sent the paperwork to you last week."

"We received the forms for Marley and the children, but nothing for Leland."

Dr. Keating waved his champagne flute in the air. "No problem. I'll check with Doris on Monday and ask her to make sure you have everything you need." Turning to Leland, he added, "Assuming Tom's agency doesn't drop the ball, you should be insured by the end of the week. Now, has anyone seen Sandra Stokes? I heard she's passing around a tray of steamed clams."

He wandered away, more interested in finding my mother with the steamed clams than in talking business with Tom Burquest. I'd been a patient of Dr. Keating's since I was born, but he hadn't recognized me. Smiling to myself, I tipped my head back and finished the last drop of champagne in my glass. Sensing someone was watching, I looked up to see Leland staring at me. I blushed, perhaps due to the effect of the champagne. Then again, maybe it was something else that brought the color to my cheeks.

Chapter 14

"Marianne Weede lied."

My statement was met with silence, and I wondered for a moment if my cell phone was dead. "Did you hear me Adam? I said Marianne Weede lied."

"Yeah. I'm thinking about what you just said. Are you sure the Witness Interview Report wasn't in the binder?"

"Absolutely certain. When we went to lunch, Weede told us that she interviewed Dr. Keating herself. She said Dr. Keating claimed he never gave Leland a check-up. At the time I thought there was something wrong there but I couldn't put my finger on it. It just hit me. I recall overhearing a conversation between Dr. Keating and Tom Burquest at a 4th of July party at the club. Not only did Leland have that exam, the doctor knew Leland wanted his medical records sent to the insurance company. When I looked for the interview report in Weede's files, it wasn't there. Something's not right."

"Are you suggesting Weede destroyed evidence? Why would she do something like that?"

"I don't know, but if she did throw the report away, do we have a case for suppressed evidence?" I was hoping we finally had something tangible, but I yielded to Adam's familiarity of criminal law.

"We'd have to prove it. And that isn't going to be easy. You told me Dr. Keating died a few years ago. What was the name of that insurance agent, Burquest, right? Give me a minute and I'll see if I can find him." In the background I heard him tapping on his keyboard. "While I'm looking, can you tell me if there was anyone else who heard the conversation at the club?"

"You're wasting your time looking for Tom Burquest. He's also dead. And no, no one else was there when I heard him talking with the doctor."

The lie came easily. I wasn't about to bring Jack into this whole thing. The less Adam crossed paths with Jack, the better. Adam went silent again, but I could still hear him tapping the keyboard. As long as he was searching for Tom Burquest, I threw out another name for him to find. "You might try looking for Doris Keating, the doctor's wife. She was his office manager, the person who sent the report to the insurance company. If she's still around, we can ask her what she remembers."

The tapping ceased as Adam found what he was looking for. "You're right about Burquest. I found his obit. Died five years ago, survived by a wife and son. I'm guessing that's your friend, Jack?"

"Right. I attended the funeral."

"Well, looks like the insurance company folded after he passed away. That makes this another dead end—no pun intended. Let's see now . . . Doris Keating."

He went back to work typing. "Nothing in New Hampshire, but there's a Doris A. Keating, age eighty-six who lives in Venice, Florida. Do you think that might be her?"

"Could be. Do you have a phone number?"

"Yep, right here. If this is the same Doris Keating, the old lady might be a bit more open to speaking with you than me. That is, if she remembers you. At her age, we'll be lucky if she remembers her own name."

"Careful there, kid. I'm no spring chicken either."

"Sorry. You know what I mean."

"And if it's her, what's next?"

"We get her statement on record. If you're right and Doris sent Leland's medical report to the insurance company, then it would seem Weede lied about speaking with Dr. Keating."

He must have heard the excitement in my voice. "Then we have our proof!"

"Don't get your hopes up. If you follow the logical path of this argument, a judge could say it doesn't matter whether Leland intended to insure himself or not. The policy on Marley and the girls was still an incentive for murder. And we don't even know if Weede filed a report after speaking with the doctor. If she didn't, then there's no suppressed evidence." From my end of the phone I could hear Adam crack his knuckles. "On the other hand, if she perjured herself on the stand or destroyed the interview report, that goes to government misconduct. Then we could have something."

A thrill ran down my arms, my pulse kicking up a notch. Until meeting Adam, I didn't realize Leland could be released without proving someone else murdered his family. It never happened that way in the movies, but suddenly the prospect seemed very real. As I was learning, the criminal justice system was full of idiosyncrasies.

"I'll call Doris Keating today. Will I see you on Saturday?"

"Yeah, that would be good. But after this weekend, I'll have to take a break. Exams are coming up and I need the weekends to study. My professor reminded me yesterday that he wants a summary report telling him where I stand with my research about the Booker case. The project runs to the end of April, but I'm supposed to be giving him regular updates."

"Is there anything I can do to help?"

"There is one thing," Adam said.

"What is it?"

"You promised to introduce me to Henry Rusak. Could you set that up for Saturday? I want to include his interview in my summary."

As far as Adam knew, there was no reason for me to refuse his request. I let his question hang for a minute, wracking my brain for a credible excuse to turn him down. Coming up empty, I agreed. Adam was about to meet Henry.

Not only did Doris Keating remember her own name, she remembered me, my parents, the Bookers, and the day Marianne Weede interviewed her husband. I reached her by phone at her beachfront condominium on Florida's west coast.

"Of course I remember you, Cate," she sang out. She sounded like she was happy to hear a familiar voice, an old acquaintance from her hometown. "How is everything in Keene? I hear it is cold up there. I check the paper every day. Today it said you have a chance of snow flurries. It's eighty-three degrees here. No chance of a white Christmas in Venice!"

I heard her laugh at her own joke and wondered if everyone in Florida was as acutely aware of their hometown weather as she was.

"Sounds wonderful, Mrs. Keating."

"Good heavens, call me Doris. What can I do for you, my dear? I'm sure you didn't telephone me long distance just to get the weather report in Florida."

I explained the situation, told her I was helping a student with a project that involved researching the Booker murders. She didn't seem too bothered that I had no obvious reason to be working with a third-year law school student. Without pressing the issue, she said she would be happy to help me. That is, as long as I didn't interfere with her two o'clock bridge game.

"Can you remember if Detective Weede ever spoke with Dr. Keating?" I asked.

"Oh my, yes. We were very busy that day, running behind schedule when all of a sudden, this woman barges in, flashing her badge and insisting on speaking with Richard. I had to reschedule all his appointments for the rest of the day. Wasn't easy. Only so many days in the month, you know, and the children needed their annual vaccinations before school started."

"Are you saying Dr. Keating spoke with her?"

"Of course he did, dear. Richard was too polite to turn her away. Once they got started, he asked me to join them. The detective's questions were mostly about the paperwork regarding Leland's physical, and my Richard—good doctor though he was—could not be bothered with paperwork. He depended on me to take care of all the record keeping." She paused, and I thought I heard her sniffle. Following a loud honking sound, Doris picked up without missing a beat.

"Anyway, I told Detective Weede about Mr. Booker's request to send the medical reports for the whole family to the Burquest agency. A week later, those insurance people claimed they never received Leland's records. Shameful how careless they were. After all, those reports contained confidential information and who knows what desk they were sitting on for the entire world to see. When Tom Burquest—he was the insurance agent, you know—asked me to resend Mr. Booker's records, I took care of it right away. Didn't give it another thought until that detective came in to speak with Richard. That's when I told her what I just told you. Let me say now, I didn't care much for that woman's attitude. I ran a tight ship in that office and I resented her suggestion that I had dropped the ball."

My thoughts were reeling as her clipped words bounced around in my head. Not only could Doris Keating confirm that her husband spoke with Weede, she was present at the interview. In our discussion, the old lady sounded a bit quirky, but

I had no doubt her memory was still firing on all cylinders. I broached the next question with care, knowing everything depended on her answer.

"Do you happen to know if Detective Weede took notes during your discussion? Or if she filed a report of the interview with the Sheriff's Department?"

"You mean that WITREP?" She giggled like a schoolgirl. "That's what she called it. The Witness Interview Report. My, but those detectives love their acronyms. Yes, she stopped at the office the following week and asked me to initial it for her records."

I was stunned into silence. Reaching for the blue binder that sat on the desk in front of me, I flipped through some pages. Every witness interview report in Weede's files was initialed. Weede apparently verified the accuracy of her reports by having witnesses sign them. I'd spent hours reading dozens of her reports, but that small detail never registered with me. Until now.

"Mrs. Keating—"

"Doris, dear."

"Doris, you've been tremendously helpful. I'd like to ask you one last favor. If we arrange for a lawyer to take your statement, would you be willing to speak with him?"

"Certainly, Cate. As long as he can make it on a Friday. Monday, I meet with the quilting ladies, Tuesday is Bingo—"

"Thank you, I'm sure we can accommodate your schedule. I'll be in touch soon."

"Pack your swimming suit when you come, dear. My condo has a lovely pool that you're welcome to use. And if you give me a day or two, I'm sure I can lay my hands on that report."

I paused, hardly believing my own ears.

"You kept a copy of the WITREP?"

"Of course. When Richard sold the practice, I sent his patients' files to the new partnership. But our tax returns and other important documents, well I thought I should hold onto those things. I suppose after all these years I could get rid of them, but I never seem to have the time. I'm quite busy, you know. Now that I'm retired, I wonder how I ever found time to work!"

I smiled, sending a silent word of gratitude to the sweet lady at the other end of the line. Doris ended the conversation, reminding me that she didn't want to keep her bridge club waiting.

Chapter 15

I didn't know Henry Rusak before the army surgeon cut into his brain, but though the injury made Henry what he was, I doubted very much that it changed who he was to begin with. The giant man-child had always been incapable of making decisions. From the day he was born, his mother told him exactly what to do and how to do it. It was easy for him to slip from that existence to the military where I imagine his commanding officer marveled at Henry's ability to follow orders. Shortly after he returned from the war, Henry's mother passed away and Leo Bishop took over. That worked well until a few years ago when Henry was forced to retire. Leo had passed the reins of running the club to his son, and though Henry still retained most of his great physical strength, Leo Jr. couldn't be bothered managing the handicapped veteran. After that Henry seemed at a loss for what to do. He puttered around town on his three-wheeled bicycle, spending time at the park watching the children play. When the police started receiving complaints, they cautioned Henry to stay away from the children. Henry complied. He often shook his head in confusion, asking me to explain why he wasn't allowed to go to the park any longer. I realized Henry needed someone in his life to tell him what to do. He needed me.

From Main Street, Adam turned left on Baker.

"It's just ahead." I pointed to the sign. "Congress Street."

Henry was expecting us. When I spoke to him a few days earlier, I did my best to explain who Adam was, but from the confused look on Henry's face when he answered the door, I gathered that he still didn't understand.

"This is Adam, the student I told you about."

Henry studied Adam. His mouth hung open like he was trying to grasp a memory that dangled out of reach. He tipped his head to one side, trying to shake it loose. Finally, a spark of recognition lit his eyes.

"I remember now," He wagged his head back and forth. "You're big trouble."

Henry's reaction didn't bode well, and I wondered how long Adam's interview would go before Henry decided he didn't want to cooperate. But my job was to get Adam through the door. The rest was up to him.

"I brought you a jar of apple butter." I offered the paper bag to Henry. "May we come in?"

Henry snatched the bag from my hand, turned, and went back into the house. I looked at Adam, shrugged my shoulders, and stepped across the threshold.

The house was still furnished with Mrs. Rusak's things. An overstuffed sofa, sagging like a potbellied pig, stood opposite a fake fireplace. Lace antimacassars protected the arms and backs of the matching upholstered chairs. A yellowed doily covered an old stain on the coffee table and a threadbare path on the Oriental rug ran from the front door to the next room. Henry was nowhere in sight. His caged parakeet started to squawk. I took a few steps over to check and see if he had enough water. The cup was bone dry.

"He's gone into the kitchen," I told Adam. "Have a seat. He'll be back."

Henry soon reappeared, the open jar in his hand, a spoon protruding from his mouth. A drop of brown apple butter dribbled down his chin.

"Yummy."

"Do you think you could get us each a glass of water?" I asked.

"Okey dokey." Henry removed the spoon and returned to the kitchen.

"You have to be a little patient with him, Adam. Sometimes Henry has trouble understanding things. Just go slow, and I'll try to help if he gets stuck on something."

"What's with the apple butter?"

"He gives me the apples from the tree in his backyard and I use his mother's recipe to make apple butter. The first year I brought him a dozen jars which he finished off in a single week. The following fall he gave me two more bushels of apples. By then I'd learned my lesson and started to ration the stuff. This jar will be gone before we leave, but he'll have to wait until I see him next week for more."

Henry walked slowly, eyes focused on the two glasses that he had filled to the brim. The jar of apple butter was tucked under his arm, the spoon back in his mouth. Water sloshed on the table as he set the glasses down. I reached into my purse and pulled out tissues to wipe the spill, then tipped a little water from my glass into the bird's dish. Settling back down on the couch, I passed Henry the tissue and pointed to my chin, indicating that he should wipe his own.

"Adam wants to talk to you about the Bookers," I said.

"Lissa and Robin." Henry's head bobbed up and down. "Lissa was my very best friend."

Adam looked at me, then glanced down at his notes. I could see he was searching for a place to begin. After starting things off, I left him on his own.

"Right," Adam said. "You knew the whole family pretty well from what I understand. You went to their house every week to clean the pool. Cate told me you also did odd jobs for Marley. Right?"

The question seemed to confuse Henry. He knitted his brows and frowned. "You already know that."

"Okay then, I'll get right to the point. I need to hear about the Aldicarb."

"The what?"

"Aldicarb—the insecticide you used to kill the bugs."

Henry nodded. "Spiders. Marley hated spiders. They gave her the shivers."

"Where did you get the Aldicarb?" Adam asked.

Henry wrung his hands. Adam didn't appear to notice the signs of stress in the old man. Maybe he didn't care. In any event, he pressed on.

"The insecticide. Where did you get the spray to kill the spiders?"

"First you fill the bottle with water, then the powder goes in and you hafta mix it real—"

"No, I mean where did you find the box of Aldi . . . the box of powder that you used?"

"In the shed behind the clubhouse. Leo said I hafta put things back where I find them. That way I can find them when I need them again. That's what Leo said."

Henry stole a glance at me. I nodded encouragement.

"If Leo told you to put everything back where it belonged, why did you leave the box of insecticide in the Bookers' garage after you finished spraying?"

"Marley said I might have to spray again if all the spiders didn't die."

"Okay," Adam shook his head. He glanced back at his laptop and consulted his notes before continuing. I sensed this wasn't going as well as he hoped.

"Tell me, Henry. How did you feel about Marley? Did you like her?"

A grin lit the old man's face. He raised his shoulders

around his ears and giggled. "Marley was real pretty, glittery all over. She was always nice to me. That is, until . . ." Henry relaxed his shoulders and hunched over, his chin resting on his chest.

"Until what?" Adam asked.

"Leo said I couldn't go there no more."

"Why?"

Henry's voice dropped. "I dunno."

"Yes, you do Henry," Adam insisted. "You must have done something wrong."

"I didn't do nothing." Henry looked into his lap and shook his head. He reached up to the back of his head and started pulling on a lock of hair. "Lissa was my friend."

"Then why did Leo tell you to stay away from Marley?"

Henry jumped to his feet and paced the room, muttering to himself. I recognized the signs. Placing a reassuring hand on his arm, I tried to stop him from spiraling out of control.

"Please sit down, Henry. He is almost finished, aren't you, Adam?"

"Just a few more questions. And if you don't want to answer any of them, you don't have to."

Henry looked at Adam. The distrust was clear in his eyes, but he nodded once, a slight dip of his massive head.

"After you sprayed for spiders, for some reason that you don't want to talk about, Leo told you to stay away. But then, a few weeks later, you went back to fix a broken window."

"Leo said fix it quick." Henry nodded. "That's what Leo said."

"I was there when Marley phoned Leo," I interrupted. "He told her that Henry was the only person available. But she made it clear that she wanted the pane in the door fixed before Leland came home. When Henry arrived, Marley sent me upstairs with the girls. I started to clean up the mess in the bedroom while she stayed downstairs."

"Are you the one who broke the window, Henry?" Adam asked. "Did you mess up the house to get even with Marley for sending you away?"

Henry's silence filled the room. He glared at Adam with a palpable hatred. Adam was unfazed. He looked away and typed something into his computer. Of course, I knew Henry didn't break into the house all those years ago. I already knew who did. As I was about to remind Adam that Henry probably had a key to the house, he spoke again.

"Last question, Henry. Did you put Aldicarb—the bug spray—in the orange juice?"

Henry's chin dropped back to his chest. When he looked back up, there were tears in his eyes. "Lissa was my very best friend."

———————————

I shivered in the cold, waiting for Adam to start the engine so we could get some heat into the car. Adam stared straight ahead, tapping the keys against the steering wheel. I could see he was frustrated. But his frustration paled compared to the anger that boiled inside me. If I had known what Adam had in mind, I never would have brought him there.

"He's hiding something," Adam said at last. "I'm sure of it."

I snapped back at him. "Oh, come on. You saw what he's like. He became confused. The very idea of Henry killing anyone is absurd."

"No, there's something there . . ."

"He loved those people. You're way off base."

Adam reached into his coat pocket, carefully extracting an object. When I saw he held Henry's water glass with two fingers pressed against the inside, my anger flared.

"What are you doing with that?"

"I assume some of the unidentified prints on the Aldicarb are Henry's. But I want to know if he also handled the juice carton."

I held Adam's penetrating stare. As the weeks went by, I had learned he wasn't exactly the malleable student I first judged him to be. But this was too much. Adam was veering off in a dangerous direction, and I felt I had to protect Henry from an injustice equal to what Leland had suffered.

My words escaped in a hoarse whisper. "Leave Henry alone."

"I'm telling you, there's something going on with that guy. Erika Tripp told me that if I could get his prints, she'd have them tested. If Henry is as innocent as you think he is, then he'll be cleared and I will owe you an apology."

I willed my shoulder muscles to relax, breathing deeply to slow my heartbeat. After all, I knew Henry's prints wouldn't be found on the juice carton. I faced forward and buckled my seat belt, deciding to change the subject.

"Have you been able to arrange for the meeting with Doris Keating?"

"Oh, didn't I tell you? It's all set up for the Friday after Christmas. I've got a few weeks off between semesters, so the timing is perfect. My dad's paying for the trip. He even contacted a lawyer in Venice who agreed to witness Doris's statement. I have a very good feeling about this. It could be the break I've been hoping for."

The break I handed you, I thought. But Adam didn't even think to invite me to the meeting with Doris Keating. Unable to shake my disappointment, I sat in silence as the car pulled away from Henry's house.

"What's wrong? Aren't you excited?" Adam asked.

"Sure," I said. "Excited."

Adam reached into his overcoat and pulled out an envelope. He stole a quick glance in my direction, his face breaking into that irresistible smile of his as he flicked the envelope onto my lap. "Go ahead, open it."

Inside was a travel itinerary, a round trip booked from Manchester to Sarasota. At the top of the page I saw my name on the reservation.

"I hope you don't already have plans for that weekend," he said. "We're staying at a hotel on the beach. Doris specifically asked for you. She said to remind you to bring your bathing suit."

I carefully folded the paper and stuck it back into the envelope. Then, looking straight ahead I reached out and slapped Adam's arm.

"Don't ever mess with me like that again."

Chapter 16

The next time I went to the courthouse, the visitor's parking area was full. I left my car at the far end of the lot. To save time, I popped the trunk and tucked my purse inside before locking up. No point in allowing the security people to root through my things again. In ten, maybe fifteen minutes I'd be in and out with what I'd come for.

Two weeks had passed without a word from Adam, and while he warned me that he would remain cloistered until his exams were over, I didn't realize how much I would miss him. When my cell phone pinged with his message I read it eagerly. "Trial stats at dad's office. Need to check for racial bias. Are you still willing to take a look?"

I responded with a single word. "Yes."

Inside I nodded to the security guys who waved me through without any fuss. As I turned to make my way down the hall, Erika Tripp appeared. The earrings that lined the cuff of her left ear were all silver, a gold cross dangled from her right lobe. Recognition registered on her face when she saw me.

Without any explanation she said, "Last office on the right. I'll take you there."

"How do you know where I'm going?"

"You're here to see the kid's father. He's expecting you."

I followed her down the hall and through the door labeled Computer Crimes. Tripp sat down, picked up a magazine, and held my gaze. There was no warmth in her smile.

Though my business often brought me to the building,

I never had occasion to visit this department. The chair at the front desk was empty. While I stood waiting for someone to appear, my attention wandered to a poster on the wall. A young girl, perhaps six or seven, stared out from the picture. Her stringy blond hair hung over one large brown eye, her other was swollen shut and bruised. A bright red line marked her split lip, and crusty, circular scabs covered the tops of her bare arms. What struck me most was the defiant look in her good eye and the challenging tilt of her chin. The caption at the top of the poster read, "Mommy said she's sorry."

Then I saw her. In the background stood a woman, her thin face a remarkable likeness of the child. She was staring at her daughter, one hand held in the crook of her arm and the other holding a lit cigarette between her two fingers. The small print at the bottom of the poster said, "Child Protection Services—Saving Lives."

I wondered how Erika knew I was there to pick up the trial statistics from Adam's father. Just as I turned to ask her, a young man emerged from one of the back offices. He wore a polo shirt, Cheshire County Justice embroidered on the pocket. His ears protruded from the sides of his head, and he bore bright red acne blemishes on his chin.

"Can I help you?"

"I'm here to see Investigator Bennett," I replied.

"And you are?"

"Cate Stokes. He's expecting me."

"Oh yes, Mrs. Stokes." The young man reached into a desk drawer and extracted a plain, white envelope with my name on it. "The boss was called away to an emergency meeting. I believe you'll find everything you need in here."

From the feel of the envelope he handed me, I could tell there was nothing more than a small lump inside. Tearing open the envelope, I discovered a flash drive, no bigger than my finger.

"I saved the documents in PDF format," the young man said. "If you have any problems accessing the information, you can give me a call and I'll talk you through it."

Obviously, due to my age he thought I was some kind of dinosaur.

"That won't be necessary." I turned, ready to make my exit. Tripp, who was still hanging around, held the door for me.

"Most visitors stuff money in the donation box when they see that poster."

"I left my purse in the car."

"I noticed. Let me buy you a cup of coffee."

"I wasn't planning to stay . . ."

"Won't take long. I want a word with you."

Upstairs, the Sheriff department's employee break room smelled of liverwurst and onions, probably someone's leftover sandwich tossed in the overflowing trash can next to the sink. The Formica tabletop was chipped and stained, the plastic chairs irreparably scratched, presumably from god-knows-what equipment that policemen strap to their bodies. But the coffee was hot and strong, and I accepted the Styrofoam cup that Tripp offered.

She watched me over the rim of her coffee cup. "I saw you staring at that poster. In case you're wondering, the guys in that department pride themselves on doing what they can to help abused kids. Next time you go down there, be sure you bring some change for the box. It'll go a long way to get the geeks cooperation when you need it."

"Okay, thanks." I knew that wasn't the reason I was sitting there. I didn't have to wait long for Tripp to get to the real point of why we were sharing coffee like we were the best of friends.

"What've you got there?"

Before I could stop her, she reached over and took the envelope off the table. I grabbed it back, scowling at her.

"This is none of your business."

A half-smile played at her mouth. "You'd be wise to keep me on your side."

"If you must know, Adam asked me to pick up some data that he wants analyzed."

"Analyzed for what?"

"Racial bias."

Erika snorted. "Good luck with that. Judge Rothenberg sat on the bench for Booker's trial. You're going to waste a lot of effort learning that he was a real straight-shooter. Totally colorblind. Adam is barking up the wrong tree there." She drummed the table with her acrylic nails. Electric pink. Weirdly, they suited her.

"On the other hand," she said, "I think the kid might be on to something with the pervert. Forensics is taking their own sweet time with the prints on that glass, but you never know. Rusak fits the profile."

I looked down at my cup, my self-control stretched to the limit. It was bad enough that Adam suspected Henry of killing the Bookers. Now he had Erika Tripp convinced too.

"Henry's not a pervert," I said between clenched teeth.

"Oh, I don't know about that. Any guy who sneaks around, jerking off outside a woman's window, is a pervert in my book."

"What are you talking about?"

She nodded, a satisfied smirk on her face. "I wondered if you knew about that. Adam tells me you're a real fan of old Henry. I suggest you watch yourself with that guy. Tell me, Mrs. Stokes, what's your interest in all this? I get that Adam's father has had a bee up his ass with the Booker case for years.

When Adam needed a project for school, it made perfect sense that the kid picked this one. But I still can't get a read on your involvement here."

"I knew the family."

"Yeah, so you said." Tripp stared at me, her eyes reptilian cold.

I met her gaze. "And what's your angle, Detective? Why are you interested in Leland Booker?"

"Me? I'm a detective. When something doesn't add up, it's like poking a bear. I get interested. When Adam first started nosing around this case I figured I'd get him a copy of Marianne's murder book as a favor. No big deal. Then, after you guys left, I had nothing else going so I cracked the cover of the original and took a closer look. I saw a few things that didn't feel right. Enough to poke the bear."

"Are you saying you want to get involved?"

"I already am involved. When Adam mentioned Rusak, I told him to get something with the old guy's prints on it. I slapped a fake case number on the evidence ticket and sent the glass down to Forensics. In the meantime, I'm thinking about those unidentified latents and asking myself why Marianne didn't get ten-cards of other people in the mix. Like you, for example."

"What's a ten-card?"

"Inked prints of all ten fingers. Enlighten me. You were in the house as much as anyone. Why didn't she get yours?"

"You'd have to ask her."

"I just might do that. In the meantime, I hear you and Adam are making a field trip to meet with the good doctor's wife. What's that all about?"

I paused, wondering how much she knew about the missing interview report. Taking a moment to decide what I should tell her, I chose to be vague.

"For some reason there was no record of Mrs. Keating's interview in the files. She's offered to tell us what was in it."

"Why do I get the feeling that you're not telling me the whole truth? I promise you, whatever Adam is up to, I'll find out in time. For now, let me be clear. Marianne Weede taught me the ropes around here. She was a damned good detective, the best. But that doesn't mean she didn't screw up now and then. Like Adam's father always said, there's something hinkey about this case. If Leland Booker didn't kill his family, I'll do whatever it takes to track down whoever did. On the other hand, if you and the boy wonder are trying to twist the law to get a murderer out of jail on a legal technicality, then you're going to find I'm a force to be reckoned with."

Sitting there, under Tripp's steely stare, I didn't doubt that for one minute.

Chapter 17

Back in my office, I ran through my divorce client's financial statements, her father's last will and testament and all the other documents I needed to convince Jack that he should recommend mediation as the path forward. His client didn't have a prayer of getting everything he wanted. Then again, I now knew that wasn't Jack's objective. All he wanted was to bleed his client dry with inflated fees.

Tipping my head back, I squeezed eyedrops into my tired eyes. Yesterday I worked late into the night, sorting through five years of court data on the flash drive Adam's father provided. After reading through hundreds of criminal trials from that period, I built a database and spent hours analyzing the results. So far, all I could confirm was that Erika Tripp was right about Judge Rothenberg. His conviction rate of nonwhite defendants was in line with all the other judges of the court, and what the demographic pool suggested it should be. After all that work, I had nothing that could be used to support our theory that racial bias played a role in Leland's conviction.

The door to my office opened, and Jack Burquest entered. He looked relaxed, happy, and sober.

"Hey, guess what?" he said. "My sons called last night. They want to see me over the holidays. Can you believe it?"

"I'm happy for you." I blinked, my vision slightly blurred by the eyedrops.

"Have I ever told you that you have the most beautiful, blue eyes of any girl I ever knew?"

He sounded strangely like a schoolboy with a crush. I couldn't decide if I liked him better drunk or sober.

"For starters, I'm not a girl, I'm a woman. And not a young one at that!"

"You're still as beautiful as the day I first set eyes on you. We were in third period chemistry class together. Remember?"

"That was a long time ago, Jack. Would you like some coffee before we get down to business?"

"No thanks, I've had my quota for the morning." He tipped his head to one side. "Do you feel okay?"

I wiped an excess eyedrop from the corner of my eye. "I'm fine. I probably shouldn't admit this to you, especially since we're on opposite sides of this divorce, but for the first time in my career, I'm working on autopilot. Maybe it's time to quit."

"Nonsense. You just need a break."

I wondered. The past few months I spent my evenings on the Booker case instead of driving myself into the ground with an impossible case load.

"You're probably right," I said.

"The boys are coming over for dinner Christmas Eve." He looked at me, and it didn't take much to read what was going through his mind. "I was wondering, maybe you could . . ."

"There is no way I am cooking dinner for you and your sons. No way."

"Help me Cate. I told the boys I quite drinking. I want to show them I mean it this time."

"Jesus, Jack. Are you saying you can't spend one evening with your own kids without getting drunk?"

"You don't understand. This is important. I want them to see I've changed."

I looked at him, knowing I was about to ignore the voice shouting in my head. I'd seen it all before. Jack didn't need much of an excuse to fall back, and family stress was one of the many buttons that would send him straight to the bottle. And it wasn't as if I had anything else going on that evening.

Traditionally my husband and I spent Christmas Eve together, just the two of us. The following day we always went to my sister's house where we watched her son, Ben open his presents. Though neither of us cared much for Nancy's husband, we both adored Ben. Arnie and he had a special relationship and I always got a pang in my chest when I saw them together. For Arnie, Ben was the son I could never give him. After Arnie died, Ben put his life on hold to stay with me, helping me get through those terrible first days. Our combined tears could have filled buckets. When Ben returned to Manhattan to finish his final year at NYU Law, my house felt emptier than ever.

With a sigh, I figured Christmas Eve with Jack and his kids was better than spending the evening alone.

"Okay, here's what you're going to do," I said. "You're going to call a restaurant and make a reservation. I'll join you for dinner but don't expect me to hang around while you open presents around the tree. You did buy presents for the boys, didn't you?"

"Oh shit! Maybe you could help me . . ." My cold, hard stare stopped him. "Yeah, well I guess I can buy something for them. Hey, this is great. We can eat at the club."

I froze at the mention of the club.

"The club? Isn't there someplace else we can go?"

"No, the club is perfect. That's the one place in town I'm sure we won't run into Cindy. That bitch wants my membership as part of the divorce settlement. I told her lawyer that's non-negotiable. I inherited the KCC membership from my father, and I'll be damned if I'm going to let Cindy have it.

We'll swing by your place and pick you up on the way. Be sure to wear something nice."

"I know how to dress for dinner at the club," I snapped. "And I'd prefer to meet you there."

"What kind of gentleman allows his date to drive herself to dinner?" His face broke into a big grin. "I'll see you at six."

I should have reminded him that I wasn't his date. Or if I was, it was a pity date, the kind he shouldn't be proud of. I let his comment go, chalking my silence up to an act of charity.

Nick and Justin Burquest had matured in the few years since I'd seen them. They were in college now, Nick in his fourth year and Justin a junior. Nick was good-looking, and according to Jack he was popular with the girls. Perhaps that had to do with his status as a sports hero, standing tall in his father's long shadow. Justin was more academic in nature, a sweet kid who seemed to favor his mother. Both boys were quiet, having said very little in the car on the drive over. After we were seated at our table, I tried to jump-start the conversation.

"Are you still playing football?" I asked Nick. He was the star quarterback of the team during his last two years in high school. I couldn't recall Jack ever telling me what his older son had been up to since. Other than knowing he was a senior at Keene State, I didn't really know much about the boy.

"No," Nick replied. He turned his head and stared out the window, making it clear he wasn't interested in small talk.

Jack drummed the white table cloth with his fingers. Justin unfolded and re-folded his napkin. I decided to try again.

"How about you, Justin? Have you declared a major at school?"

Justin mumbled. "Not yet."

The weight of the evening pressed down on me like stones. It was going to be a long night.

"May I take your drink order?"

I turned to see our waitress standing by my side wearing the same kind of uniform my mother used to wear. Her appearance was a welcome relief from my failed attempts at conversation. I suggested the boys and I could share a bottle of wine. Jack ordered tonic water. Watching the waitress walk back to the bar, I took in our surroundings.

Leo Bishop's son had transformed the place. The dining room was tastefully redecorated. Gone were the old velvet drapes, the crystal chandeliers, the overstuffed chairs. Now the windows were covered with chain mesh blinds, cold but trendy. Halogen lamps cast a pink glow over the white leather chairs. I liked the new décor. It helped put some distance between now and the past.

"So, are you and my dad hooking up or what?" Nick's question shook me from my thoughts.

"No!" The word came out of my mouth too forcefully. Fixing a smile on my face, I added, "Your father and I are old friends, that's all. We've known each other since high school and . . . well, I didn't have any plans for tonight and he was kind enough to invite me . . . that is, he asked if I'd like to join you this evening and . . . well, since I haven't seen either of you for some time I thought it would be nice to . . ."

Nick sensed my discomfort. His grin bordered on a sneer.

"I'll let you in on a little secret, boys. Cate and I dated back in high school." Jack smiled at me. "She's the one who got away."

Nick sat up in his chair showing some interest for the first time that evening. "So, now that her husband is out of the way you decided to try again?"

I didn't like the smirk on Nick's face. I nailed him with a wilting stare and enjoyed an unhealthy pleasure when he started to squirm. He cast his eyes downward, the smile wiped from his face.

"No, Nick. I told you, we're just friends."

"What happened?" Justin asked. "Did he dump you or did you dump him?"

"Neither. Things sort of ended between us before he left for 'Nam."

What I didn't tell him was why I stopped returning Jack's calls before he shipped out. Why I never answered any of his letters sent from the jungles of Vietnam. I let the romance die a cold, silent death, and Jack and I never spoke about it since.

Jack was watching me. He placed his hand over mine.

"The important thing is, we can still friends," he said. "I don't think you guys really want to hear about our ancient history. Let's get down to more serious stuff. What does everyone want to eat? The turkey dinner looks good to me."

With our brief discussion over, silence descended. I pulled my hand back, picked up the menu and waited for the waitress to reappear.

"Service sure is slow here tonight." Having exhausted the subject of our history, Jack seemed unsure how to start a new conversation with his sons. I could almost see him searching his brain for the next subject. His face brightened as something occurred to him.

"Cate, why don't you tell the boys about that project you're working on? You know, the thing with the murders."

"What murders?" The expression on Nick's face changed from moody to interested. All eyes turned on me.

"It all happened a long time ago. A woman and her children were poisoned. Her husband ultimately went to jail for the murders. I'm helping a law student who is trying to prove he was wrongfully convicted."

The waitress reappeared with the wine. Removing the cork with ease, she poured a bit into Jack's glass. I reached across the table and passed it to Nick.

"Why don't you take a sip and see if it's okay," I suggested.

Nick downed the wine in one gulp and nodded. The waitress got the message and poured some wine into the remaining three glasses. She set the tonic water before Jack and pulled out her pad. Touching a pen to the tip of her tongue, she started making her way around the table.

"So, did the guy kill his family or not?" Nick asked.

"I don't believe so," I replied. "The prosecution steamrolled him. By a unanimous vote, the jury found Leland guilty after only three hours of deliberation. Getting him exonerated won't be easy but there are some legal issues that we are pursuing. We think he has a chance."

"What do you mean? Booker may go free?" The shock in Jack's eyes was unmistakable. On the day he met Adam, he must have assumed that I was simply assisting a student with a research project. From the expression on his face, the possibility that we might actually clear Leland's name never crossed his mind.

"Yes, as a matter of fact. We're going to Florida next month to interview a potential witness. Do you remember Doris Keating?"

"The doctor's wife." Jack shook his head. "Are you telling me she is still alive?"

"Very much so." I was warming to my subject and encouraged by my audience. Deciding it wouldn't do any harm to spice things up a bit I said, "It appears that Doris has evidence that could prove Leland Booker's innocence."

The waitress had finished with everyone else's order and was waiting by my side. I folded my menu and asked for the turkey dinner.

"Awesome," Justin said. "Just like on TV. Did you know those people, Dad?"

"Of course." Jack started telling his boys about the Bookers, a family he barely knew. He spoke about his time working in Gordon's Market, remembering how cute the girls were, how beautiful Marley was. I listened as he recalled Robin's fondness for the color purple. And as he spoke, I remembered how good Jack was with my girls.

Through all the years, Jack and I never spoke about the Bookers. His face was animated as he recounted the story about the day he and Billy found us on the beach. The boys were in stitches when their father told them about Kenny kicking Billy in the groin.

"Billy had it coming after what he said about Kenny's mother." Jack explained the feud between Kenny and Billy escalated to a point where Marley got involved. "Billy cooked up a scheme to get even with Mrs. Booker, but I can't remember the details."

For the life of me, I couldn't understand how Jack could smile and wink at me when speaking about Billy. What's more, I didn't believe for one second that he lost all memory of the disaster that followed.

Chapter 18

On the 5th of July, Kenny appeared at the house with a burlap bag slung over his shoulder. He dropped it at his feet, the unmistakable clank of glass a dead giveaway.

"What are you planning to do with those bottles?" I eyed the grubby sack with more than a touch of skepticism.

"Are you kidding? I can get a shitload of money by returning these to Gordon's."

I cringed at his language. Though I'd promised Marley to cure Kenny of his filthy mouth, I struggled for weeks with no result. Kenny didn't appear to know the difference between words that were socially acceptable and words that were best used in a dockside bar. It was only a matter of time before one of the girls slipped and repeated one of Kenny's choice expressions in front of their mother. If that happened, I knew Marley would hit the roof and Kenny would be banished from the house for good.

"What?" Kenny saw the look on my face, but seemed clueless as to what the problem was. "It's Tuesday. We are going to Gordon's for ice cream, right?"

Then it occurred to me. Bribery. Mulling it over in my head, I realized it wasn't ideal but by that point I was ready to try anything to get Kenny to clean up his act. Fishing through the kitchen trash, I pulled out an empty mayonnaise jar. After rinsing it, I cut a slot in the lid and dropped in twenty-five pennies.

"Every week I'm going to put twenty-five cents in this

jar," I explained. "At the end of the summer, whatever money is in there will be yours."

"What's the catch?"

"With every swear word, I'm going to take a penny out."

"That's all? Shit, that's easy."

I unscrewed the lid and took out a penny.

"Hey, what the fuck are you doing? That's my money!"

I removed another penny. He opened his mouth, started to say something, then closed it and peered at me from the corners of his eyes.

"Now you're getting it. Let's see how this goes."

By noon the jar was empty.

After lunch, with Kenny's bottles stuffed in the basket on my bike, the four of us set out for Gordon's Market. Jack smiled as the bell rang and Robin ran up to the counter.

"Hello, princess," Jack said. "I ordered a fresh batch of grape sherbet just for you." I was glad to see Jack had developed a nice rapport with Robin. Most people in town gave us a cool reception, but Jack seemed to have a natural way with the children.

Robin giggled and jumped from one foot to the other as Jack scooped the purple ice into a sugar cone. Handing it across the counter with a flourish, he turned to Lissa.

"Will it be strawberry today? Or cherry?"

"Strawberry, please." Lissa gave him a shy a smile. "I always pick strawberry. You know that."

Jack waved the scoop in the air. "Chocolate for the Mazza kid, right?"

I glanced outside to see Kenny keeping a safe distance from the store.

"Right. He asked me to return these bottles for the deposit." I hoisted the bag on the counter. It occurred to me that Kenny might have stolen the empties from the wooden trays that sat out back behind Gordon's, but I didn't say anything. Reaching to take the chocolate cone, our fingers touched. Jack held on a fraction longer than necessary. Brushing back his bangs with his free hand, he looked at me and smiled.

"Are you free tonight? After work, that is."

Where he was going with this was obvious. I felt my heart picking up the beat.

"I'm staying at the Bookers. Leland and Marley have something going on at the club tonight."

"What about tomorrow, then?" He counted the Coke bottles, shooing aside a yellow jacket that crawled out from one.

"Cate doesn't watch us on Wednesdays," Robin piped up. "That's Mama's day off."

"Let's go to the lake," Jack said. "I'll pick you up around noon for lunch at Timoleans. After that, we can hit the beach."

"Take me too!" Robin squealed. "Please?"

I looked down on the top of her head. "I don't think so. I have other plans."

"Sure." Jack dropped Kenny's deposit money into my open palm. "Maybe next time."

I mumbled a feeble "thank you" and made my exit, leading the girls to the picnic bench outside where Kenny waited for his ice cream. When I transferred the coins into his outstretched hand, the boy gloated over his newfound wealth. He seemed to forget—at least momentarily—his lost opportunity in the mayonnaise jar.

Marley came home to change after work. She found me in the kitchen as I put a pot on the stove for our hot dogs.

"Hello darlings, I'm home. Come give Mama a kiss."

Lissa and Robin stopped what they were doing and

paused long enough for her to plant kisses on their foreheads before they turned back to setting the table.

"The girls look like they've been making mud pies," Marley said to me. "They need a bath before they go to bed."

"No problem." I did my best to wipe the ice cream from their mouths and faces, but Marley must have noticed the purple stain on Robin's shirt.

"Did you have a good day?" I turned the stove off, deciding to wait until Marley went upstairs before the girls and I sat down to dinner.

"My feet are screaming. I don't know what I was thinking, wearing these heels today. Truth be told, I am not looking forward to sitting next to Mildred Bishop at dinner tonight, listening to her squawk all evening about her—"

Marley froze in midsentence when Kenny burst into the room. Blood flowed from his nose, crimson drops spreading on the front of his torn T-shirt. Both his knees were skinned raw, and he cradled his right arm with his other hand. Of all the terrible damage done to the child, what shocked me most were the tears running down his cheeks. Kenny Mazza was bawling his eyes out.

My mouth fell open as Marley dropped to her knees, pressing Kenny against her pristine golf dress. She stroked his back and murmured to him in comforting tones.

I grabbed a towel to staunch the bleeding. "What happened?"

"Billy took my money." Kenny choked between sobs. "An' he busted my bike all to hell."

Marley took the towel from my hand and told Kenny to hold it to his nose. He winced as she gently touched his arm. I saw the spark of anger in her eyes.

"That bastard," she growled.

Aside from the occasional hiccup, Kenny quickly regained

his composure. The boy looked at Marley, eyes wide. Turning
to the girls, he realized they were watching. Taking one
step back from their mother he stood straight, his shoulders
thrown back.

Marley took control of the situation. "Kenny needs a
doctor. Call Doris Keating and tell her to send her husband
over." Turning to Kenny she said, "Where can I find Billy?"

"In the park. What are you going to do?"

"Never mind that. Do you want to call your mother?"

Kenny shook his head. He locked eyes with Marley.
Some kind of understanding seemed to pass between them,
and she nodded.

"Okay then. Stay here with Cate until the doctor arrives.
I'll be back soon."

"But what about your dinner at the club?" I said.

"Leland will just have to entertain the Bishops
without me."

I peered out the window and watched her march into
the garage. Seconds later she came out with a golf club in her
hand. Tossing it into the trunk of her car, she got behind the
wheel and peeled out of the driveway. A shiver ran down my
arms. I stood there, staring out the window for a few minutes
before I remembered to pick up the phone and call the doctor.

By the time Marley returned, Dr. Keating had finished
bandaging Kenny's cuts and bruises. He glanced at her in
surprise. Marley's dress was stained with Kenny's dried blood
and strands of her platinum blond hair had broken free of her
French twist. There was a nasty scratch with little beads of
fresh blood running down her arm. The doctor rested his hand
on Kenny's head and told Marley that he was taking him to the
hospital for x-rays. Marley nodded and told Kenny to hold out
his hand. She dropped some coins into his outstretched palm.
His deposit money for the Coke bottles.

A few days after Kenny's run-in with Billy, I stopped at Gordon's on my way home from work to pick up a carton of milk. I hesitated before going in. Billy's motorcycle was parked out front, headlight smashed, rearview mirrors shattered. The chrome muffler was a mangled twist of metal and stuffing leaked out of the slashed leather seat. When I stepped through the door, Billy, one arm held in a sling, glared at me with dark recognition in his eyes. He pushed himself away from the counter and limped by, passing close enough to bump me with his good shoulder. I reckoned there were only a few weeks before Billy reported for boot camp on Parris Island. He couldn't leave town soon enough for me.

Chapter 19

Arriving early at the airport, my travel jitters eased once I found where to park and how to get to the main terminal building. Looking around, I tried to get my bearings. Every flight to Florida had long queues of gray-haired people waiting to check in with their luggage.

I spotted Adam standing by a bank of check-in kiosks. Despite the arctic temperature outside, he was dressed for the beach, T-shirt, shorts, and sandals on his feet. He guided me through the process of obtaining my boarding card from the machine, a welcome alternative to waiting in line. I hadn't flown since before the 911 terrorist attacks. Passing through security was a whole new experience for me. When we got to the waiting lounge, we discovered every seat was taken and several other passengers milled about. A gentleman stood, offering me his seat while Adam dropped to the floor and pulled out his cell phone. From where I sat, I watched him play a word game with someone at the other end of the line.

"Coupons," I said.

"What?" Adam asked, looking up in surprise.

"C-O-U-P-O-N-S," I repeated. I pointed to the space where he should place the word. "It's worth eighty-five points."

Adam tapped in the letters on the board and smiled up at me. "Jennifer won't be happy. She usually beats me at this one.

"Who is Jennifer?"

"My blind date. The one my mother set up for Thanksgiving."

"I guess that went better than you thought it would. She must be special or you wouldn't allow her to beat you at that game."

"Are you kidding? I never let her win."

"Let me get this straight. You have a two-year advantage in law school, but she still beats you at a simple word game?"

I could see a smart comeback on the tip of Adam's tongue, but he was interrupted by our boarding call. We fell in line with the rest of the passengers who shuffled onto the plane. Adam and I settled into our seats across the aisle from each other.

As I pulled my winter coat tight against the blast of cold air from the overhead vent, Adam's phone pinged. He gave it his undivided attention, tapping in a reply before looking across the aisle at me.

"Jennifer wants to know if you want to join her online to play the game too."

I cracked open my paperback and shook my head. "Tell her thanks, but no thanks. But you can bring her over one evening for a home-cooked meal and I'll get out my Scrabble board."

The attendant passed down the aisle and asked Adam to turn off his phone until we were airborne. As the roar of the engines increased, I leaned back and lost myself in my novel. Two hours later we landed at our destination.

The air in Tampa smelled of the tropics, warm and moist. We picked up our rental car and Adam drove south. As we passed over the Skyway Bridge, the water of Tampa Bay sparkled.

"When will you get your exam results?" I asked.

"Not until mid-January, but I think I did okay."

"And how did the meeting with your project advisor go?"

"He was interested in the missing WITREP. Gave me lots of advice for how to handle Doris Keating's statement. If we ever get to submit a request for judicial review, the record of this deposition will be submitted as evidence. He said my question phraseology needs to be carefully constructed. Funny, but it occurred to me that after three years of studying the law, I don't really know much about actually practicing it. There are standard procedures for everything, but none of that is covered in our lectures."

"They expect you to learn on the job. Don't worry, you'll be fine. Doris is a sweetheart. She'll make this easy for you."

"My professor also suggested that I speak again with Marianne Weede. If I'm going to accuse her of police misconduct, I should give her a chance to explain."

We shared an uneasy silence. I didn't envy Adam having to face Weede with what amounted to an accusation of poor detective work. It would be even worse if we accused her of intentional wrongdoing, but so far there was no evidence of that. As we merged onto Interstate 75, I thought Adam might be thinking the same but when he spoke, I realized his mind was elsewhere.

"I received a copy of the trial transcript yesterday. You'll find your copy attached to an email I sent you."

"I'll have to wait until I'm home to read it."

"You should invest in a laptop or something if you want to keep your job as my research assistant." I glanced over at him and saw he was teasing.

I smiled, playing along. "Like I would ever give up the thrill of being a divorce lawyer. Did you see anything of interest in the transcript?"

"One thing caught my eye. Remember Tom Burquest?"

"The insurance agent." My heart rate kicked up a notch. There was something in the eager tone of Adam's voice that resembled the bray of a bloodhound.

"Right. Are your ready for this? Thomas Burquest was also the jailhouse snitch that swore Leland confessed to killing Marley and the girls."

I sat stunned into silence. My mind raced. Nothing about this made sense. I couldn't picture Mr. Burquest, a pillar of the community, locked up for DUI. Even if he had been stopped for reckless driving, based on the way things worked in Keene, the local police would certainly let him go with a warning. I tried to recall if Jack ever mentioned anything about his father's involvement in the Booker case, but came up empty. Maybe he wasn't even aware. Not that Jack and I ever discussed the trial. The subject of the Bookers never came up until our dinner a few nights ago. My thoughts were interrupted when Adam spoke again.

"They briefly shared a cell while Leland was held in the Keene jail. There's no record of Burquest ever being charged. He was released right after Leland was transported to the county prison. And for some reason, Burquest wasn't present for the trial. He was deposed in advance and his testimony was read aloud by the court clerk. Do you remember my list of reasons for wrongful conviction?" Adam kept his eyes on the road, but he was wearing a full-blown smile now.

"Sure." I ticked the reasons off on my fingers. "Eyewitness error, government misconduct, mishandled or suppressed evidence, racial prejudice, community pressure to solve the crime, inadequate legal representation and . . ."

"And snitch testimony given for a reduction in sentence!" Adam laughed out loud and slapped the steering wheel. "When we get back, I've got to ask Leland what went on in that jail."

I couldn't share his excitement. After all, Tom Burquest passed away years ago. There was no way he could be questioned about his testimony. I didn't see how Adam's latest discovery would help Leland now. Something told me Tom Burquest was literally a dead end.

Arriving in Venice, I felt like I'd stepped onto the *Cocoon* movie set. The town Doris Keating chose for her retirement was teeming with senior citizens. Everywhere I looked, snowbirds—retirees wintering in Florida—walked, biked, and jogged through the parks. Even the public tennis courts were filled with retirement home candidates. We drove down Venice Avenue where quaint shops lined both sides of the street and restaurant tables spilled out onto awning-covered sidewalks.

Our hotel was located directly across from the public beach. From my room I watched a large group of elderly people practice yoga on colorful blankets spread on the sand. I needed to adjust my old-fashioned concept of retirement.

On the third ring, Doris picked up her phone.

"Hello dear. I hope you and that young lawyer haven't already made plans for dinner. We have a reservation at the Crow's Nest for five thirty."

Five thirty. I imagined how Adam, city dweller that he was, would react to the early dinner schedule, but I accepted her invitation anyway. After getting directions—turn right and keep going to the end of the road—and hearing her say everything in Florida was 'casual dress,' I hung up and dialed Adam's room.

"Five thirty? What is that, a late lunch?" he asked.

"There are still a few hours before we have to leave. Want to join me for a walk on the beach?"

"No thanks. I'm going to give Jennifer a call."

I had the beach all to myself. The sand squished between

my toes and I rolled up the cuffs of my pants to venture into the gentle surf. A rogue wave rose up and I darted out of the way, laughing out loud when I was too late. Wet pants and all, I couldn't remember the last time I felt so free. Though I pretended otherwise, in the past few months I could feel my love for my business fade away. I pushed back the concern and decided to enjoy this short holiday in paradise without giving the firm another thought.

With a sigh, I turned and slowly made my way back to the hotel where I discovered Adam sitting on the veranda. He faced west as the sun hovered over the Gulf of Mexico. Though he appeared to be sleeping, when my shadow crossed his path he opened his eyes.

Adam stood and stretched. "I could get used to this place."

I noticed he'd changed into long pants and a button-down shirt, but the sandals were still strapped to his feet. "Me too. But duty calls. It's time for you to meet Doris."

Chapter 20

Rising from a small spit of land, the Crow's Nest faced the sea.
Adam and I arrived a few minutes early to find there was already a queue of customers waiting for the restaurant to open.
People chatted congenially, perfect strangers drawing Adam
and me into conversation as if we were old friends. When a
young man finally opened the doors, I glanced at my watch.
Five thirty-five. No one seemed bothered that it was later than
the posted hours.

The front doors led to a dark cavern-like room with a
low ceiling. Booths with vinyl-covered benches lined the walls.
Given we were on the beach I was hoping for a view overlooking the water, but the interior of this place looked more like a
common bar back home than a seaside restaurant. I gave the
receptionist Doris's name, and she checked the register, waving
us up a narrow stairway before turning her attention to the
next person in line. Looking at Adam, I shrugged and led the
way, emerging at the top into a large, bright dining room. The
view caught my breath.

The sky was aflame, the clouds painted red and orange
by the setting sun. Pelicans circled above, dive-bombing the
choppy sea, shaking their beaks in frustration at the fish that
got away. Below, boaters returned from the Gulf, their sails
catching the westerly breeze as they glided through a channel
and into the marina below. I could have stood there for hours,
just taking in the scene, but the hostess soon appeared and led
us to our table.

"Jeremy will be your server this evening." She set three oversized menus on the table. "I'll send him over to take your drink orders while you wait for Doris."

I glanced around the room. Not quite six o'clock and every seat in the place filled. Still no sign of Doris. Adam must have been reading my mind.

"I wonder where she is," he said. "Do you think we should give her a call?"

I started to nod when out of the corner of my eye I caught sight of Doris, earrings bouncing to the beat of her steps as she hurried toward us.

"Hello Cate dear. Sorry I'm late." I caught the smell of lavender and roses as she bent down to kiss my cheek. Old-age spots marked her arms, wrinkles on her face spoke of years in the Florida sun.

Adam stood, offering his hand. "Pleased to meet you, Mrs. Keating. I'm Adam Bennett."

She wiggled her fingers as if to brush all formality away. "Call me Doris. Everyone else does." She slipped into the chair that Adam had pulled out and allowed him to push it in under her. "Oh my," she said. "Such good manners, dear boy. Your mother must have raised you right."

Doris Keating was smaller than I remembered, and decidedly thinner, but by all appearances she was as energetic as ever. She still wore her hair in a bun at the back of her neck, but the bright ginger color that I remembered had turned silver. Her eyes, magnified behind a pair of wire-rimmed spectacles, reflected a keen intelligence unaffected by her age.

She blew out a little puff of air. "My, my what a day this has been. Our condo association meeting ran late, and . . ."

The waiter appeared by her side and whipped her linen napkin off the table and onto her lap. "Why thank you, Jeremy." Doris looked at him, the corners of her mouth turned up in appreciation. "I'm hoping you have some of that pompano tonight."

"You not foolin' nobody, Doris," Jeremy said. "You commin' here all the time to see me, not our fish." The rhythm of his Jamaican accent played like music floating in the air between us. A smile flashed out of his black face revealing a gap between his front teeth.

Doris giggled, "I declare, Jeremy. Your wife is about ready to give birth to your first-born and here you are, flirting with an old lady. Have you decided on a name for the baby yet?"

"Laurel, she set on namin' the baby after the president's wife. And my woman, she know what she want."

I glanced around, noting the nautical décor. The walls were covered with fishnets, weathered oars, and wooden crab traps. Jeremy returned with the wine and told us he put in three orders for pompano. When my meal arrived, the whole fish lay on the plate, staring up at me from a bed of rice. Doris allowed Jeremy to filet her dinner while Adam and I decided to tackle the challenge on our own. Taking a forkful of flakey, white meat into my mouth, I let it rest on my tongue before swallowing. Soft, salty, buttery. I had never tasted anything quite as wonderful.

"Why haven't I heard of this fish before?" I asked.

"Local catch," Doris said. "Pompano is only available this time of year, and then only at restaurants near the coast. I've always found that the things you treasure most are the things you can't get enough of. Don't you agree?"

I thought about that and nodded agreement. Sage words from a lady who seemed to have everything in life she could possibly want. A heavy gold necklace hung around her neck, several gold bangles on one arm, and an expensive, diamond-encrusted watch on the other. It looked like Dr. Keating left his widow in good stead.

"I'm looking forward to tomorrow." Doris reached across

the table and placed a hand on Adam's arm. "This is exciting, just like my TV shows. You're never too old for new experiences, isn't that right?"

"I don't know if it's going to be all that exciting," Adam replied. "We're scheduled to meet in the lawyer's office at eleven. I'll ask the questions that I emailed to you last week. Mr. Martinez will be present to witness your statement. Shouldn't take more than an hour."

"Oh, I almost forgot . . ." Doris pulled her wicker handbag, large enough for a week's groceries, onto her lap and started rummaging through the contents. In addition to her wallet and sunglasses, she pulled out several tubes of lipstick, bits of fabric, and a craft book. At last she extracted a folded sheet of paper. An old-fashioned carbon copy. Doris handed it across the table to Adam. "This is that report I told Cate about. She said you might want to see it."

Adam's eyes caught the light from the table's candle as he scanned Marianne Weede's witness interview report. "I can't believe you held onto this."

"Well, you never know when you might need something." Doris bobbed her head. "Like that report, for example. Who would have guessed that would come in handy after all these years?"

"This is a big help. I don't know how to thank you." Adam carefully refolded the paper and passed it to me. I tucked it into my purse.

"I'm just glad to know you're trying to get to the bottom of that business with Mrs. Booker and her children." Doris lowered her voice to a conspiratorial whisper. "I always had my doubts, you know. Seemed to me the police were in too much of a hurry to pin those murders on Mr. Booker. And why would such a nice man kill his family? Just didn't make sense to me, but then, none of it did, if you know what I mean. Those murders were simply terrible. Nothing like that ever happened in Keene before. Not since, either. It's a nice town. Good people, mostly."

"Cate has been telling me a little about the Booker family," Adam said.

"Well, she knew them as well as anyone." Doris turned to me, patting my hand in an affectionate way. Her bracelets clinked together. "Cate was wonderful with those girls. You'd think they were her own, the way she looked after them. She brought them all around town on their bikes. The Booker girls and that other one . . . the Mazza child. Oh my, that poor boy. Do you remember, Cate? That night when you called for my Richard to come and set the boy's broken arm? And then there was the time with his mother . . . well, all I can say is, what would that child have done without you?" She shook her head as if to free her mind of the ugly memories. "I wonder what became of him."

"I don't know," I replied. "After the state stepped in, Kenny was sent away to live with a relative. A month later I left for college. I never heard about him again."

What I didn't tell her was that losing track of Kenny was one of the biggest regrets of my life. A few years ago, I tried to track him down but came up empty. Given the circumstance of his removal from his mother's home, the records were sealed. Even searching on the Internet, I found no trace of Kenny Mazza anywhere. It was like he vanished from the earth.

"One of life's mysteries." Doris shrugged. "Now, if you still have room after the fish, the key lime pie here is wonderful."

The next morning, I woke in time to take a walk on the beach before getting ready for the deposition. Strictly speaking, I didn't need to be present to hear Doris give her statement, but

Adam insisted that I join them. Maybe he wanted an audience. Maybe he needed emotional support. Whatever the reason, I was happy he asked.

I found Adam in the hotel's café. His hand was wrapped around a half-empty mug of coffee. He glanced up and gave me an appraising stare.

"You look nice."

I was flattered that he noticed. I rarely wore makeup or bothered to fix myself up in any way. But this was a special event, and I took the opportunity to dress for the occasion.

"You too." I noticed he tucked his tie between two buttons of his dress shirt. His suit jacket was draped over the back of his chair. "How do you feel?"

"Great. I'm glad I had the chance to get to know Doris before taking her statement. She's really something, isn't she? I want to tell you again how much I appreciate your help with this. I looked over her copy of the WITREP that you gave me after we got back to the hotel last night. The report supports what she told you on the phone. Doris Keating may just be the most significant lead that we've found so far."

It was nice to be appreciated. And I did feel like we were on to something. If not by itself, Doris's testimony would at least prove Detective Weede lied on the stand. And that fell into the category of government misconduct. Maybe not enough to justify a judicial review of the case, but it was a step in the right direction.

I picked at my breakfast. Adam speared my untouched sausage and washed everything down with a glass of juice. We arrived at the law office fifteen minutes early. The receptionist, Carol, showed us into a conference room and promised to return with coffee. The décor was Law Office Anywhere. Walnut chairs waxed to a high gloss were arranged in perfect symmetry around a matching table. An etched crystal Chamber of

Commerce award commemorating "Law Practice of the Year" from three years prior sat on a credenza pushed against the wall. Original watercolors were mounted in expensive frames, a mirror on the world just outside the building.

Carol returned with our coffee, pulled out a chair, and joined us. Placing her laptop on the table, she explained that she would be taking notes during the meeting. When we were done, she would print out Doris's statement, ready to be signed and notarized. As the clock on the wall chimed eleven, Ed Martinez, a junior partner of the firm, slipped into the room. He joined us at the table with nothing more than a yellow legal pad and an expensive-looking pen in his hands. We made small talk, filling the time while we waited for Doris to arrive. Adam and Ed chatted amiably. They covered a range of topics including law school, job opportunities in the legal profession, and of course, the Booker case. Every now and then I glanced at the clock. It was one thing for Doris to be late for dinner, another for her to arrive past the scheduled time for this appointment. As the minutes ticked by, it seemed that I was the only one in the room who was anxious about Doris's absence.

"I'm going to give her a call." I opened up my cell phone and selected her name from my contact list. Six rings later I was kicked into voice mail. Puzzled, I left a brief message.

"Doris, it's Cate. We're here with Mr. Martinez, waiting for you. I hope you're on your way. See you soon."

"What do you think?" Adam asked.

I shrugged my shoulders, noting the time. Even by Doris's standards, she was unexplainably late.

"I think we should go to her condo and see if she's there."

While Adam drove, I tried reaching Doris on the phone several more times. The door to her building's lobby was locked, instructions printed on a security panel for how to gain access. Punching the buttons, I could hear the phone ring at the other end. No answer. As I pondered what to do next, a woman bearing four canvas bags filled with groceries arrived. I stepped away from the panel so she could tap in her security code. The lock on the door clicked, and Adam jumped to hold it open for her to pass through. We both followed her in.

"Apartment 505," I said as we stepped into the elevator.

"You must be here to visit Doris." The lady with the groceries pursed her lips. "I didn't see her at the gym for our nine o'clock aerobics class. It's not like Doris to miss without calling me."

"We're picking her up for an appointment downtown," Adam said.

"Well, tell her to call me when she gets back. I need a ride to Bingo tonight."

After the lady got off on the fourth floor, I turned to Adam. "Doris missed her aerobics class this morning."

"Maybe she overslept."

"I have a terrible feeling that something is wrong."

No one answered the bell. I hammered the door with my fist with no result. I was about to suggest we find a maintenance man with a key when Adam reached out and turned the knob. The door opened on silent hinges. With a shrug, I stepped into the air-conditioned apartment. Calling out her name, I made my way down the hall. I could hear the crash of waves five stories below. A wall of windows at the far end flooded the apartment with light, and relief washed over me as I saw the back of Doris' head resting on the sofa.

"Doris!" I cried. "We've been worried about you. Did you forget . . ."

She still wore the outfit from the night before. Both hands curled into balls on her chest. Her glasses were skewed slightly, as though they were knocked awry when her head fell back on the couch. Pale, lifeless eyes stared straight ahead. I didn't need to touch her to know her skin was cold. With all of the indignity death dealt Doris, what bothered me most was her hair. Ragged strands had broken free of her bun, giving her an unkempt look that she would never have permitted in life.

I drew in a raspy breath, shoving the side of my hand into my mouth to keep from crying out. Only then was I aware of Adam standing behind me, bracing my arms to keep me from buckling under my trembling knees.

"Oh, Doris!"

Adam pulled out his phone. "We need to call 9-1-1."

I nodded, turning my head away from her sightless eyes. My attention swept over the coffee table where I noticed a tray bearing a plate of cookies, a sugar bowl and creamer. The smallest of silver spoons sat next to the bowl. A thin skin covered the cream.

"She must have fixed herself a cup of coffee after she got home from dinner last night." I shook my head. "She seemed absolutely fine when we left her."

"I know." Adam's face was drained of color. "Let's get out of here. We'll wait downstairs for the EMTs to arrive."

Soon two medical technicians appeared. Adam led the way to Doris' apartment, returning minutes later with the EMTs right behind. They explained that a doctor needed to pronounce Doris dead before they could move the body. One of the technicians called the hospital, and an understanding physician with the air of a man who had seen this all before showed up in minutes. The EMTs told us to send the police up when they arrived.

With blue lights flashing, the squad car came to a screeching halt by the front door. The cop stepped into the lobby, taking both of us in with a curious sweep of his eyes. He then instructed us not to leave until he came back down.

A small crowd gathered. Residents from the building came down to ask us what was going on. Aerobics Lady
clucked away, stating that she knew something was wrong
when Doris didn't show up for their class. I was relieved
when the policeman came back down and cleared everyone
else out of the lobby. I noticed his shoes were covered in blue
paper booties.

The questions came fast. He wanted to know what
our relationship was to Doris. When I said she was an old
friend from my home town in New Hampshire, he gave me a
funny look.

"You came here to visit her?"

"No . . . that is, yes we did."

"When did you see her last?"

"We had dinner together at the Crow's Nest last night."

Adam stepped forward. "We came by this morning
because she didn't show up for our appointment with Ed
Martinez."

The cop peered at Adam over his logbook. "I thought
you were here on a visit. Now you're saying you had business
with a lawyer?"

I didn't like the tone of his voice. "Yes."

"How did you gain entry to the apartment?" he asked.

"We rang the bell," said Adam. "When Doris didn't answer, I tried the door. It was unlocked."

"Um-hmm." The officer clicked his ballpoint pen repeatedly. "I'm going to need contact information from both of you."

After we gave him what he wanted, he slapped his logbook shut. He pushed the digital camera that hung on a strap
around his neck to one side so he could stuff the logbook into
his right breast pocket.

Removing his radio from his collar, he keyed the mike

and said, "Hey, Sal. We're going to need a Forensics team over here."

The cop pulled his logbook back out. Scanning his notes, he unclipped the ballpoint pen from the cover and started to write again. "I have a few more questions. Did either of you touch anything in the apartment?"

"No. What is this all about?" A rising panic rose in my chest. "Why did you call for a forensics team?"

"What time did you leave the Crow's Nest?"

"Around eight," Adam replied. "Doris drove herself home and Mrs. Stokes and I returned to our hotel."

"Was she wearing the same clothes she's in now?"

Adam and I nodded in unison.

"Listen," Adam said, "what's going on?"

"Nothing for you to be concerned about, sir. Looks like a common robbery gone wrong. Given her age and the state of the body, I'd venture to guess Mrs. Keating suffered a heart attack during the attack. If we can determine the time of death, that will help us define the window of time when all this went down. My guess would be it was right after she got home from the restaurant. The autopsy will confirm."

I wrapped my arms around myself, shivering in the sun-drenched lobby. My eyes fell on the cigarettes sticking out of the officer's breast pocket. He followed my gaze, pulled out the pack, and passed it to me. I didn't hesitate.

"Of course, you wouldn't know about the robbery." The officer held the lighter for me while he continued to explain. "Her bedroom was tossed. Did you happen to notice if she was wearing any jewelry when you were at the restaurant?"

"Yes." I blew out a stream of smoke. The nicotine gave me the jolt I needed to keep my nerves in control. "A necklace, watch, bracelets . . ." Even as I spoke, I pictured Doris on the couch without her necklace.

"I'm guessing someone spotted her at the restaurant and figured her for a soft target. Unfortunately, that sort of thing happens. The guy probably followed her home, forced her to let him in, and then . . ."

Something wasn't adding up. I closed my eyes and tried to focus. It took me a few beats before I realized what was wrong.

"What about the coffee?"

It was one of those details that registered in my head. On the way out of the apartment, as I passed through the kitchen, I noticed the coffee pot was full, the red light on.

"The coffee, ma'am?"

"There were two cups," I said.

"You think she was expecting someone?"

I shrugged my shoulders. "She didn't mention anything last night."

"We'll check with the owners of the other units and see if they saw anything." The officer made one last note on his logbook and shoved it back into his pocket. "Thank you both for your cooperation. We'll take it from here. I'm very sorry for your loss."

"You have to catch this guy," I said.

The officer tipped his head to one side. "Unfortunately, this kind of thing is all too common. We'll do our best, but I can't promise anything."

I glanced at Adam whose shoulders slumped. Only then did the realization sink in. Doris, the one bright light in our effort to free Leland, was gone.

Chapter 21

Back on the second floor of the Courthouse, Adam and I waited. The same conference room where we met Detective Tripp
months ago felt even more cramped, the heating system blast-
ing hot, dry air into the small space. We didn't speak. Adam's
chair was pushed back from the table as far as the wall allowed. His forearms rested on his legs, hands clasped together,
his head bent toward the floor. I winced at the sound of him
cracking his knuckles. Only when Tripp opened the door did
he look up. Marianne Weede filled the space behind her. A re-
freshing stream of cooler air came in with the two of them.

"Let's get started," Tripp said. No one had offered us
coffee, not that I would have welcomed any in the stifling
room. But a glass of cold water would have been nice.

Adam straightened when the two detectives stepped
into the room. Sitting erect, he waited until Tripp settled into
her own chair before speaking.

"Do you think you could get us some water before
we begin?"

Tripp glared at him. She pushed her chair back with a
grunt and left the room.

Weede took the seat opposite Adam. From my vantage
point I could see her ample thighs hanging over the sides of
her chair. Her midriff sagged onto her lap. The gray roots of
her hair suggested she was overdue for a visit with her hair-
dresser. It occurred to me that someone should have told her
tight perms went out with disco. But despite her gone-to-seed

condition, she still projected an air of substance. Weede could probably wrestle an elephant to the ground if she wanted.

"Come on, kid. I told you you're wasting time on this Booker guy." She shifted in her seat. "Here I thought I'd sent you on your way when what do you know, I get a call from Tripp telling me you want to meet. What's up?"

Erika Tripp returned with a tray weighed down by a pitcher of ice water and four glasses. She set it on the table—none too gently—and dropped down in the chair opposite me. When no one else moved to pour, I reached over and picked up the pitcher, offering Adam the first glass.

"Is this your handwriting?" Adam slid a copy of Dr. Keating's witness interview report across the table. Weede picked it up, held it at arms' length, and nodded sharply before sliding it back to Adam.

"Yeah, sure. That's one of my WITREPs."

"Can you explain why the original isn't in the Booker file?"

"I dunno." She shrugged. "Stuff gets misfiled all the time. I worked hundreds of cases a year. Could be in one of my other books. Maybe you should check on that."

"I don't need to." Adam gave her a satisfied grin. "As you can see, I have the witness' copy."

"Good for you."

While she and Adam were sparring, I mulled over her suggestion of what happened to the original report. On the surface, hers was a plausible explanation. On the other hand, if Weede wanted to lose some paperwork, misfiling it with another case would have been a smart move. If she was ever accused of destroying evidence, she could produce the missing report—after making a show of looking through all her other files—and claim an honest mistake. I decided Weede was either very careless or very, very clever. And nothing I'd heard about her suggested careless.

"I'm having some trouble reading your handwriting." Adam slid the WITREP back to Weede. "Could you read this for me?"

Weede gave him a hard stare before reaching for the paper again. She pulled a pair of reading glasses out of her purse. I saw her eyes moving down the page.

"Start here." Adam reached across the table and pointed to the first line. "Out loud, please."

"November 5, met with Dr. Richard Keating in his office at 61 Washington Street, Keene, New Hampshire. When asked if he examined the Booker family for the purpose of getting life insurance, he answered in the affirmative. I asked witness to confirm Leland Booker was also examined. Again, he answered in the affirmative."

Weede pushed her reading glasses to the top of her head and gave Adam a poisonous look. "Are you screwing with me, kid?"

Adam leaned forward in his seat. "Just read the report, Detective."

With a heavy sigh, Weede flipped her glasses onto the bridge of her nose and resumed reading. "I asked then what forms were sent to the insurance company. Witness stated his wife would know. The wife, Mrs. Doris Keating was asked to join the interview. When asked about the medical forms, she confirmed that she sent them to the insurance company. She further stated Tom Burquest, owner of the insurance agency, called sometime after. (note: Mrs. Keating was unable to provide the exact date of the call.) Burquest denied receipt of aforementioned form. Witness stated insurance agency now has two copies. She refused to provide copy for my files on the basis of doctor/patient confidentiality."

Adam snatched the report out of her hands. "Thanks, Marianne. That clears things up." It was the first time I heard him call her by her first name. She didn't look too pleased.

"You didn't drag me all the way down here to have me read to you, kid. Get to the point."

"The point is, there seems to be a conflict between this record of the Keating interview and what you testified to while under oath at the trial. At that time, you said the exact same thing you told me a few months ago. That the doctor told you Leland never asked for his records to be sent to the Burquest Agency."

Weede pounded the table with both fists. Startled, I nearly jumped out of my seat. She was on her feet, glaring at Adam. Swinging her head, she caught Detective Tripp in her furious glare. "What kinda game are you playing with this asshole?"

Tripp placed a hand on her arm. "Calm down, Marianne. I'm sure there's a good explanation for all this. Did you uncover some additional information after the interview? Something that altered your testimony?"

Weede jerked her arm away but sat back down. "How the fuck should I know? That investigation was a hell of a long time ago." She took a deep breath, fighting to gain control over the tide of anger that overwhelmed her. "Maybe, yeah. That could be." She turned to Adam with a penetrating stare. "I'm warning you kid, you're messing with the wrong person here."

"I'm not messing with you, Marianne," Adam kept his voice calm, his normal pitch, but against the ranting of Weede, it sounded like a whisper.

"No? Let me tell you something, you little shit. I was closing cases long before you were out of diapers. And I was good. I was the fucking Mariano Rivera of the squad. The absolute best, just check my record. You wanna know what my secret was? Instinct. I could smell the guilt on someone a mile away. And your guy, Booker, stunk to high heaven. I knew he was the killer long before I had proof. My job was to give the DA what he needed to put that goddamned murderer behind bars, and I delivered. How dare you come in here to threaten me? I don't care who your old man is, I don't have to take this shit from you."

She pushed her bulk out of the chair and turned her angry glare on Tripp. "The next time you want to talk to me, get a subpoena. We're through here." With that, she hauled open the door and left, her heavy footsteps receding as she stomped down the tiled hallway.

Tripp remained in her chair, a pensive look on her face as she gazed at Adam. She blinked once before speaking. "That was interesting."

"She's a liar," Adam said at last.

"Maybe." Tripp shrugged. "Maybe she just did what she needed to do to short-circuit the justice system. Tell me, Adam. What is the greater crime? Perjury or murder?"

Adam leaned forward. "What if Booker is innocent?"

"I haven't made up my mind about that yet." Tripp ran her fingers through her hair, picked up a pen, and started tapping the table. "I'll give your theory the benefit of the doubt. Eventually we'll get the results of Rusak's prints and then we'll know more."

"It's been more than a month," I said. "What's taking so long?"

"Let me give you a lesson in fingerprinting," she replied. "Back in the day, we had a bunch of techs peering through magnifying glasses all day long. They worked with a grid system, matching the lines at defined points to the inked prints on a ten card. Usually they needed more than one latent to get a positive ID, and they always needed at least eleven points to match. It took time, and we only had so many techs.

165

Unless a detective had a pretty good idea in advance that there would be a hit, he or she didn't bother jamming up the system with a bunch of prints just for grins. That would explain why Marianne didn't submit all the latent prints they found on the evidence at the scene."

I took exception to the detective's condescending tone. "But everything's on computers now, right?"

"Sure, but here's the thing. It still takes time, and not only do the lab rats have to worry about checking fingerprints, they're swamped with DNA test requests. They're under-staffed, and there's a hiring freeze. These days everyone shows up for work more pissed-off than normal. Of course, when a detective wants something, it's always urgent and you know how the saying goes about how shit runs. In this case, the crime lab techs are at the bottom of the hill. I swear to God they're working slower than ever just outta spite. You won't want to hear this, but I can't very well go down there and expedite a case that's been closed for forty years. And remember, I put a false case number on Rusak's sample to get it processed in the first place. I can't risk my career by calling attention to this one."

"Now what?" Adam's jaw worked in frustration.

"You just have to be patient. They'll get to it eventually. The good news is that I requested they run the crime scene prints through our own system and VICAP, the FBI's database. I figured we were only going to get one shot at this. Why not go for the whole ball of wax when we have the chance?"

Adam sighed. Patience wasn't one of his strong points. But even I could see there wasn't much we could do to speed things along. Besides, this was an exercise in futility as far as I was concerned. No way could I be convinced that Henry Rusak had anything to do with the murders. Absolutely no way.

The idea hit me in the middle of the night. "Check the record," Weede had said. Why hadn't I thought about that before?

Not bothering to turn on the lights, I made my way downstairs. Minutes later I was bathed in the glow of my laptop, struggling to figure out how to re-sort the database I had painstakingly built. Pressing my lips together, I took a deep breath and pushed the button. A slow smile covered my face as I scanned the results.

Chapter 22

It didn't take me long to learn Marley always got what she wanted. When she didn't feel like cooking, she convinced Leland to bring the whole family to the club for dinner. New dress, new shoes, a piece of jewelry, Marley put it all on the charge cards. Leland would blow his stack, rant and rave about her spending habits. All to no avail. She continued to do as she pleased. In the middle of July, she decided she wanted more free time, and set about getting Leland to grant her wish.

Marley claimed things around the house were slipping. She needed one morning a week without the girls underfoot so she could tend to housework. Never mind that I emptied the dishwasher every morning, pushed the vacuum through the whole house, cleaned the ashtrays and folded the laundry. She apparently wasn't satisfied. Leland objected, saying he couldn't afford part-time help at the pro shop to cover her hours. Marley negotiated a compromise. She signed the girls up for tennis lessons at the club, saying it would be good for them to socialize with children their own age. That freed my schedule for me to work Tuesday mornings in the pro shop, giving Marley more free time.

Leland seemed happy with the new arrangement. The plan wasn't going to cost him any additional money, and he knew his wife would keep pestering him until she got what she wanted anyway. As for me, I wasn't crazy about the arrangement, but Marley didn't ask my opinion. She raided her closet, emerging with an armful of Lacoste skirts and tops so I could dress appropriately for the job.

Aside from getting her handed-down clothes, the new schedule did have one advantage. Marley suggested I use her car on Tuesday mornings. I could bring the girls with me to their tennis lesson, then drive them home for lunch. It made some sense since biking from my house to the country club in my new clothes wasn't a really great idea. And I truly loved driving her Mustang. It almost made up for having to work in the pro shop.

On my first morning behind the counter, Leland took a few minutes to show me how to work the register before leaving with Mrs. Bishop for her ten o'clock lesson.

He placed his hand on my shoulder and gave a reassuring squeeze. "You'll be fine, Cate. I'll be back in a few hours to see how you're doing."

After he left, I wandered around the empty shop familiarizing myself with the stock. A few golfers dropped in to browse while they waited for their scheduled tee time. They barely paid me any attention before leaving. Having nothing better to do, I sat behind the counter, poked my nose in a book and started to read. Before I finished the first page, the bells above the door rang. A familiar voice called out.

"Hiya, Marley."

I peaked out from behind Agatha Christie with a warm smile. Henry's bottom lip dropped, giving him that confused, befuddled look I'd seen so often before.

"Uhh . . ." He swung around, staring for a few minutes at the Mustang in the parking lot. Turning back to me, he said, "Where's Marley?"

In Marley's handed-down clothes, with my hair pulled back like hers, I understood Henry's confusion. He looked disappointed when he realized Marley wasn't there.

"Marley is home," I said. "I'm covering for her."

"I brought her these." He raised his hand, displaying a

bunch of wild flowers clutched in his fist. They were just weeds really, daisies, black-eyed Susans, Queen Anne's lace. I thought it was sweet of him.

I reached out for the flowers. "I'll put them in water so they stay fresh until she comes in this afternoon."

Henry pulled back. "No thanks."

The bell rang again and a customer dressed in plaid pants, a striped shirt, and white shoes stepped into the shop. Even on a golf course, dressing like that pushed the boundary of self-respect. I put on my friendliest face and wished him a good morning. Henry continued to stare at me, flowers dangling from his hand. "You look different. Pretty, like Marley. But not as sparkly."

"I have to get to work now, Henry. I'll see you later, okay?"

"Okie dokie. See 'ya later."

I smiled as I watched him shuffle out of the shop, climb into his golf cart, and drive off.

When Plaid Pants asked me to suggest one brand of balls over another, I was lost. My knowledge of golf was pathetically limited. I couldn't even tell a nine iron from a hockey stick. He left empty-handed and I began to wonder what I was doing there.

Leland returned from his lesson, a bead of sweat trickling down his temple. He pulled off his cap and ran his fingers through his hair. I watched him close his eyes as he drank in the cool, conditioned air.

"Any problems while I was gone?" he asked.

"I'm afraid one of the members wasn't very happy with me." I told him about Plaid Pants, how I made a mess of not knowing what I was doing.

"Don't let that old goat intimidate you. He never buys

anything. Like a lot of the guys around here, he only comes in to flirt with Marley."

"I don't know anything about golf," I said. "One of the members told me he shot an eagle this morning. And I actually thought he shot an eagle. He looked at me like I was some kind of idiot or something."

Leland laughed, saying some people have no sense of humor. He flashed his million-dollar smile, put his arm around my waist, and guided me to the wall where dozens of clubs hung on display.

"Let's start here."

He led me through the entire shop inventory, returning to the clubs. Taking one off the rack, he demonstrated how to hold a driver. When he passed it to me, I tried to mimic his grip, but got it all wrong. Turning me around by my shoulders, Leland wrapped his arms around me and placed his hands over mine so I could get the feel of the club. His body was warm from being out in the sun, the smell of his cologne rising from his skin.

He stepped back and shook his head. "This isn't really the best way to go about this. Let's go outside where you'll have some room to swing."

"I'd love to, but I can't. The girls are waiting for me at the tennis courts."

"Oh, right. Another time, then." He gave me a wink, took the club from my hands, and hung it back on the display rack. "Get here early next week so we can hit a few balls before the shop opens."

After collecting the girls from the courts, I got behind the wheel of Marley's car. I drove with the top down, my body holding the memory of Leland pressed against my back, his arms wrapped around me. I stepped on the accelerator, expecting to quickly shed the sensation, but even with Robin in the seat next to me, chattering nonstop, the warmth of Leland's skin against mine lingered.

When we arrived home, I found Marley humming to herself in the kitchen. She smelled of Chanel and hairspray, wearing an outfit I'd never seen before. It seemed to me that the heat made her cheeks a bit rosier than normal, the skin on her neck flushed. I looked around, wondering what she had done with her morning. The house looked the same as always, though I glimpsed Henry's wilted flowers sticking out the top of the trash can.

"Did you have a good morning?" I asked.

"Yes, perfect." She flashed me a smile. "And how were things at the shop?"

"Fine. Quiet."

Robin tugged at her mother's skirt.

"Mama?"

"What is it, darlin'?"

"I want to go to the lake."

Our plan was hatched in the car on the way home from the club. When I asked the girls if they had fun at their tennis lessons, Lissa replied, "All right, I guess," and retreated into a sulky silence. I sensed there was some trouble, but decided to let her tell me about it in her own time. To cheer her up, I suggested we could go to the lake that afternoon. Both girls jumped at the idea.

Robin hopped from one foot to the other, waiting for her mother's answer.

"Well, I don't see why not. As long as Cate doesn't mind taking you, that is." She looked at me, her eyes scanning up and down. "You can keep my car for the afternoon as long as you drop me off at the club before you leave."

"Give me one minute to change." In no time I was back

downstairs, tugging at the bathing suit that I wore under my jeans and T-shirt. Marley reached into her purse and pulled out a few dollars.

"This is for lunch money. They do have sandwiches and such at the lake, don't they?"

"There's a snack bar there. I'm sure they have burgers and hot dogs."

"Well, that would be fine. Just keep the girls away from sweets."

"Go get your sunglasses," I said to Robin. I'd noticed Lissa's were perched on the top of her head, holding back the curls that had grown at least an inch since I first met her. Robin disappeared to search for hers.

We threw towels and a blanket in the car. As I slammed the trunk shut, Robin stood by my side, her sunglasses propped on her head exactly like her sister's. I gave them a swipe with my hand and they dropped down, caught on the tip of her nose. She leaned her head back, looking up at me through the dark lenses with a toothy grin.

The children climbed into the back of the Mustang. Marley slid into the passenger's seat and we were off. After I dropped Marley at the club, Lissa scurried over the console and buckled up.

"Hey, I want to sit up front," Robin whined.

"You'll get your turn on the way home," I replied. Lissa sat still, eyes turned down, lost in thought. It worried me that she was quieter than normal. I reached over and gave her an affectionate poke on her arm. "Everything okay, kiddo?"

"Yeah."

I could tell from the pout in her voice that she was still bothered by something.

As we passed Gordon's, I hit the brakes. It occurred to me that the snack bar may not have apple juice for the girls. Making a U-turn I turned into the store's parking lot. Instructing the girls to wait in the car, I ran in. Jack sat behind the counter, the radio tuned to a Red Sox game.

"Hey, I haven't seen you around lately." He reached for the dial and turned down the volume. Staring at the halter strap of my bikini that protruded from under my T-shirt, he said, "Good day for the beach. Are you going back to Swanzey Lake?"

I picked up the bottle of juice and handed it to him. "The girls want to go for a swim."

"Have a good time."

I paid for my purchase and headed south. The road to the lake ran alongside the Ashuelot River, twisting and turning through the thick woods. I stole a glance at Lissa, glad to see she was acting more herself. Her troubles seemed to have blown away in the summer breeze. When we got to the covered bridge, I waited for a car coming from the opposite direction to cross. With the top of the Mustang down, we could hear the wooden boards clacking under his wheels. The driver smiled and waved, hitting the gas after he passed us. Robin and Lissa waved back, laughing as I maneuvered the car through the nineteenth-century bridge.

On the beach, I spread the blanket in our usual spot. Robin squirmed while I smeared Noxzema on her back. When it was Lissa's turn, she held her arm next to mine, comparing shades of brown. I'd been working on my tan all summer, but while the sun had turned my skin the color of strong tea, Lissa had darkened too. Robin, not to be outdone, wedged herself between her sister and me, pressing her arm against mine.

"You'll never catch up to us," Robin said with a giggle. "Mama either!"

"Well, look who I found." Jack, dressed in cut-off jeans

and unbuttoned cotton shirt, stared down at me. I leaned around to glance behind him.

"Billy's not with me," he said.

I hated that he could read my mind.

"Jack!" Robin shrieked. "How did you know where to find us?"

"When Cate came into the store she practically begged me to join you," Jack said with a wide grin.

"I did not!"

Jack dropped on the blanket next to me. Pushing back the bangs from his face, he kicked his sandals onto the sand.

"I got off early and thought it would be nice to spend the afternoon with you. . . and the kids, of course."

Robin pulled on Jack's sleeve to get his attention. "Will you carry me into the water on your shoulders like Daddy does?"

"Who do you think I am? Superman?" Jack pulled Robin onto his lap and started to tickle her ribs. She wriggled and squirmed, struggling to keep her breath as she laughed.

Jack's attention diverted, I took the opportunity to strip down to my bathing suit. When I pulled my head free of my T-shirt, I blushed to find Jack staring at me.

"Don't be a creep," I said.

"Just enjoying the view."

Avoiding the sharp stones that littered the beach, I guided the girls over the hot sand. Jack raced ahead, diving straight into the spring-fed lake before returning to scoop Robin onto his shoulders. Lissa stayed with me at the water's edge where we inched our bodies into the cold water. Holding Lissa's hand, I kept my eyes trained on Robin who had climbed off Jack's shoulders and was now stretched flat like a surfboard, her feet kicking up a white spray while Jack gently steered her into deeper water. I called out, worried that she couldn't stay afloat if he let go.

With a shrug of his shoulders, Jack guided Robin back to us, setting her back on her feet. He whispered something into her ear, and with a whoop he picked me up and ran a few steps into the lake where he dropped me with a splash. I came up sputtering to the sound of his laughter. Jack reached over and brushed the streaming water from my forehead.

"That wasn't funny!" My words came out like a croak.

Robin giggled. "Yes, it was."

I turned and made my way up the beach, tracking wet sand onto the clean blanket where I wrapped myself in a towel and nursed my ego. After five minutes of watching Jack clown around with the girls, I found myself wishing I was back in the water with them. When lunchtime rolled around and the three of them returned to where I sat alone, I was glad. All four of us slipped into our sandals and trudged through the sand to the snack bar.

The girls filled their bellies with hot dogs and chocolate bars. I insisted they wait for thirty minutes before going back into the water. They complained, but Jack stepped into the void, offering to let them bury him in the black sand. As I sat and watched, I started to notice something. This wasn't the Jack I thought I knew, the arrogant football jock from school. I could see no trace of the hell-raiser who hung out with Billy Reynolds.

On the way back to the car, Jack took my hand. "Are you still mad at me for throwing you into the water?"

"I may have overreacted. You're really good with the girls. I didn't know you were so . . ." We reached the car and he turned to face me. We stood close enough that I could see the black rings around his blue irises.

Behind the shield of the open trunk, while the children

spread their towels on the car's leather seats, Jack leaned over and pressed his lips to mine. When he pulled away, I drew a deep breath. Then, with a start, my eyes snapped open.

"See you here next Tuesday?" Jack said when he pulled away.

"Sure . . ."

Jack's shoulders swung from side to side as he jogged away. I stood watching until he got in his car and drove away.

Chapter 23

Before we parted ways at the Courthouse, I invited Adam to my house for another home-cooked meal. As I had promised Jennifer a good old-fashioned game of Scrabble, I extended the invitation to include her. I spent the next three days in preparation, fussing over the menu, selecting the wine, shopping for food. I wanted everything to be perfect when I told Adam of my recent discovery.

Standing in front of the stove, I inhaled deeply, savoring the basil-scented steam. Picking up my wine glass, I joined my guests in the dining room.

"Five more minutes."

I scanned the table, checking to be sure I hadn't forgotten anything. Salt, pepper, butter dish, whole-grain rolls. Earlier, I'd folded the linen napkins in the shape of swans. In my rush to set the table, I'd faced one the wrong way. Reaching across Adam's shoulder, I set it right.

With everything ready, I ran through my mental checklist one more time. Examining the spread, I decided to wait until dessert before discussing business with Adam. That way, I figured we could enjoy the osso buco without distraction.

"This tastes awesome," Jennifer said.

Acknowledging her compliment with a nod, I mentioned that the tomatoes and spices came from my garden. "Take a few jars of sauce home," I said. "I have more than enough to last me until next summer's crop."

Jennifer shook her head. "I don't cook. Like ever! There

are at least fifteen restaurants within walking distance of my apartment. But thank you anyway."

Her refusal didn't bother me. I found it admirable that she spoke her mind, yet tempered her speech with good manners. Now that I'd met Adam's girlfriend, I could understand his attraction to her. She wasn't what you would call beautiful—short, curly hair, a sharp nose—but her freckles and ready smile softened her appearance. She was almost as tall as Adam with a dancer's body. I could picture her running the New York marathon just for fun.

"I don't have a lot of choice," I said. "Unless you count pizza parlors, there aren't too many restaurants in Keene. I guess that's the price we pay for living in a college town."

"Adam told me you grew up here," Jennifer said. "And that you knew the Booker family. I understand you loved those girls. And Ken too, of course."

Adam caught her eye and she paused. The moment passed so quickly that I wondered if I had imagined it.

"You mean Kenny? Yes, he was a handful but there was something endearing about that boy. That poor kid didn't get a lot of breaks in life."

Jennifer broke off a piece of her veal with a fork. "Tell me something about him."

I told her about the day Kenny kicked Billy in the groin, and the story of their ongoing feud. I explained that things got worse when Billy ambushed Kenny, giving him the beating of his life. Then I told her Marley evened the score with her golf club.

"She went wild." I took a sip of wine. "Billy certainly deserved it, but Marley destroying his motorcycle only made matters worse. Billy struck back right before he left for boot camp."

"How exactly?" Adam asked.

"I already told you." I set my wine glass down. "He

waited for a time when none of us was around, then broke in through the back door."

"Actually, you haven't told me. Every time I ask about that day, you brush me off, saying you aren't ready to talk about it."

I still wasn't. Pushing back my chair, I gathered up the dirty plates. Jennifer stood to help, following me into the kitchen with the leftover vegetables. Loading the dessert dishes on my mother's black lacquer tray—the one she never used in fear of leaving water rings—I handed everything to Jennifer and asked her to carry it into the living room.

"I'll join you as soon as the coffee is ready."

She stood for a moment, watching as I measured beans into the coffee grinder.

"You should tell Adam," she said. "Now."

I gave her a hard look. She held my stare, her chin slightly uplifted. I wasn't used to such arrogance in a person who was young enough to be my daughter. I was about to tell her to mind her own business when she relaxed and took a step back.

"Of course. It's your story to tell. All I'm saying is, you made the decision to help Adam. And from what little I know about you, I expect you'll want to finish what you started." With a shrug of her shoulders, she turned and left the kitchen.

When the coffee was done, I joined them in the living room. Jennifer sat pressed against Adam on the couch, her hand resting on his leg. I set the mugs on the table and took the seat opposite them.

"This Dame Blanche looks perfect." When she caught my eye, I saw the challenge was still there. She cracked the chocolate shell with her spoon, offering Adam the first taste.

I cleared my throat. "I should have told you long before now. I know who murdered Marley and the girls."

"That's easy." A crease formed between Adam's eyebrows. "It was Henry Rusak. But knowing is one thing, proving it is a whole different ball game."

"It wasn't Henry," I said. "Billy Reynolds killed them."

Adam's eyes opened wide.

"I've always told myself Billy didn't mean for it to go that far. Certainly he didn't want to hurt the girls. Not even Billy would . . ." I stopped, took a breath, and started again. "Billy is the one who broke into their house the day before they died. He wanted to get even with Marley for going after him with that golf club. He must have found the insecticide in the garage and got the crazy idea to make her sick by pouring some into the juice."

Adam frowned. "You don't know any of this for sure, right? You're just guessing."

"It had to be Billy. What he did inside the house was awful. Flour and sugar smeared all over the kitchen countertops, broken jars smashed on the floor. Upstairs, he pulled everything out of Marley's dresser and tossed the room. His anger was definitely aimed at her. I can't think of anyone else who would have written WHORE on her bathroom mirror."

"Why didn't you tell someone about the break-in?"

"The first time the police spoke to me about the murders was when Marianne Weede came to my parents' house to interview me. That was two weeks later."

"You could have said something then," Jennifer said.

I let the silence hang over us like a shroud while I searched for an answer.

"Marley never told me why she didn't want Leland to know about the vandalism. Even now I think it was strange. Of course, Leo and Henry knew there was a break-in but Marley told them nothing was taken and no damage was done. By the time I sat on my mother's couch and faced Marianne Weede, I was the only one alive—other than Billy—who knew what he did to the house. I just wanted Weede to go away."

"What do you mean?" I could tell by Adam's expression that he was confused.

"My parents didn't want me to get involved. They told me to keep my mouth shut. They said whatever happened in that house had nothing to do with us. I was only eighteen and though I've always had a mind of my own, I was shaken up by the whole thing and figured they knew best. The following week I left for college and didn't hear from Weede or anyone else about the murders until forty years later when you came knocking on my door."

What I told Adam was mostly true. And since Billy was dead and unable to tell the rest of the story, I wasn't worried that my omissions would ever be discovered. In the end, I didn't think it mattered. Adam always said we didn't have to find the real murderer. We only had to prove prosecutorial overreached.

"After all this time, I don't think this will help," I said. "But when Marley and I were cleaning up, we looked all over for the lipstick that Billy used to write on the mirror. I remember the color was called Very Berry. Funny, isn't it, that I can remember something like that after all these years. Anyway, we couldn't find the lipstick. Maybe Billy kept it as a trophy. Of course, with him gone we'll never know."

"Now what?" Jennifer made use of the time while I was speaking to set up the Scrabble board. Taking turns, we each drew a tile. Since I held the letter "A," I went first. I picked another six tiles and set them on the rack before me.

Adam studied his tiles. "None of what you just told us changes anything. I still aim to convince my professor that Leland is a strong candidate for the Defender Project."

Jennifer wrote down my score. "Twenty-two points. Do you have enough evidence to submit the case to them?"

"No. Not even close." Adam tacked his word onto the end of mine, scoring thirty points. I would have to step up my game if I was going to keep up with him.

"I invited you over tonight to tell you I've got something that might help."

Adam spread his replacement tiles on his rack. "What?"

"The County trial records. It took me forever to enter all that information your father provided, but I downloaded the entire database to my computer. The nature of the crime, verdict, age and race of the defendant, prosecutor name, judge, everything."

"You told me weeks ago that racial bias was a dead end," Adam said. "Leland's judge was clean."

"That's true. But it wasn't the judge we should be looking at."

Adam leaned forward on the edge of the couch. Jennifer withdrew her hand from his leg and took her turn on the board. To my amazement, she added her word to his, hit all the right bonus squares, and scored forty-three points. I was way out of my league.

"Nice one." Adam beamed at Jennifer before turning to me with a smile. "I warned you she was good. Now, let me guess what you're talking about. Marianne Weede's record wasn't as pristine as the good judge's, right?"

"How did you know?"

Comparing Weede's results to those of the other detectives on the force, I discovered an anomaly. Her conviction rate of nonwhite defendants was off the chart. If her suspect was African American, Hispanic, Asian, anything other than white, ninety-nine times out of a hundred, the jury returned a "guilty" verdict. By comparison, her conviction rate for white defendants was below average. The Scrabble game stalled while I explained the results to Adam. A smile played at the corners of his mouth.

"This is great! I can't wait to tell my professor."

"Not great. Not great at all."

I turned to Jennifer, wondering what the problem was.

"Don't you see? This makes matters worse for Mr. Booker."

"What do you mean?" I held up my hand, counting my fingers as I touched on each point. "Weede improperly with-held evidence, lied under oath, and—as the record shows—was racially biased. That's three counts of police misconduct. All grounds for wrongful conviction."

"Jen is right." Ben set his cup back on the coffee table and slumped against the couch. "No judge in his right mind is going to air the county's dirty laundry. It's one thing to prove Weede corrupted this investigation because Leland was Black, but another to suggest it was a career-long habit. The lawsuits against the county would start stacking up like planes at Logan airport. We're screwed."

A chime interrupted the discussion. Pulling his phone from his pocket, Adam checked the caller I.D. He glanced at his watch before answering.

"Hey, Erika. What's up?"

I heard Erika Tripp on the other end of the line, heard the excitement in her voice, but couldn't make out the words.

"Wait a sec," Adam said. "I've got Cate here. Let me put you on speaker."

He took the phone from his ear and set it on the table. Jennifer and I leaned in. Tripp was in midsentence when Adam tapped the glass.

". . . bitch of a day. Dragged away from my desk for one of those sorry-ass sexual harassment workshops. Waste of time if you ask me. The Neanderthals I work with all think it's a big joke. Anyway, before I went home I stopped by my desk to check my inbox. What do you know, up pops this email from some cop in Florida. At first, I didn't get what he was trying to say. Then I put two and two together and realized my techs finally got around to submitting those prints to IAFIS, the FBI's national fingerprint system. This Florida cop got a match with a thumbprint lifted from a murder scene down there."

"Murder scene?" He rose to his feet. "What are you talking about?"

"I'm talking about your dead witness. Turns out Doris Keating didn't have a heart attack after all. Autopsy results indicate she was smothered. Probable weapon is a couch cushion. Can you believe that?"

I heard a soft chuckle coming through the line, but I didn't see anything funny about what Tripp was saying. Adam stared at the phone. I started to speak, but my voice came out as a sort of croak. Clearing my throat, I tried again.

"Detective Tripp, this is Cate," I said. "Are you saying that the fingerprints Adam gave you—Henry Rusak's fingerprints—were found in Doris Keating's apartment?"

"What? Hell no! I'm talking about the other prints, the unidentified prints from the Booker home. Pay attention to what I'm saying here, people. My guys took the prints that were lifted off the Aldicarb from the Bookers' garage and entered them into IAFIS and came up with a match."

My heart raced, wondering who she was about to name. Adam didn't wait for her to say.

"Whose prints were they?" he asked.

"No idea," Tripp said. "They came back as 'unknown.' But whoever put their paws on that poison just left his thumbprint on the rim of Doris Keating's cookie plate. Is that weird or what?"

"So, it wasn't Rusak?" Adam asked.

"Well, I was getting to that . . ."

There was a gap in the conversation that neither Adam nor I jumped to fill. I closed my eyes, aware of my thumping heart as I waited for the detective to finish saying whatever it was she had to say.

"Here's the thing," she continued. "Those guys in the Forensics lab? Bunch of juveniles. Anyway, one day last week they were fooling around during lunch, and well, bottom line is, the bag with Russak's glass was knocked off the bench. Broke into like a million pieces. You gotta get me another sample."

My stomach lurched. Henry was not capable of traveling on his own to Doris Keating's apartment and killing her but without his fingerprints, Tripp couldn't eliminate him as a suspect.

"Erika?" I said.

"Yeah?"

"I'll get you that sample."

Adam turned to me and smiled.

Chapter 24

Steam rose from the mugs of black coffee sitting on the glass coffee table next to six neat stacks of papers. The air in the room was charged with the promise of progress, but nothing was going the way I intended.

"Getting Henry's fingerprints is the only way to clear him," Adam said. "If he's innocent, that is."

I glared at him. "Of course he's innocent! That is why I told Tripp I would get them for her. Still, I hate sneaking behind his back."

I held Adam's gaze as he picked up his coffee.

"Give me a few days to figure something out."

"Don't take too long."

I slammed my hand down on the table. "Where will that leave us when Henry's prints don't match?"

Adam shrugged. "At this point, all I've got is enough material to write a report and turn it in to my professor for a passing grade. Jennifer was right about Weede's history of racial bias. No county judge will let us get very far with that, given it would put every other case she handled at risk. I know you were hoping for more, but unfortunately, I'm out of ideas." He eyed the stacks of paper on the table. "If you've found something else, now is the time to tell me."

"I did a lot of thinking last night after you left, trying to figure out how to hold Marianne Weede accountable for her actions. So, I started again from scratch."

Adam shook his head. "I've read every police report,

every interview, and the entire court transcript more times than I can count. If there's something else in there, I missed it."

"We have to go back to Weede's partner," I said quietly. "Lou Bragg."

"I told you weeks ago, he won't speak with me. I can't force him."

"He'll talk to me."

Adam leaned forward on the couch, giving me his full attention. "Why would he do that?"

"Several years ago, he and his wife asked me to prepare their last wills and testaments. Shortly after that, their son, Louie Jr. was stopped for driving with a broken taillight. The cop would have let Louie go with a warning if it wasn't for the small bag of marijuana sitting on the passenger seat of the car. Still, that wasn't a big deal. Getting caught with less than ¾ of a gram of grass is a civic violation, punishable with a $100 fine. But as his lawyer, Lou asked me to get involved."

"Why?"

"Because Louie was in the process of applying to Keene State. A black mark on his record, even something as trivial as a civic violation would have prevented him from being accepted. I contacted a friend of mine at the college admissions office and explained the situation. I told him that I gave Louie a job in my office so he could pay his parents back. As his employer and family friend, I added my name to his reference list."

"Let me guess . . . Louie Jr. was accepted to Keene State."

"Parents don't forget that kind of thing. Lou will talk to me."

Adam leaned back on the couch and grinned. "Great. Set up a time when we can go see him."

"Lou already said he didn't want to talk to you. It might be best if meet with him alone."

"You're probably right."

I could see the disappointment on Adam's face. He reached for a donut and took a big bite. Wiping the powdered sugar from the corners of his mouth he said, "When you meet with him, make sure you get Bragg to confirm what we already know. That Weede was out to nail Leland. Hopefully he knows if she did anything wrong at the time that falls into the category of police misconduct."

"I'll do my best." I glanced at the stacks of documents. Everything was there with the exception of the medical examiner's report. Having no stomach for the photos in the sealed envelope, I kept the whole package in the side drawer of my desk. Of the six folders, the one marked Racial Bias was the thickest. With a bit of luck, it would be fatter after my interview with Lou Bragg. My gaze shifted to another folder, one that featured Lou's direct involvement. In my careful handwriting, Snitch Testimony was written on the tab. Inside was a printout of Tom Burquest's testimony. Lou was the detective who took Tom's statement. I figured it wouldn't hurt to ask him about it. For some unknown reason, Jack's father was not present at the trial. Instead, his deposition was read into evidence. At the very least, I hoped to learn why the insurance agent didn't testify in court.

At the time of the trial, Lou Bragg was in his early thirties and one of the youngest detectives on the force. The Booker case was his first assignment to a murder investigation. With Marianne Weede as lead detective, the records suggested that Lou mainly contributed by researching telephone records, bank accounts, and hospital reports. From everything I'd read, there was only one exception to the grunt work and that was the interview with Tom Burquest. But Lou was Weede's partner. If she broke the rules of police conduct while investigating the case, he would know.

We agreed to meet at his home on Winter Street. Now seventy-something, he looked closer to my age, more like sixty. A generous dose of silver at his temples softened the severity of his still thick, black hair. He was dressed in running clothes that hung loosely on his long, lean frame. His appearance was the opposite of what I thought an old cop should look like. No soft paunch, no broken blood vessels on his nose, no scars on his face. Lou smiled as he opened the door.

"You're right on time. I was hoping we could chat while I take my daily walk down to the park and back."

The humorless February wind whipped against the backs of my legs. I glanced down, instantly regretting my decision to wear heels and a skirt.

Lou followed my gaze and waved me into the house. Closing the door behind me he said. "I guess I should have told you to wear your sneakers. My walk can wait."

After giving him my coat, I followed him into his study. Heat radiated from the wood stove plugged into the fireplace. I stood in front of it for a minute, warming my hands.

"How's Louie doing?" I asked.

"He sends his regards. He's on duty, otherwise he would have stopped by to say hello in person."

"You must be proud." I knew that after earning his degree in criminal justice, Lou's son followed in his father's footsteps and was now a captain in the Keene P.D.

A shadow passed Lou's face. The smile lines framing his eyes disappeared. "We are, of course. But his mother and I worry about him. Things are different from when I was on the force. Drugs have changed everything. Don't get me started on what cops are up against these days."

"It's not like you had an easy time of it. You must have seen a lot of ugly situations during your time as a homicide detective."

"Right." Lou shifted in his seat. "I know you're here to talk about the Bookers. What's going on?"

"I'm helping a law student from UNH who is researching the Booker case for a project."

Lou nodded. "He called a few weeks ago, asking if I would speak with him about it. Some cops thrive on rehashing old investigations. Not me. I told the kid I have better things to do than live in the past."

"I thought the same thing when Adam asked me to get involved. But he managed to convince me that there were some irregularities with the case. I'm hoping you could help shed light on a few details that elude us."

"Like what?" I could see Lou was curious. But that didn't mean he was comfortable speaking with me. One wrong question on my part and I suspected he would end the conversation.

"We've spoken with your partner, Marianne Weede."

A warry look crept into his eyes. For the first time since I arrived I could see the cop in the man. His guard was up.

"The Booker case was the only time Marianne and I worked as partners." He spoke slowly. "She took the lead on this one. If you have any unanswered questions, I suggest you go back to her."

"Was there some reason you never worked with her again?"

"Let's say there wasn't a lot of chemistry between us and leave it at that." Lou crossed his arms across his chest. I sensed the door closing on our interview so I decided to get to the point.

"She lied on the stand," I said. "And we suspect she destroyed or buried evidence that didn't support her case. Weede was determined to put a Black man behind bars for the murder of his white wife and kids, even if the facts didn't fit her theory. I just can't prove it."

Lou stared at me, unmoving. His steely expression told me I was right.

"Partners don't rat on partners. Marianne and I had our differences, but she was a damned good detective. Now, if you don't mind, I think I'll take that walk." He rose to his feet, ready to show me the door.

I held my ground, unmoving. "I respect your loyalty, Lou. But there is one more thing I need to ask. There was a witness, a jailhouse snitch. If I'm not mistaken, you handled that aspect of the investigation personally."

"That's not a question." Lou remained standing, but at least he didn't hand me my coat.

"You arranged for the DA to offer Tom Burquest a plea agreement. In exchange for his testimony, you managed to get all charges against him dropped. Mr. Burquest gave you sworn testimony that while they shared a cell, Leland confessed to poisoning Marley and the children."

Deep wrinkles formed on the ridge between Lou's eyes. "You've got it all wrong."

"What do you mean?" My heart raced.

"*Jack* Burquest was the snitch, not Tom. You must know him. I believe he practices law in town."

In my mind, everything clicked into place. I recalled the opening lines of the deposition. Q: Please state your full name and spell your last name for the record. A: Thomas John Burquest. B-U-R-Q-U-E-S-T. Thomas John Burquest. I couldn't believe I missed the connection. After a few moments, I realized Lou was still talking.

". . . stopped for DUI in the early morning hours by a cop named Keith Sterling," he said. "You may know him too. He's retired now, lives in those condos on Arch Street. Anyway, that night Jack was so impaired that Sterling brought him in to the police station. Someone called the parents to tell them to come and get the kid. When he got the call, Tom Burquest told Sterling to let Jack spend the rest of the night in jail. Some father, right? The next morning, before anyone showed up to claim the boy, Leland Booker was brought in and put in the cell with Jack."

"What did it take to get Jack to lie? What kind of deal did you strike with him?"

"Hey, hold it right there." The anger I saw in Lou's face a few minutes earlier returned. "I never told him to lie."

"But you must have suspected."

Lou dropped his gaze and I knew once again I had guessed right.

"When I first laid eyes on him, Jack was pacing the cell, begging me to let him go. Said he had just signed up with the Marines, and if the military got wind of his arrest, they'd kick his ass back home. He said he had to get out of there before his dad showed up. Go figure. Seemed more afraid of the old man than of getting shipped off to Vietnam."

"So, you asked what he had to offer?" I prompted.

"I did what we were trained to do. Jack Burquest was charged with DUI and resisting arrest. As soon as his father showed up I took them both into a conference room and laid out Jack's options. I knew the kid had just spent a few hours with our primary suspect for the Booker murders, so I asked if Jack had heard anything we could use. Tom, the kid's father, got the hint right away. He suggested Jack might have something to trade. I called Marianne and told her what was happening. She jumped on it, made the call to the DA's office, and within an hour we had a deal."

"But something about it didn't sit right with you," I said quietly.

"Hell, the murders were no secret. Everyone at the station was talking about them. Every time the phone rang or someone called in on the radio the whole place heard what was going on. With Booker sitting in the same cell, it must have taken Jack about two minutes to put it all together. The kid would have heard enough of what was going on to sell us a story. If you read his deposition, you'll see there's nothing there except what every living soul in the station already knew. So yeah, something didn't sit right with me. It was too easy. But Marianne was the lead detective on the case, and she wanted to go with the kid's story. And it worked. Only one little hitch, and we figured that out without breaking a sweat."

"What was the hitch?"

"The kid was scheduled to report for duty in a few weeks. We knew the trial wouldn't get underway for months. The DA's office fixed it so Jack could give his deposition before he shipped out. He didn't have to make a personal appearance in court. Everyone came away happy."

I met his eyes. "Everyone but Leland Booker."

Lou nodded. "Everyone but Leland Booker."

An uneasy silence hung between us until he spoke again.

"What you said earlier is true. This case never did sit right with me."

"Now is your chance to fix things."

Lou shook his head. "If Booker was innocent . . . well, if that's the case, no one can fix what we did to him."

I took a deep breath, releasing it slowly.

"We have to try."

When Henry didn't answer the bell, I checked and found the door unlocked. With Lou Bragg's comments about the rise in drugs fresh in my mind, I decided to tell Henry to be more careful. Not that he had anything of value to protect, but an old man like him would be an easy target for someone looking for cash to feed a habit. I called out, letting Henry know I was there. I found him stretched out on the couch.

"Henry? Are you okay?"

He was dressed in his pajamas, a moth-eaten afghan covering his legs. Chocolate crumbs stuck to the corners of his mouth and littered the two-day stubble on his chin. More crumbs spilled onto the carpet from the empty cookie package on the floor. He blinked, and it seemed for a moment that he couldn't remember who I was.

"You're back," he mumbled.

It had been two full weeks since I'd seen him. From the look of things, he hadn't fared well in my absence. Guilt washed over me as I realized I should have checked on him the previous Sunday evening after I returned from Florida.

"I brought you something." The paper bag I handed him contained a fresh jar of apple butter. Henry propped himself up and peered inside. A spark of life came into his eyes. He threw the cover from his legs and shuffled into the kitchen. I flinched inwardly as he called out his thanks.

"Bring me any empty jars you have kicking around. I'll need them when I make the next batch."

He reappeared with three empty jars, each bearing his fingerprints. I felt like a rat.

Standing face-to-face, a sour smell hit me. I wondered how long it had been since his last shower. But something else bothered me more than his hygiene. Close up he looked worse than merely disheveled. He looked emaciated.

"When was the last time you ate a healthy meal?"

"I dunno. You were gone a really, really long time. I thought you forgot about me."

"I told you. I made a trip to visit Doris Keating. Don't you remember?"

He mumbled something that I couldn't catch.

"Well, never mind. I'm back now. Let me fix you something to eat."

In the refrigerator I found a jar of pickles and an empty bottle of V8 juice. The freezer didn't yield anything but a few ice cubes. Two cans of vegetable soup were tucked on a shelf in the pantry behind a bag of rice. I pulled one down, added a handful of the rice for substance and turned on the stove. While I waited for the soup to warm up, my eye caught Henry's pill dispenser on the counter. Two weeks earlier, prior to leaving for Florida, I made sure to fill the tray with the correct number of pills for each day. Half of the sections were still full. No wonder Henry was acting strangely. Not only did he forget to take his cholesterol medication and blood thinner, he had skipped taking his anti-depressant as well.

"I saved the mail like you said."

I turned with a start, not realizing he had followed me into the kitchen. Sure enough, sitting on the counter was a basket overflowing with envelopes. I poured his soup into a bowl, scooped up the mail, and set everything on the kitchen table. Before sitting down, I tipped one day's worth of pills into my palm and handed them to him with a glass of water.

"I'm sorry, Henry. I should have asked someone to check on you while I was gone."

While Henry slurped his soup, I sorted through his mail. I tossed three introductory offers for credit cards into the trash together with an invitation for a free luncheon where Henry could listen to a financial advisor tell him how to invest his money. Out of habit, I set aside the sales fliers from Sears and Hannaford's to save for the bottom of the parakeet's cage. My hand froze in midair. The house was too quiet. I slipped into the living room to check. Seed overflowed the food dish. The water dish was bone dry. The parakeet lay dead on the bottom of the cage.

"Do you think maybe you forgot to give the bird some water?" I asked when I returned to the kitchen.

"Maybe." Henry pulled a shank of hair on the back of his head.

"Don't worry." I reached over and pushed his hand away. "We'll get you a new one."

Tears filled his eyes. "You were gone a really, really long time."

I finished sorting the mail, holding onto the bills and a bank statement. Running short on time, I stuffed them together with his checkbook into my purse, planning to take care of paying the bills when I got home.

"I'm know, Henry. I promise not to leave you alone again. Okay?"

A goofy grin broke out on his face. "Okie dokie."

I got rid of the dead bird and left, promising Henry that I would be back soon with some food. Placing the empty jars on the seat next to me, I reflected on the visit. Henry was obviously lost while I was gone. His age was catching up with him. For the first time, it occurred to me that he may no be safe living alone.

Chapter 25

In the country club's dining room, surrounded by Keene's elite, I waited for Jack. The venue was my idea. It seemed like the appropriate place to confront Marley's killer with the past.

For over four decades, I chose to blame Billy. His hatred of Marley burned red-hot and I believed it was his hand, and his hand alone, that added Aldicarb to the orange juice. Whether or not he intended harm to the girls, I would never know. Only one thing was for sure: Jack was in the house with Billy that day. After they broke-in, Jack sent me Marley's diamond bracelet. There were two sets of unidentified prints on the Aldicarb. And one of those sets belonged to the person who was in Doris Keating's condo the night she was killed. That left me with a bitter truth. Billy didn't act alone.

With misguided loyalty, I protected Jack by holding my tongue. Now, I seethed in anger at being played for a fool. I aimed to set things right by destroying the man I once thought was my friend.

The undercurrent of chatter died. I glanced up to see all heads turn as Leo Bishop made a royal entrance, his wife, Mildred, on his arm. With his free hand, Leo waved his cigar to the members in the room. As he guided Mildred to their table by the window, he stopped to have a word with old friends. To my surprise, he paused when he reached my table.

"Well, look who's here, Mildred. You remember Cate, don't you?"

Mildred Bishop, her chin slightly raised, looked down.

Her neutral expression suggested she had no idea who I was. She said nothing, waiting.

"Cate's mother waited tables at the club for years," Leo continued. "Surely you remember Sandra Stokes?"

"Oh yes, of course." Mildred's smile seemed to chill a few degrees. "And how is your mother?"

"She passed away five years ago," I replied. "You sent flowers."

Mildred's face paled. Leo turned up the wattage on his smile. "It's nice to see you again," he said. "We just returned from our second home in Florida. I see you became a member of the club while we were gone."

"Jack Burquest invited me to be his guest this evening."

"Ah, of course."

Mildred tugged on her husband's arm. "I believe our table is ready, Leo."

As they walked away, I felt the stares of those members who were seated close enough to hear our little exchange. An elderly gentleman—I recognized Plaid Pants from my days in the pro shop—sat at the next table with his trophy wife. I forced a smile and nodded in this direction, then turned my attention to the menu.

I watched in disgust as Jack crossed the room, holding himself erect. He worked hard to appear sober but even from a distance, I could see he was drunk. When he bent down, I turned my head and caught his kiss on my cheek.

"Sorry I'm late," he said. "After everyone else left, the boss called me into his office to tell me I am no longer a part of his firm."

His head swiveled around the room. "Where is the waitress?"

"Jack, look at me. There's something important that I need to tell you."

"Not now, Cate. We are going to celebrate."

He slapped the table, waving his hand in the air as he shouted. "What does it take to get a drink in this place? I need a waitress over here."

For the second time that evening, all eyes in our section of the dining room turned in my direction. A waitress—the same one who served Jack and me the last time we were there—appeared by Jack's side.

"May I take your drink order, sir?" she asked.

"Thought you'd never ask. Ketel-One, straight up. Make it a double. And for the lady?"

"Tonic water, please," I said.

Jack thought there was something funny about that. With an explosive laugh, he reached across the table and took both my hands. Rubbing an old-age spot on my wrist, he raised his eyes to meet mine.

"Why don't you wear that bracelet I sent you?"

"Jack, don't . . ." I tried to pull back my hands, but he held tight.

"Listen, I've made a lot of mistakes in my life, but hell, I never understood what went wrong between us. Now that Arnie is gone, maybe we can—"

"Jack . . ."

"Shit." He released his grip on me and ran both hands down his face. The waitress reappeared, placing our drinks in front of us. Without looking up Jack said, "Bring me another. This one will be gone by the time you get back."

After the waitress left, Jack took a long swallow of vodka. I wondered how many drinks he had before arriving at the club. Taking in the situation, I knew it would be best to cut the evening short. I would have to find another time to convince Jack to tell the truth about his testimony regarding Leland's so-called confession.

"You didn't answer my question." He set down his glass and stared at me through blood-shot eyes. "About the bracelet, that is."

Stealing one quick glance at my wrist, I looked up to catch his leering smile. Something inside me came unleashed.

My words shot out like a missile. "That bracelet belonged to Marley!"

Jack winced and reached for his drink.

"You're a thief and a liar and I'll never forgive you for what you did."

"We were just having a little fun. It was all Billy's idea." Jack actually smiled at the memory, but the expression on my face stopped him cold. He wiped his mouth with the back of his hand and cleared his throat. "Billy was pissed as hell at Marley. He wanted revenge. You didn't see how she came after him. She could have killed him with that golf club. And for what? Teaching that Mazza brat a lesson? Give me a break, that little bastard had it coming. Anyway, Billy gets this great idea. He says we can break into the house and mess things around a little. You know, just to let Marley know she didn't have the last word. Billy was itching to get even, and he needed to work off some steam. It was no big deal."

"No big deal? You think stealing Marley's bracelet was no big deal?"

"Okay, I'll admit that was wrong. But, Jesus, this was like a hundred years ago. She's dead, right? It's not like . . ."

I looked at him, incredulous. "Jack, you killed three people."

"What? No way! How can you possibly think that?"

Until then, Jack and managed to keep our voices low so the people around us wouldn't hear. But those last words burst out of his mouth, reaching the far corners of the room. Plaid Pants turned around and shushed us.

"Sorry," I mumbled. I glared at Jack.

"How can you possibly think I'd do something like that?" Jack repeated in a hoarse whisper. He suddenly appeared sober, a genuine look of shock on his face.

"What am I supposed to think?" I spoke through clenched teeth. "You're forgetting that I saw what you wrote on the bathroom mirror."

"I have no idea what you're talking about."

"You used Marley's lipstick to write the word, WHORE."

Jack grew quiet, staring at the empty glass in his hand. "That sounds like something Billy would do. At least now I understand why you never answered my letters from 'Nam. Why you refused to see me when I came home. You actually thought I killed those people?"

I had a tight feeling in my chest. Our conversation had taken an unexpected turn. Gathering my bag, I stood to leave. Jack rose too, knocking his chair over as he grabbed the table for balance. By the time he caught up with me I was outside, waiting for the valet to return my car.

"You have to believe me, Cate." He grabbed me by the arm and twisted me around to face him. "I didn't kill those people."

My breath caught with a hitch. Seeing the look in his eyes, I tried to believe him. For a few beats I considered that Leland might have murdered his family after all. The valet brought my car to a stop in front of me. Shaking free of Jack's hold, I shoved a few dollars into the boy's hand. Turning to Jack, I said, "Tell me this. If you didn't do it, then who did?" I slipped behind the wheel of my car, slammed the door, and floored the gas. Glancing back, I caught sight of Jack, his image in the mirror shrinking as the distance between us grew.

I couldn't sleep. Slipping on my bathrobe, I stepped

outside and leaned against the railing of my back deck. The
moon threw eerie shadows across the yard. My garden lay fal-
low, a few errant leaves trapped in the furrows. A gust of wind
grabbed the hem of my robe, the last arctic breath of winter
raising goose bumps on my bare legs. I heard something rustle
in the dead leaves under the bushes. A raccoon? A mouse?
Perhaps the neighbor's cat. I held still. No sound now but the
wind sighing in the oak branches. Shielding a match in the cup
of my hand, I lit a cigarette.

Shivering in the cold, I drew smoke into my lungs. A
rush of nicotine cleared my head and I could feel my heart
pounding in my chest. I realized I had to face Jack again—
sooner rather than later. For Leland's sake, I needed to focus on
the fact that Jack lied to Lou Bragg about Leland confessing to
the murders. Everything else—the bracelet, the break-in, everything—had to take a back seat. Without Jack setting the record
straight, Adam's wrongful conviction case didn't have a prayer.
And after coming this far, I couldn't let Adam down.

Two cigarettes later, I returned to the warmth of the
house. Shedding my robe, I crawled under the covers. My path
was clear. Tomorrow I would call Adam and tell him what I
learned from Detective Bragg. Then I would have to contact
Jack and somehow persuade him to tell Adam what happened
when he was locked up in that cell with Leland. After our scene
at the club, I doubted Jack would ever speak to me again. But
if there was any truth to what he told me, I hoped against hope
that he would help Leland now. And if Jack cooperated, Adam
would have enough evidence to file for Leland's wrongful
conviction hearing. Best of all, I would finally be done with the
ghosts of the past.

Closing my eyes, I tried to relax. Sleep refused to come.
Memories of the distant past kept playing in my mind.

Chapter 26

I loved golf. Leland was a patient teacher, smiling encouragement when I missed the ball on my first three swings. When I made contact on the fourth stroke, the ball veered crazily, pinging off one of the electric carts parked nearby. The ring of Leland's laughter stung. I felt the heat rise to my face. He stepped closer, covering my hands with his to correct my grip. I felt the warmth radiating from his body. Despite the distraction of his touch, under his guidance my next few shots flew true.

"Impressive." Looking up, I was surprised to see Mildred Bishop leaning against a gleaming golf cart, her heavily made-up eyes fixed on Leland, a mocking smile on her red lips. "Am I early?"

Leland glanced at his watch. "Right on time." He warned me earlier that he was scheduled to coach Mrs. Bishop through a round of eighteen holes that morning. I checked my own watch and realized I needed to open the pro shop.

"Thanks for the lesson." Slinging Marley's borrowed clubs over my shoulder, I lugged them back to the clubhouse. After unlocking the door, I turned on the lights and propped the "OPEN" sign in the window. Alone for most of the morning, I had plenty of time to work on my putt with one of the practice pads in the shop.

Several hours later, Leland stood in the open door, waving as Mrs. Bishop drove off in her cart. When I asked how the lesson went, he shook his head.

"Mildred owns the best golf clubs money can buy, has

played this course for years, and today she managed to break one hundred for the first time."

"Is that good?"

"Not really, but she thinks I'm some sort of genius. And as long as she believes that, I have a job. How'd it go here while I was gone?"

"I put price tags on those new sweaters, and moved the sale items to the rack in the back of the store." I watched as Leland ran a towel across the back of his neck. A trickle of sweat run down his temple following the line of his jaw. He wiped the side of his face and tucked the towel into his back pocket. "I also sold Plaid Pants a Ping driver."

"Plaid Pants?"

"You know, that guy who was in last week. He wears the plaid pants . . ."

Leland laughed out loud, and I blushed all over again. "You must mean Stan Robinson," he said. "I can't believe you got him to finally buy something. Maybe you should work with me full time while Marley stays home with the kids."

"But . . ."

"I'm just kidding." He pulled a bottle of water from the refrigerator and took a long drink. "The girls would kill me if I took their favorite babysitter away. Bad enough that you're leaving for college soon."

I thought about Robin and knew she would adjust to my departure without any problem. But I suspected Lissa would truly miss me. Marley was too busy to notice Lissa's brooding silences, and I doubted that Leland was aware his older daughter was having trouble adjusting to the recent changes in her life. With his next words, I realized my mistake.

"Lissa is going to be heartbroken when you leave. I think you know she hates the fact that I uprooted the family to take this job. Don't get me wrong, since you started working for us, she's been much happier here. But she still misses her friends back in Georgia."

"Have you thought about taking her back for a visit?"

"Marley will never go back."

I glanced at the clock on the wall and realized it was time to leave. Promising Leland I would see him the following week, I left to pick up the girls.

Robin and Lissa were waiting for me courtside, tennis racquets sticking out of their bags. When I approached, Robin was smiling from ear-to-ear, jabbering away with a red-headed girl who sat next to her. Lissa sat apart, staring into the distance.

"This is my new best friend Kelly," Robin said. "I invited her to come to the lake with us this afternoon."

The bright morning sun fought a losing battle against angry storm clouds. Even as I turned my face skyward, the rumble of thunder sounded in the distance.

"We won't be going to the lake today." I turned to Kelly. "You're welcome to join us next week if your mother says it's okay."

I wrote down Kelly's phone number, vowing to give her mother a call and make the arrangements. Robin was disappointed, but after she waved goodbye to Kelly, she skipped ahead, leading the way to the car. I took Lissa by the hand and followed.

Fat drops of rain splashed against the Mustang's windshield. Robin turned up the volume so she could hear Michael Jackson belt out "Rockin' Robin" over the din of rain beating the canvas roof. I clutched the steering wheel, focusing on the white lines that ran down the center of the road. After I pulled to a stop in the Bookers' driveway, the girls and I counted to three and burst from the car, making a mad dash for the house.

Marley watched from the porch, laughing as we sloshed across the lawn. She jumped out of the way when we shook our heads, the three of us spraying water like wet dogs.

"Not exactly a good day for the lake," she said.

I dropped the car keys into her outstretched hand. "There's always next week."

The spent storm spit the last few drops of rain. Marley, taking no chances with her carefully teased hair, looked to the sky and opened her umbrella. With mincing steps, she avoided the puddles on the driveway as she made her way to the car. A short time later, while the girls were still upstairs changing into dry clothes, someone raised a racket at the back door.

"Where were you?" Kenny glared at me from under the fringe of his dripping bangs. Soaked to the bone, he cradled a new batch of muddy golf balls in his drenched T-shirt. By the scowl on his face I could see he was angry, fighting mad. The sight of him made me smile, which only made him madder still.

I realized he wasn't aware of the new schedule. "The girls are now taking tennis lessons at the club on Tuesday mornings. How long have you been waiting out there?"

"A long time." His tone lost some of the sharp edge. His angry expression morphed into a pout.

I told him to stand there, just inside the door, while I retrieved the old bucket from the garage. When I returned I saw a muddy puddle spread on the linoleum beneath his feet. After he dropped the balls into the pail, I grabbed a clean towel and started to rub him dry.

The cold rain had washed the color from his face. I worked my way down his scrawny body, glad to see no trace of the awful black and green bruises that Billy had dealt him. The cast on Kenny's arm was gray with grime. Above the plaster

I thought I saw the hint of some fresh marks. He caught me staring and pulled away, twisting his body to block my view.

"I remembered his mangled bike. "Did you walk here all the way from your house?"

"What do you think? How else could I get here?"

"What's wrong with your flip-flop?" I grabbed hold of his left ankle and removed the sandal that didn't look quite right to me. After a quick inspection, I realized the thong had ripped away from the cardboard-thin sole. Freeing my pony-tail, I wrapped the rubber band several times around the knob of the thong. It wouldn't hold for long, but Kenny gave me a small smile of gratitude when I passed the sandal back.

"You could catch a cold from standing outside in the rain. Marley was home the whole time we were gone. She would have let you wait inside until we got back."

"I knocked like a million times but no one answered. I was about to go when that old pervert showed up. I couldn't let him catch me red handed with those balls so I hid in the bushes until he left."

I saw a spot of grime on his hand that I missed on the first pass. Grabbing hold of his arm, I wiped the dirt off with the damp towel.

"Mr. Bishop is afraid of a lawsuit if somebody gets hurt on the course. It's part of Henry's job to keep you kids out of the water hazards."

"Yeah, well, I guess that creep wasn't looking for me anyway. He was too busy snooping around and playing with himself." A sly smile crept across his face. "Besides, them balls didn't come from old man Bishop's precious ponds. I found 'em on the grass."

"Not the driving range!"

"Hey, finders keepers, that's what I say. I would've taken more, but I couldn't carry 'em all. There must have been

a hundred balls out there. Two hundred. Maybe more. Them
pussy golfers just leave 'em there."

"You just lost another penny from your jar."

Kenny's eyes opened wide. "I didn't mean those kinds
of balls."

"You said, 'pussy,'" I fought the urge to smile. "You can
only use that word when you're talking about a cat."

———————————

Though the sky soon cleared, the ground was sodden.
I insisted on keeping Kenny and the girls inside. They entertained each other in the family room, fitting pieces of a jigsaw
puzzle together while I warmed a can of tomato soup and
prepared grilled cheese sandwiches for lunch. Spatula in hand,
I went to see who knocked on the door.

"Hmmm, something smells good." Jack kissed me lightly before tucking a loose strand of hair behind my ear.

"I was hoping you would stop by. The kids will be happy to see you."

"Wasn't looking for the kids." He pulled me close and
kissed me again. I leaned into him, lost in the moment. When
we separated, he pushed his bangs off his forehead and peered
over my shoulder.

"The girls are in the family room, putting a puzzle together with Kenny."

"When will we have a chance to be alone?"

"I have to mind the girls until Marley gets home from
the club. I was just about to give the kids some lunch. Do you
want to join us?"

"Thanks, but I promised Mr. Gordon I'd help him
restock the shelves this afternoon. I'll pick you up here after
I leave work. We can grab a burger at Timolean's and catch a
movie. *The Godfather* is playing at the drive-in."

After he left, I closed my eyes and leaned against the

door for a few moments, thinking of the evening ahead. I loved being the object of Jack's attention, something that amazed me given his popularity at school. But it occurred to me that our timing was off. In a few short weeks he would be leaving for boot camp and I was starting college. With a sigh, I decided to just enjoy whatever time we could spend together. Take it day-by-day. After all, there was no telling what the future would bring.

Calling the kids to lunch, I returned to the kitchen just in time to catch the soup before it boiled over.

Chapter 27

"Why would you give your bike to that Mazza boy?" Dad asked. "You know how those people are. Junk cars and broken toys all over their lot. The bike that you took such good care of will be trashed in no time."

It was my day off, and I regretted getting up in time to have breakfast with my dad. Over a bowl of cereal, I announced I decided to give Kenny my old bicycle.

"I feel sorry for him, Dad. Kenny doesn't even own a decent pair of flip flops. And you should see the clothes he wears. Billy Reynolds beat the poor kid for no good reason, then destroyed his bike. My old bicycle has been in the garage collecting cobwebs for years. What else am I going to do with it?"

"Place an ad in the classifieds. Sell the thing. God knows you could use the extra money for school."

Frustration rose in my throat. It was my bike, and I felt I should be able to do whatever I wanted with it. My father was treating me like a child. I turned to my mother who hid behind the morning edition of the *Keene Sentinel*.

"What do you think, Mom?"

My mother lowered the paper and peered over the top of her reading glasses. She smiled, a sure sign that she had been following the discussion while pretending to read.

"I say it's your bike." She gave my father a pointed stare. "You can do what you like with it. Personally, I think it's nice that you want to help that poor boy. God knows he can use all the help he can get."

Dad glared at my mother. "Okay, Cate. Give the boy your bike if you want. But don't expect me to give you a lift to the Mazza place in my truck."

"Here." Mom grabbed her keys from the rack by the door and tossed them to me. "Be back by ten. I need the car to get to the club in time to work the lunch shift."

I found Kenny in his yard amid the junk that my father so accurately described. He stopped sawing an old wooden wine crate long enough to glance at me before going back to work.

"What are you making?" I asked.

"A cage for my hampsters."

With his arm still in a cast, he wasn't making much progress cutting the wood. I took hold of the crate to hold it steady. His tongue stuck out the corner of his mouth as he concentrated.

"I didn't know you had hamsters."

"I'm gonna buy me some soon as I finish making this cage. They have lots of babies, you know."

"And what are you going to do with the babies?"

Kenny threw me a look that suggested I was a complete idiot. "Sell 'em. What else would I do with them.?"

"Do you have enough money to buy the first two?"

"I got some in that cussin' jar, don't I?" He paused, glancing at me out of the corners of his eyes.

"Some, but not enough." I stood up to stretch the muscles in my back.

Kenny studied the crate only to discover that for all his effort he had only made a small cut in the wood. Looking totally defeated, he threw the saw into the weeds and gave the crate a solid kick with his bare foot. He yelped, hopped a few steps and dropped to the ground to check for splinters. Finding none, he jumped back on his feet.

"Why did you come here?" he asked.

"I brought you something. Come and see."

Kenny watched with interest as I opened the trunk of my mother's car. When I produced the bike, he grimaced.

"What do you expect me to do with that thing?"

"I thought you could use it. You know, since your bike is broken."

"But it's pink!"

I never thought about that. Staring at my old bike, a solution came to me.

"Where's your bike?"

"What good will that do?"

"You'll see. I have an idea."

"Wait here."

When he disappeared behind the back of the house, I took the opportunity to look around. Kenny and his mother lived in a dingy mobile home perched on cinder blocks. Turning away, I studied the assortment of items in the front yard. Weeds grew up around a rusted Ford, also propped up on blocks. A freezer chest, coils of barbed wire, and a baby carriage were among the inventory strewn about. Before I could take it all in, Kenny emerged from the back of the house pushing his bicycle. The front wheel was bent beyond repair, the seat was gone entirely, and one pedal dangled by a screw. He let the bike fall to the ground and looked from one to the other, then back again.

"What's this great idea you have?"

"Look, the two bikes are the same size. We can strip mine down and use the parts to fix yours."

Head tipped to the side, Kenny made a full circle around my old bicycle.

"We need a wrench or something." Kenny scanned the yard. I was pretty sure there was no wrench amid the detritus.

I walked back to my mother's car and reached into the emergency toolbox that my father insisted she keep in the trunk. Straightening up, I held up the wrench before tossing it to Kenny. He caught it easily, squatted down in front of the bicycle and set to work. He'd only managed to free the handlebars when the sound of a squeaking hinge caught my attention.

"Hey, what's going on out there?" Kenny's mother stood on the wooden stoop, wrapped in a faded satin robe. Her hair was bleached blond and looked like she hadn't run a comb through it in weeks. Black smears of mascara ringed her eyes. In one hand she held a plastic tumbler. Squinting in our direction she shouted. "Where'd you get that bike, boy? If I find out you stole it, I swear I will beat you black and blue to Sunday."

"Hello, Mrs. Mazza," I called out. "I hope we didn't wake you." I'd never laid eyes on the woman before, but my mother's gossip stuck in my head. Everything I'd ever heard about Theresa Mazza appeared to be true. Though I wasn't surprised by her appearance, I was shocked to see that Kenny's mother seemed to be no more than five years my senior, placing her somewhere around thirteen when she gave birth to Kenny.

Kenny shouted back at her. "I didn't steal nothing, Ma. This here is Cate's old bike."

"Well, she can take it right back." Theresa Mazza glared at me with bloodshot eyes. "We don't take charity."

"It wasn't charity, Mrs. Mazza. Kenny bought this bike from me."

She snorted. "Yeah? How much did the little shit pay you for that old thing?"

"Five bucks," Kenny chimed in.

"Liar. Where would you get that kind of money?"

"I earned it." Kenny stood with his legs planted apart,

hands on hips, chin raised in defiance. "And it's all gone now, so don't bother looking for where I keep my money hid."

"Don't sass me, boy." Mrs. Mazza shifted her suspicious gaze back to me. "You should be ashamed, selling him that heap of crap for so much money."

With another squeak of the door hinge, Kenny's mother disappeared into the trailer.

"Where's my five dollars?" I asked.

"You'll get it when fuckin' pigs fly."

"I should charge you two cents for that one."

"Are you gonna help me fix my bike or not?" Not waiting for an answer, Kenny got back to work.

Long before I was due back with my mother's car, Kenny's bike was restored to working order. He left the remaining pieces of the cannibalized bicycle strewn about, destined to eternal rust. With a wave of his hand, Kenny jumped on his bike and tore down the street, a cloud of dust rising in his wake.

Chapter 28

I tapped a Marlboro out of the box. Adam's eyes followed my hands as I lit up. After taking a deep drag, I politely turned my head and blew the smoke into my garden. As always, I held the cigarette the way Marley taught me, like the Pope giving benediction.

We sat on the back deck overlooking the lawn, still heavy with early morning dew. Tender leaves adorned the oak in the back corner, the pussy willow clothed in a soft, furry bloom. While we waited outside for Jack to arrive, Jennifer remained in the living room, her nose stuck in a book titled *Rules of Evidence*.

"Do you think he'll show?" Adam asked.

"I don't know. He's drinking again." I glanced at my watch before pushing aside dozens of butts in the ashtray to clear space for my spent cigarette.

"I haven't seen you this nervous since we were in Florida. What's wrong?"

I was afraid Jack wouldn't show. But more than that, I was afraid if he did turn up, the whole truth would come out. Earlier, when I told Adam about my discussion with Lou Bragg, I didn't mention my failed dinner date with Jack. If Adam learned I lied about Jack's involvement in the break-in, he would never trust me again. And losing Adam's trust bothered me more than I cared to admit.

"I'm worried about what Jack will say," I replied.

"You told me he is willing to admit Leland never confessed to the crime."

"With Jack you never know. Now that he's had time to think about it, he might change his mind."

Two days earlier, I found the courage to call Jack. I felt the chill in his voice coming through the line. After a long pause, he confessed to everything Lou Bragg always suspected concerning the plea bargain. Jack agreed to meet with Adam at my house and go on record to help Leland. I knew Jack better than almost anyone, and while I could never forgive him for lying to save his own skin, I wanted to believe he told me the truth when he said he wasn't involved in the murders.

Now Adam shrugged. "My professor's project deadline isn't negotiable. And I can only include verifiable facts in my report. That excludes Detective Bragg's comment that he thinks Jack Burquest lied. I need an admission directly from the source. If Jack doesn't show, then I can't include that in my report."

"But what about all the other information we uncovered? Police misconduct, suppression of evidence, racial bias. That's got to count for something."

"My professor has already mentioned Leland to his friend in the Defender Project, the organization that accepts wrongful conviction cases. What we've got is good, but without Jack's testimony, it won't be enough for them to consider Leland's petition for representation. When you agreed to help me with this project, I warned you not to get your hopes up. The odds of this helping Leland are a million-to-one. But if Jack admits he gave false testimony at the trial, then maybe we'll be able to file for a judicial hearing. There would still be a long road ahead to freeing Leland, but that would be a start."

I was beginning to appreciate the enormity of what I didn't know about criminal law. I had no real notion of the

legal gyrations in wrongful conviction cases. As I was about
to ask Adam more about the process, I head the front doorbell
chime. Jack Burquest had arrived.

He smelled like he hadn't showered in days. The air
around him turned like sour milk. I crossed the rug and opened
a window before taking orders for coffee. Jennifer jumped up
to help me in the kitchen.

"Jack isn't what I expected," she said when we
were alone.

"He's been going through a rough time."

"Obviously. But what I mean is, something just occurred
to me. The fact that he's a total wreck works in our favor. Look
at him. When he says he lied to save his own skin, the whole
world will believe him."

I sent her back into the living room with a serving plate
stacked with warm snicker doodles. Following with a full
carafe, I filled three cups with black coffee and passed them
around. Jennifer lifted her glass of ice water to her lips, took a
sip, and stood. She walked over to where Adam had mounted
a video camera on a tripod across from where Jack sat in my
Eames lounge chair.

Jack didn't seem like he was up for small talk, but Adam
did his best to thank him for showing up and reassure him
that he was doing the right thing by speaking with us. As Jack
dipped his face to the steam rising from his cup, for the first
time I noticed a bald spot on top of his head. He looked up,
caught me staring at him, and pushed back what was left of
his bangs from his forehead. His eyes revealed no sign of the
affection I used to see there.

"I guess we can get started," Adam said. "If you don't
mind Mr. Burquest, I'd like your permission to record our discussion here today."

When Jack nodded his approval, Jennifer swiveled

the camera toward him. She pushed a button and a red light appeared. Adam stated the date and location of the meeting, followed by the names of all those present. I could tell by the confident tone in his voice and the flow of his script that he had rehearsed before arriving at my house.

"Mr. Burquest, can you confirm that you are here as a willing witness to give testimony regarding what transpired between you and Leland Booker on the morning of August 9, 1972?"

Jennifer kept the camera trained on Jack.

"Yes."

"And you understand that you have a right to legal counsel during this deposition, but that you have waived that right."

"That's right. I mean, yeah, I don't need a lawyer."

"Great. Now could you please state your full name, and spell your last name for the record."

I remembered reading the introduction to Jack's testimony from the original trial transcript. Adam had copied the legal jargon word-for-word. He wasn't yet a full-fledged lawyer, but he was getting the hang of the language. I hid my smile behind a sip of coffee.

Not wasting time, Adam jumped back to the day when Jack met Leland in jail.

"On that morning, while you were being held at the Keene police station, did you speak with Leland Booker?"

"Yeah, they put him in the cell with me. It's not much of a jail, really. Each cell has two cots and a sink. I got the impression that they only use the place to hold people short term. You know, until they were released or sent somewhere else."

"Was there anyone else with you that morning?"

"No, just us two."

"You and Leland Booker."

"That's right. I spent the night waiting for my old man to get me out of there. Some time that morning they brought Leland in."

"And how would you describe Mr. Booker's condition when you saw him?"

"He looked like shit. In shock, I guess you could say. I didn't know the guy well, but I'd seen him around the club and he was usually pretty upbeat. Friendly like. But that morning he acted like I wasn't there, even after I said hello."

"So, you initiated a conversation?"

"I wouldn't call it a conversation. I asked him if he was all right, and he said no, that his wife and kids were dead. All he wanted was to get out of there and go see their bodies for himself."

"Do you remember his exact words?"

"Something like, 'They told me they're dead. I need to get out of here.' I can't tell you his exact words. You need to understand I was a little preoccupied. I had my own problems to think about."

Adam scrolled down a few lines on his tablet. After a short pause he continued.

"Before Mr. Booker was put in the cell with you, did you overhear the police discussing the murders?"

"Sure. Everyone was talking about it. It's a small place and that was big news."

"Were you surprised when they brought Mr. Booker in?"

"Not really. That is, I could guess he was a suspect. Why else would they lock him up?"

"What happened next?"

"Nothing until my father showed up. Then this county detective—Lou Bragg was his name—he took my father and me into a small room. Dad was giving me a hard time, saying how the Marines wouldn't let me in with an arrest record. I never even thought about that until then, but I believed him. He was on a slow burn and I knew from experience I was going to be in some serious trouble when we got out of there."

"What do you mean?"

"Aren't we getting a little off track here?" Jack's eyes darted to me. "The thing is, when my dad said that stuff about the Marines, I could feel this knot in my stomach getting bigger and bigger. All I could think was that my ticket out of this town was slipping away. I can't believe I was that stupid. Can you imagine I wanted to go to 'Nam? Hell, in 1972 most of the country knew what a bad idea that was. Life sure can be ironic."

Jack held out his hands, palm up, as if to say that he had nothing to show for a lifetime of bad decisions. He turned to me and I dropped my gaze to study the carpet.

"Anyway, Bragg left me alone in the room with my father. After a while he came back and said if I had something to trade, he might be able to get the charges dropped and my record would be clean. Sounded like a good idea at the time. Dad pressed me to give them what they wanted so I signed some papers and pretty soon we were out of there. I never saw Leland again."

"Let me understand," Adam said. "Leland Booker never told you that he killed his wife and two children?"

Jack cleared his throat. "Right. He never said anything like that."

"And you were released as part of the deal to testify that he had?"

"Yeah, that's what happened."

I poured the last of the coffee into Jack's cup and stood. "Maybe this would be a good time for a break. I'll make a fresh pot."

Adam nodded and signaled to Jennifer that she could turn off the camera. "Let me help you."

Jennifer gave him an imploring look, begging him not to leave her alone with Jack. Adam, oblivious, jumped up and followed me into the kitchen.

"How do you think it's going?" Despite the polished professionalism he had displayed in the other room, I caught a glimpse below the surface of a student who needed reassurance.

"You're doing fine. I'm not sure how much longer Jack is going to hold up, though."

"I'll wrap everything up as quickly as I can, but I still need him to give me more details about the deal with the prosecutor's office. And it would be good to get some background on why he was arrested in the first place. I only hope he's as forthcoming with that stuff as he has been with lying about Leland's confession."

"Go easy on him. Can't you see he's sorry for what he did?"

Adam studied me. A crease formed between his eyebrows. "You still have feelings for him, don't you?"

"I don't feel anything but disgust for that man," I snapped. "But I can see he's trying to do the right thing."

"But you can't forget about all the years Leland lost because of what Jack Burquest did to him."

"The difference between you and me is that you blame Jack for that. I blame whoever killed Marley and the girls." I picked up the pot of freshly brewed coffee and decanted it into the carafe, spilling a good deal in the process. Adam, sensing that I was upset, placed his hand on my shoulder.

"We have to stay focused on the end result. After what I heard in there, I believe we have a good chance to free an innocent man."

Adam took the carafe out of my hands. As he turned to go he spotted the brown bag sitting on the counter. With a black marker, I had written Adam's name on the flap.

"What's that?"

"I stopped to see Henry last weekend. There are two jars with his fingerprints all over them in that bag. I was planning to give them to you before you left."

He may not have believed me. I wasn't sure I believed myself. I could have delivered those jars to Erika Tripp a week ago. For some reason, I always found an excuse not to. Though I didn't think for one minute that Henry's prints would match those from the Aldicarb found in the Bookers' garage, it still felt like a betrayal for me to turn the jars over. With a sigh I picked up the bag and handed it to Adam.

"The only reason I did this was to clear Henry's name."

Adam shrugged and returned to the other room.

One long and painful hour later, Adam brought an end to the deposition. Inquisition would better describe the process he put Jack through. After the break Adam was relentless. At first Jack ducked the issue of who came up with the idea of a plea deal. But in the end, he admitted it was his father who told him to lie about Leland's so-called "confession."

"Okay, I admit I lied." His voice cracked like a teenager's. "I know it was wrong, but I wanted my life to go on exactly as I planned."

"Are you willing to testify in court as to what you just told us here?" Adam asked.

"Yeah, I need to make amends." He caught my eye. "Not just to Leland, but to everyone else I hurt when I lied."

Adam stood up. "Thanks, Jack. I guess we're done here."

Jennifer remained behind the camera. The red light stayed on.

Adam stuffed his notebook into his briefcase. "I'm curious about something. Why did the cops pick you up in the first place?"

Jack's hands trembled. I could see he was desperate for a drink. "What?"

"It not important, but I was wondering why you were arrested."

"Because we were being stupid. Story of my life. I got stopped for speeding down West Street in my dad's Lincoln." Jack glanced at me again, addressing his next comment directly to me. "Sometimes I wonder if it's too late to change, but a friend of mine tells me I have to keep trying."

Adam snapped his briefcase closed. "It would be unusual for them to lock you up for speeding. Were you drinking?"

"Billy bought a few six packs after we left the Bookers' house, and then . . . to be honest, I'm a bit unclear as to what happened. The cop claimed I resisted arrest. Said I took a swing at him while he was shoving me into the squad car, but I don't remember that."

Jennifer turned to look at me, the dawn of understanding lighting her face. When I raised my eyes to met Adam's, I saw no trace of surprise. I couldn't explain how, but I had the feeling that Adam already guessed Jack was in the Bookers' house with Billy that day.

Chapter 29

Henry was dead. I found him sprawled face down on his mother's Oriental rug. The faded vines in the weave of the carpet seemed to wrap around his body, ready to enshroud him where he lay. My whole body trembled as I stepped closer to see his blackened lips, swollen face, open eyes. I later learned that the dried, chalky substance running down his chin was his own saliva. Though I never saw the photos right after Marley died, over the years I learned enough about Aldicarb to recognize the signs of poison.

On his mother's ring-stained coffee table, written in his crooked printing, was a note. I'M SORRY. I stood frozen, trying to absorb his meaning. The note was written on a plain sheet of paper. The pen set neatly beside it was one of those cheap promotional ballpoints that businesses pass out. This one came from the Veranda Inn. Seconds passed. I tried to remember where I'd seen that name before. Then it hit me. Adam and I drove past the place on the way to our beach hotel in Venice. The Veranda Inn was one of those old Florida motels on Route 41 that had seen better days but survived by attracting travel-weary vacationers on their way to somewhere else. In what seemed a long wait for the ambulance to respond to my 9-1-1 call, I tried to get my head around an explanation for how Henry came by that pen. Nothing.

On the heels of the EMTs came the police. They shot questions at me rapid-fire.

What brought you here today?

What was your relationship to Mr. Rusak?

How long has it been since you last saw him?

Have you noticed a recent change in his behavior?

Between questions, I stole glimpses at that pen. Numb, I provided the cops with answers. It seemed to me that the important question was the one they didn't ask. How did that pen get here?

I told them Henry skipped a few Zolofts while I was in Florida. He was clearly depressed the last time I saw him. One of the officers went searching for Henry's medication tray. The previous day's pills were still in their compartment.

The only question remaining was why, but no one else seemed to care.

When at last it appeared that I was of no further use to the police, they asked me to step outside. A short time later the EMTs exited the house, pushing a gurney bearing Henry in a black bag. The reality of the situation—surreal until then—hit me. As I watched them haul Henry's body away, I tried to stifle the sob that rose from my chest. I had no control over the silent tears that ran down my cheeks.

Nothing about the scene resembled the crime shows on television. No teams of gloved forensic experts, no fleet of cars with blue strobe lights, no squads of detectives shouting orders, no medical examiners in their white lab coats. The quiet unnerved me. After the emergency vehicle pulled away from the curb, the two uniformed policemen stepped out of the house.

"Thank you for your assistance, Mrs. Stokes." The cop's nameplate read PISONI. On his belt he carried a holstered pistol, a stun gun, a radio, and what appeared to be a can of mace. A stray thought crossed my mind that it must be uncomfortable for these guys to ride in their cars with all that stuff hanging around their waists. At that point I was willing to think about anything but Henry.

"What do you have in there?" I raised my chin to indicate the nylon roller board he pulled behind him.

"Evidence."

"Evidence?"

"Yes ma'am," Pisoni said. "To verify our finding."

"What finding?"

"Suicide, Mrs. Stokes. There was a note . . ."

"Do you have a list of everything you took?" I was still in shock, but my head was beginning to clear.

"Yes ma'am." Pisoni eyed me up and down, no doubt weighing the pros and cons of showing me. He shrugged, pulling the folded paper from the notebook he carried.

I scanned the list. An empty jar, one spoon, suicide note, pen, prescription drug bottles, and Henry's pill tray.

After they left, I reentered the house. Eager to escape the image that came to mind when I stepped into the living room, I climbed the stairs. A narrow hallway separated two small bedrooms. Turning right I peered into Mrs. Rusak's room. Even though the old lady died twenty years earlier, Henry left his mother's belongings in place. Reflected in the mirror I could see her jewelry box and hairbrush on the dresser. A cross-stitched quilt covered the bed. A shiver ran down my arms when I noticed her shoes lined up neatly under a dress that hung on the closet door.

Turning, I made my way into Henry's room. His smell lingered. Not the putrid odor of urine and feces downstairs, but his familiar aftershave. Everything was neat and tidy, his bed made, his pajamas folded on the chair. I felt like an intruder. As I turned to leave, an object on the chest of drawers caught my eye. Moving closer, my knees grew weak. Not trusting my legs to hold me, I slumped down on his bed, reached for my cell phone, and dialed.

Erika Tripp answered on the first ring.

Chapter 30

Erika wasted no time. The detective pummeled me with questions until she was satisfied. Fortunately, I had answers. He was face down on the carpet, left a suicide note, a pen from the Veranda Inn . . .

"Okay, I get the picture. Let's go upstairs."

Erika snapped her notepad shut and stuck the pen behind her ear. I counted five earrings, all silver, all studs.

I pointed to where I discovered Doris Keating's necklace in the small crystal bowl on Henry's dresser. Erika used her pen to push the necklace aside, exposing an object buried underneath.

"What have we got here?" She lifted the necklace with her pen. My eyes were riveted on the silver tube of lipstick.

"Mrs. Stokes, are you sure this belonged to Doris Keating?"

"What? Oh . . . yes, I'm sure."

"Good. I suppose this was hers too." She poked the lipstick. "Can't imagine what the old guy would be doing with her makeup. Of course, I've heard rumors . . ." She started to let the necklace fall back into the dish when I stopped her.

"Wait." Bending to have a closer look, I read the label. Very Berry by Revlon.

"That looks like Marley's lipstick."

At the mention of Marley's name Erika raised her eyebrows, gum snapping in overtime.

"Did you touch anything up here?"

"No, nothing. Oh wait, I sat on the bed while I called you."

"Okay. I'll get in touch with Investigator Bennett's office. He needs to send some techs down here ASAP."

"Do you think they will find Marley's fingerprints on the lipstick?"

"That would seal it, wouldn't it?"

I nodded. As improbable as it seemed, it looked like Henry was somehow involved in the Booker murders.

"Hell, don't look so disappointed. A few weeks ago, you were running around telling anyone who cared to listen that Booker was innocent. Well, if it wasn't him, then somebody had to kill those people, and Rusak is—make that was—as good a suspect as any. I'll contact the sheriff's department down in Florida to let them know what's going on. If this is Doris Keating's necklace, that makes Rusak good for her murder too. But first I've gotta make a call to the Keene police station. What did you say the name of that cop was?"

"Pisoni."

"Right. He won't be too happy. The locals really hate it when County steps in. Any idea where they took Rusak's body?"

I shook my head.

"No problem, I'll find him. Nobody works in the city morgue on Sunday. We'll get the body moved to the county facility tomorrow. The ME can do the autopsy there."

She wrote everything down in her logbook as she spoke. When she reached the end of her list, she looked up at me with a smile on her face. "Well, it looks like Adam's dad was right about this thing all along."

"His dad?"

"Who did you think put the kid on the case in the first place?"

Something scratched the surface of my memory. Something Erika said months ago that didn't sit right at the time. I couldn't quite put my finger on it, but all I needed was a few more minutes and then . . .

"Now clear out." She snapped the logbook shut. "I need to contain this scene."

I followed her down the stairs, but instead of heading for the door, I turned toward the kitchen.

"Where the hell do you think you're going?"

"I want to pick up the mail. Henry puts it in the basket so I can pay his—"

"Nothing leaves this house until my investigation is complete."

"Of course." I retraced my steps. "After all, the electric bill could be the last piece of evidence you need to prove Henry was a murderer."

From the look on her face, I could see she didn't appreciate my sarcasm.

———————————

Erika left me in Henry's front yard. Before departing, she admonished me not to return to the house. She even went so far as to dig a roll of crime scene tape from the trunk of her car. Crisscrossing both the front and back doors with the yellow tape, she gave me one last warning glance before leaving me alone. Then I called Adam.

I caught him driving east on Rt. 202 as he made his way back to school. Jennifer left an hour earlier in her own car and was probably halfway to Durham. When I explained where I was and why, Adam told me stay there and wait for him. He estimated that it would take him twenty-five minutes. He made it in twenty.

Adam brought the car to a screeching stop. I could almost hear the words *I told you so* hanging in the air between us. To his credit he didn't say them out loud.

"Tell me everything." His face was flushed with excitement. "Start from the moment you stepped into the house."

I repeated the events of the morning. With every detail, Adam grew more animated.

"And you saw Marley's lipstick in his bedroom?"

"Since Erika left I've been going over and over everything in my head. I still can't figure out what Henry was doing with that lipstick. Or, for that matter, why he had the pen from the Veranda Inn."

"Maybe he kept it as a souvenir. That's possible, isn't it?"

"I guess so. But there are other things that don't make sense. I know you only met Henry once, but you said it yourself. He simply wasn't capable of flying down to Florida on his own. The whole thing is implausible."

"But Henry knew Doris had evidence that we hoped would prove Leland was innocent. Maybe that scared him into going down."

"He knew Doris kept the police report from forty-four years ago. Hardly the stuff that would have been a threat to Henry."

"He didn't know that. Maybe he thought you were on to him."

"You're still assuming he killed Marley and the kids."

"He had access to the poison, and he had motive. Not to mention his creepy obsession with Marley. When she let him into the house to fix the door, he had an opportunity to slip some Aldicarb into the juice."

I shook my head. "Henry would never hurt the girls."

"But we always said whoever killed them only meant to poison Marley."

I closed my eyes and took a deep breath. "That's true. He

knew the girls didn't like orange juice. Marley told me to pick some up, but then . . . well, nothing went right the day before they died. Marley and Leland were fighting, the girls were sulking. Then Kenny called and everything went from bad to worse."

"What do you mean?"

"Get in the car. I want to show you something."

Adam gave me a curious look, but climbed into the passenger side without asking any questions. Shifting into gear, I eased away from the curb. As we headed up Court Street, I slowed for the turn onto Sparrow. I hadn't been down Kenny's street in years. Not since that horrible day when I last saw him. On the lot where the trailer once squatted, there now stood a new mobile home. It didn't appear to be very old, but there were already signs of wear. One of the porch railings was broken. A faux shutter hung crooked, ready to fall off. Broken toys littered the yard. A mongrel crept out from his tar-papered crate and stood staring at us from the end of his chain. The sound of a woman shrieking at her child penetrated the closed windows of my car.

My voice came out in a whisper. "Some things never change."

"What are we doing here?" Adam asked.

"This is where Kenny lived. The Mazza's' trailer is long gone, but I thought you might want to see the place."

"Why?"

"It's time I told you the rest of my story."

Chapter 31

Leo Bishop's birthday party was the gala event of the summer season. My mother had to work serving drinks and canapes that night, but Marley and Leland were invited guests. Marley wore a new dress, a tight-fitting silver number that accentuated her figure. She came down the stairs in a cloud of Chanel, her platinum blond hair swept up in a French twist. She beckoned the children to "come give Mama a kiss," and then she and Leland were gone. It was only after the door closed behind them that I realized something. In the entire time since Leland had been home from work, Marley hadn't said a single word to her husband. And from what I could tell, he wasn't speaking to her either.

I knew from past experience that the Bookers would be out late. Marley told me not to wait up. After watching Johnny Carson, I went to bed. Sometime in the early morning hours I woke to an angry crescendo of voices. Marley and Leland were downstairs arguing. Again. For the past few days, every time I saw them together they were either not speaking to each other or engaged in open warfare. From my bedroom—I had come to think of the Bookers' guest room as my own—I caught fragments of their argument. At first it seemed they were fighting about money, but I soon realized this was about something more than that.

"You're out of your mind!" Leland shouted. "Exactly how do you propose going about that?"

Marley said something about speaking with Dr. Keating at the party.

"I don't care what he said. We barely make ends meet as it is. We can't afford another kid."

Marley lowered her voice to a purr. I couldn't make out what she said next, but Leland's reply soon made it clear.

"Forget it. That's not going to work with me this time. I mean what I say. We're not having another baby."

I heard his heavy footsteps climbing the stairs. After Leland slammed the bedroom door, the house went quiet save for the muffled sounds of Marley crying downstairs. The smell of cigarette smoke reached me from below.

The next morning, Robin's normal chatter barely covered the sound of Marley retching in the upstairs bathroom. I stole an anxious glance at the kitchen clock. It was getting late, and still no sign of Leland. Robin babbled on about her friend Kelly and how much fun they were going to have at the lake that afternoon. Lissa wanted to know if Jack would meet us there. I wondered if Marley was sick from being hungover.

"What a night!"

I looked up to see Leland leaning against the door frame.

He took the cup of coffee I offered, tossed back some aspirin from the palm of his hand, and washed them down with a single gulp. "My head is killing me. Would you mind if we skip your lesson today?"

"No problem." I tried to hide my disappointment with a smile, but couldn't keep it from my voice. "I'll fix Marley some breakfast, bring the girls to their tennis lesson, then meet you at the shop in time to open at nine."

"Yeah, well, I don't think Marley is going to want breakfast this morning." Leland drained his coffee cup and picked up his keys. After planting a kiss on each of the girls' foreheads, he stood before me. For a fleeting moment I thought he was going to kiss my forehead too, but he just looked down at me and smiled. "Thanks for the coffee."

Lissa dressed herself without any fuss. I knew Robin would take forever if I left her to her own devices so I gave her a hand.

"Arms up, Robin." I slipped her sundress over her bathing suit. She wiggled and fidgeted while I tied the bow around her waist. Still no sign of Marley. Anxious that I would be late for work at the club, I tiptoed down the hall.

"Marley?" I spoke to the closed door. "Is there anything I can do for you before we leave?"

I took the silence as a sign that she was either asleep or didn't want to be disturbed. With a shrug, I picked up the tennis bags, loaded the girls into the car, and drove to the club.

After dropping the kids at the tennis court, I headed directly for the pro shop. Leland looked up, the dark circles under his eyes suggesting he wasn't feeling any better than when he left the house.

"Mildred called. She wants to reschedule her lesson for tomorrow." He leaned against the display counter filled with Lacoste sweaters. "I guess she had a bit too much to drink last night like the rest of us."

"Would you like to go home and rest for a while? I can handle things here until it's time for me to pick up the girls."

He shook his head. "No thanks. I think Marley would prefer me to give her some space this morning. There is something you can do for me, though."

"Anything."

"Mildred invited me to have lunch after her lesson tomorrow. I know it's your day off but I was hoping you could mind the shop until I got back."

"Sure, no problem."

"Did you have other plans?"

"Jack invited me for a game of tennis tomorrow morning, but I can call and tell him something else came up."

"No, don't do that. I'll figure something out for tomorrow."

We took it easy that morning. Leland nursed his headache with coffee while I tended to the customers. By the time I left to pick up the girls, he appeared much better.

Walking across the lawn to the tennis courts, I spotted the girls from a distance. When I drew close, I saw Robin wore a towel draped over her shoulders and a pout on her face.

"What's wrong?" I asked.

"Kelly got a stomachache so her mother took her home."

Robin's moods rose and fell with the tides, so I didn't take her sour face too seriously. "She can come with us to the lake next week." I turned to Lissa. By her sullen expression I could see something was bothering her too.

"What's wrong, kiddo?"

"I hate it here. I wish we could move back to Georgia."

While I knew Lissa missed her friends back in Georgia, since Kenny appeared she seemed to be happier about living in Keene. I wondered what was going on.

"Did something happen during your lesson?"

The girls exchanged glances. Robin was the first one to speak.

"Cindy called Lissa the 'N' word."

"What? Wait here while I tell your father."

Lissa grabbed my arm. "Please, don't tell him."

"But Lissa, somebody needs to talk to Cindy's mother about this."

"You don't understand. Cindy's mom and dad are club members. Daddy only works here. I don't want to cause any trouble."

I pulled Lissa into a big hug. Kissing the top of her head,

I told her how much I loved her. Yet despite her concerns, I made a silent vow to tell Marley what happened, knowing full well she wouldn't let the matter drop. As I drove home, both girls stared glumly out the windows. I let them sulk in silence.

Before I brought the Mustang to a full stop in their driveway, Marley burst from the house. Yanking the passenger door open, she slipped into the car's bucket seat.

"Do you know how to get to Kenny's house?"

"What's wrong?"

"Kenny just called looking for you. He said his mother won't wake up."

While I put the car in reverse and backed onto the street, I lowered my voice so the girls couldn't hear me.

"There's something you should know about Mrs. Mazza. She . . ." I stole a look across the console at Marley's impassive face. "There's a good chance she's had too much to drink and is sleeping it off."

Marley nodded like I wasn't telling her anything new. "I'm sure Kenny has seen her like that before. This time is different. This time he's scared enough to ask for help."

Kenny had pulled the needle from his mother's arm, but I could see the angry welt marked where the heroin had entered her system. As Marley knelt next to the bed and put her ear to Theresa Mazza's chest, she shouted for me to call an ambulance. When I finished giving the operator directions, Marley pulled me aside to tell me Mrs. Mazza's heart was still beating, but barely. She spoke in a hoarse whisper.

"Take the children outside. I'll wait here until the EMTs arrive."

With all the excitement, I'd nearly forgotten the girls. They stood in the open doorway, staring at Kenny's mother who was sprawled across the soiled bedspread. Kenny was there too, seemingly frozen in place, anxious eyes fixed on Marley. I stole another glance at Theresa Mazza, her face pale but peaceful. Once again, I was struck by how young she was.

Kenny stood with his legs apart, his skinny arms crossed in determination. "I'm staying here with my mom."

Marley nodded agreement. I took Robin and Lissa by the hand and led them outside. We sat on the wooden steps out front.

"What's wrong with Kenny's mom?" Lissa asked.

I looked at Lissa's earnest face. "I don't know. We have to wait and see."

"Is she dead?" Robin asked.

"Shut up, Robin." Panic crept into Lissa's voice. "She's not dead, is she, Cate?"

"No, kiddo. She's not dead. Not yet, anyway."

Theresa Mazza stopped breathing before the medics arrived. After the ambulance left with the body, Marley called the county social services department. An uptight-looking woman with her hair pulled back in a bun appeared within the hour. The girls cried uncontrollably, their chests heaving with each sob. I wrapped my arms around them, doing what I could to calm their hysteria and fight the tears that filled my own eyes. Marley sat on the step next to Kenny, holding his hand while she spoke quietly to him. Kenny stared at his shoes until the social worker pried him away from Marley and shoved him in the back of her car.

"Where are they taking him?" I asked.

"That woman is going to call around and try find a relative who will take him. In the meantime, she'll place him in a temporary home." A deep crease formed between Marley's eyebrows. "The last thing that boy needs right now is to be dumped in some foster home until he's claimed by somebody who doesn't want him. But I'm afraid that's exactly what will happen. I offered to keep Kenny with me until more permanent arrangements can be made, but the social worker said that wasn't possible."

I thought of all Kenny's relatives in town, and wondered which one would take Kenny. I couldn't think of a single Mazza that would be better for Kenny than Marley Booker.

"Can we at least visit him?" I asked.

"I'll call and ask." Marley's eyes met mine. With her manicured fingers, she brushed a lock of my hair from my eyes. "Don't get your hopes up. These situations are never easy."

Chapter 32

After I finished telling Adam about Kenny and his mother, I sat quietly, exchanging stares with the mongrel chained in the yard. "I never did get the chance to tell Marley about the girl who called Lissa the 'N' word."

Silence stretch between us until I was ready to go on. "While we were gone, Billy broke into the house and trashed the place. When we saw what he had done, I stayed to help Marley clean up the mess. Soon Henry showed up to fix the broken window and I went home."

I felt drained after telling Adam everything that happened the day before Marley and the girls died. I had nothing more to say. Adam remained still, staring at the site where the Mazza trailer once stood. The place where Kenny's mother died of a heroin overdose.

Glancing at my watch, I was surprised to see how much time had passed since Adam and I left Henry's house. As I reached for the ignition key, Adam finally spoke.

"There's something I've been meaning to tell you." He cracked his knuckles.

I cut him off before he could say what was on his mind. "I spoke with Erika this morning. She told me your dad always suspected Henry was the killer."

"I wasn't talking about Henry," Adam said. "You should know that—"

"Let me finish. A while ago Erika told me Henry was caught hanging around the Bookers' house, peeping in the windows. I realize now she had no way to know that. I've read every word of the interview reports and the trial transcript. Nowhere in any of those documents was there any mention of Henry being seen outside Marley's window."

Adam turned his attention to the dog in the yard. I waited for him to say something but he seemed lost with his own thoughts.

"The thing is, someone else mentioned catching Henry snooping outside the Booker's house. Care to guess who told me that?" I waited a few beats. "It was Kenny. Kenny saw Henry peeping into Marley's window."

The silence in the car grew heavy.

"I don't understand why you let me talk about all of this without saying a word. After speaking with Erika this morning, I realized how stupid I've been." I drew in a deep breath. "The kid I knew as Kenny Mazza is your father."

Adam continued to stare out the window. I could tell his eyes had long stopped registering what he saw. He took a deep breath before speaking.

"When I needed a project for my class, my dad told me about a murder that happened here in Keene when he was a kid. He said there was a good chance that the man who was convicted of the crime was innocent. That's when he suggested I call you. He knew you would help, especially if I told you who I was. In fact, he wanted to call you himself, but I felt I had to do this on my own."

"That's commendable. But once I said I would help you, you should have told me."

"You're right. But I wanted something else from you. You see, Dad never speaks about his mother. It's like he can't bring himself to talk about it. I've always wondered what happened to her. I figured you could tell me but I was afraid you would hold back if you knew who I was."

"I guess I just proved you wrong," I said.

Adam nodded in silent agreement.

"What happened to Kenny—your dad—after the social worker took him away?" I asked.

"An aunt who lived across the state in Durham raised him. She and her husband, Jim Bennett, couldn't have children of their own, so when Dad's mother died and left him behind, they took him in. I didn't know they were anything other than my real grandparents until after they died. That's the first time Dad mentioned he was adopted. He never said a word to me about his birth mother. I guess he tries to block out that part of his childhood."

"I think Henry knew who you were," I said. "Remember, when he saw you said he knew you were trouble. In any event, he took an immediate dislike to you, just like with your father."

"Well, Dad suspected Henry was the killer all along."

"Your father was just a kid at the time. In this case you can't trust his judgment."

"No, but I do trust the evidence. We'll have confirmation soon. Fingerprint results should be back in a day or two. The toxicology report too. And I'm sure Dad's team will check Henry's phone and credit card records to see if he bought airline tickets to Florida. Then of course there's Doris's necklace and Marley's lipstick—"

"I know." I held up my hand in an effort to stop his litany of evidence against Henry. "It all looks bad, but I can't imagine how he could have killed them."

"I'm sorry I didn't tell you about my father. You have every reason to be mad at me."

"Not mad. Disappointed that you didn't trust me, that's all. How is he?"

"You can see for yourself. He's been asking me to arrange

for a time when you can meet. Give me a few days and I'll set it up."

We headed back to Henry's house to pick up Adams's car. Parting ways, Adam promised to be in touch. I didn't realize at the time how long it would be before I saw him again.

Chapter 33

I missed the excitement of working with Adam. I missed Henry too, and though I kept busy at work, my life seemed without purpose. To fill my free time, I worked in my garden, turning the soil in preparation for when all threat of frost was gone and I could start planting. Ordinarily that lifted my spirits, but nothing I did seemed to fill the hollow feeling inside me.

Though Leo Bishop was the executor of Henry's will, I offered to make all the arrangements for the funeral. The service was a sorry affair that left me feeling more depressed than ever. Leo and his wife stood alone with me at the grave, their grotesque flower arrangement dwarfing my small bouquet of spring flowers. When I commented on Leo's healthy appearance, he mentioned that they were just back from a month in Florida. Before parting ways, Leo surprised me by mentioning Henry left his mother's house to me. When he asked what I intended to do with it, I shrugged without answering. At any rate I had plenty of time to decide; the police wouldn't release the property until the investigation into Henry's death was closed.

When word did reach me about the investigation, it came from a surprising source. A few days after the funeral, the phone rang as I arrived home from the office. Setting my briefcase on the floor, I picked up the handset to hear Erika Tripp's voice at the other end.

"We need to talk, Mrs. Stokes."

"Right now? I just got home from work and—"

"No, ma'am." I detected a trace of humor in her voice. "I wonder if we could meet for lunch tomorrow."

"Well, yes, that would be fine. As a matter of fact, I was thinking of giving you a call to ask you about—"

She cut me off again. "Meet me at Lindy's Diner at twelve tomorrow."

I arrived ten minutes early and chose a booth at the far end of the restaurant. Erika showed up ten minutes late. I glanced up the minute she walked through the door, my eyes following as she made her way to the table. She wore a New England Patriot's sweatshirt over a pair of faded jeans. Her bottle-blond hair was pulled back as usual at the base of her neck. Five silver earrings that I hadn't seen before lined the cuff of her ear.

"This is an official meeting." She slid onto the bench across from me. "But I wanted to talk to you somewhere outside of the station."

"Why?"

"Let's just say there may be some unofficial discussion mixed in that I don't want anyone to overhear."

I looked around, spotting only a few factory workers at the counter and an elderly couple seated a few tables away. Feeling foolish for checking, I turned back to Erika.

"Oh, you meant your colleagues," I said.

"That's right." Erika gave me a cold smile. "Officially, I have a few questions about Mr. Rusak. Still, I figured you would want to know where we are with the investigation. That's information that I'm not supposed to share with you at this point, but I'm going to tell you anyway. Unofficially, understand?"

I nodded. "What do you want to ask me?"

"Did you tell Rusak why you and Adam went to Florida?"

I nodded. "I told him we were going to meet with Doris. That she had some evidence that would help Leland Booker."

"When did you tell him that?"

"The Sunday before we left. I needed to tell him because he expected . . . that is, I wasn't going to be able to visit the following week, and I didn't want him to be upset when I didn't show up."

"That fits." She pulled her logbook out of her pocket and made a note.

"Fits with what?"

She closed the book and set it aside. Catching the eye of our waitress, she nodded. Turning to me, she said, "Let's order some lunch. The club sandwich here never killed anybody."

When the waitress left with our orders, Erika used her napkin to wipe some grease off the table. She leaned across the table, looking at me eye-to-eye. "Look, I'll be straight with you. When we first met, I didn't much care for you. I figured you were hell-bent on ruining Marianne Weede's reputation just to get Booker out of jail on a technicality. But I told you, if it turned out Marianne got it wrong that I would do what I could to set things straight. Well, it looks like Marianne got it wrong, so here I am."

"You think Henry killed Marley and the girls?"

"I know he did. The toxicology report came back from the ME yesterday. You wanna take a guess at what killed old Henry?"

She didn't wait for me to reply.

"The apple butter was loaded with Aldicarb. Isn't that a kick? He killed himself with the same poison he used to kill the Bookers."

"My apple butter? You don't think that I had anything to do with—"

"Calm down, Mrs. Stokes. Nobody thinks you killed

anybody. We found other evidence to connect Rusak with the murders. His fingerprints matched one of the unidentified sets on the pesticide. And if that weren't enough, the sheriff's department down in Florida got a confirmation that the necklace you found in Rusak's bedroom did in fact belong to Mrs. Keating. No idea what he did with the rest of her jewelry, but it probably won't turn up. Never does. So we have that, plus your statement that the lipstick in Rusak's house was the same brand and shade that Marley Booker used. By the way, Revlon stopped making it about thirty-eight years ago, so that fits the time frame."

Erika leaned back in her seat. "Then there's the matter of Rusak's credit card. We found charges on his account for a plane ticket to Tampa and back. He booked on the day you told him you were going to Florida. And there was a charge on the same card for a hotel room at the Venice Veranda Inn. I haven't figured out how he got from the airport to the hotel, but I'm not too bothered by that. He could have paid cash for a taxi or something. Bottom line is, we've got a paper trail that places Rusak in Venice at the time of Doris Keating's murder. By the way, the autopsy report confirms she was smothered. Fibers from a throw pillow on the couch matched those they found in her nose and air passages. From the look of him, I'd say Rusak was strong enough to hold the old lady down until she stopped breathing."

I took a sip of ice water. My hand shook as I placed the plastic glass back on the table. "What happens now?"

"The DA hasn't decided yet. Good as it is, all the evidence linking Rusak to the murders is circumstantial. For example, he had reason to handle the pesticide in his line of work, so just because we've got his fingerprints on the container in the Bookers' garage, that doesn't say he was the one who added it to the juice. I have no clue how the Cheshire County prosecutor will want to proceed, but that's not my problem. Like I said, looks like we sent an innocent man to jail, and I want to set the record straight."

"Why are you telling me this?" I asked.

"Because I think you deserve to know." She shrugged. "I understand Booker's new lawyers are getting ready to file in federal court for a wrongful conviction. Inspector Bennett's kid is out of it now. He was told to stop talking to you because you're on the witness list and he may also be called to testify. Matter of fact, I'm taking a helluva risk talking to you now. If anyone asks, tell them we met so I could question you about the Rusak thing. Got that?"

"Sure, Erika. I really appreciate what you're doing."

"One more thing. Adam's dad wants to see you."

"When?"

"How about now?"

Out of the corner of my eye, I caught a figure approaching the table. Raising a hand to shield the sun, I found myself looking up at the smiling face of Inspector Ken Bennett.

Kenny Mazza beat the odds. Nowhere in the distinguished figure before me could I detect any trace of the wild child from the wrong side of the tracks. I made a quick mental calculation and figured Kenny was in his early fifties. A few strands of silver touched his temples, but otherwise he looked to be ten years younger. Tall, fit, dressed in a brand-name golf shirt and matching windbreaker, he projected an air of quiet confidence. It was only when he opened his mouth did I know for sure it was the same boy I knew forty years ago.

"Shit, I would have known you anywhere." He gave me a crooked grin, the same as his son. I wondered why it took me so long to connect the two. "You haven't changed a damn bit, Cate."

"Still the liar." I couldn't keep the smile off my face. "And I see you haven't managed to improve your vocabulary."

Erika slid across the bench and stood. "I ordered you a club sandwich," she said to Kenny. "Enjoy your lunch." She gave me a pat on the shoulder before taking her leave.

"Adam says hello," Kenny said as he sat down across from me. "He wanted to join us but he was advised not to."

"I know. Erika explained everything. I understand Leland's lawyers are filing a petition for a hearing before a federal judge. Do you think they have a chance? Will Leland be exonerated?"

"Unlikely." Kenny shook his head. "Exoneration requires proof of his innocence. They're going for a wrongful conviction instead. That's a condition where a federal judge rules there were problems with the way the trial was conducted. Now that Jack has confessed to lying about hearing Leland confess to the murders, it should be a slam dunk. But in the end, Leland will be freed without actually being declared innocent of the crime. Technically, the federal judge bounces the case back to the state. They could then decide to bring new charges and retry the case in front of a jury. But hell, for political reasons, the state will just let this thing die."

"Adam is going to be a great lawyer. You must be very proud of him."

"I am." Kenny looked down at his sandwich and shook his head. "Sometimes I can't believe how lucky I am. My life could have turned out to be very different."

"Adam told me a little of what happened after your mother . . . that is, after . . ."

"My aunt and uncle were great," Kenny said. "But over-protective as hell. As soon as I moved in, they cut me off from everything and everyone in Keene. I was only ten, so it was easy to isolate me from the news. My aunt never told me about

Marley and the girls. I didn't find out what happened to them until years later."

"I'm sure she was acting in your best interest."

"Yeah, like I said, they were great. But it might have been better if they told me. For a long time, I held on to this fantasy that Marley would swoop in and carry me back to Keene. I wanted her to be my mother."

"She had a special attachment to you." I fought the hitch in my throat. "That was obvious."

"Years later, I tried to find Marley. I wanted to let her know I turned out okay and to thank her for everything she did for me. I had no idea . . . anyway, that's when I found out about the murders. I still think about Robin and Lissa with their whole lives ahead of them. Not to mention Marley's baby."

"What baby?"

"Adam said he gave you copies of the file." Kenny looked at me in surprise. "I assumed you knew Marley was pregnant."

My mind flashed to the manila envelope with the autopsy reports I never read, the photos I couldn't bring myself to see. My voice came out in a hoarse whisper. "I had no idea."

"Well, thanks to you and Adam, it looks like Leland will finally be vindicated."

"Poor Henry. I wonder if he fully understood what he was doing. I still don't believe he intended to kill the girls."

"Are you kidding? He was one twisted son-of-a-bitch. Only one thing about him surprises me."

"What's that?"

"When my team went through his house, I expected they would find porn, kiddie or otherwise. Nothing. Not a single dirty magazine, no photos, not even pay-for-sex calls on his phone records. I would have bet the ranch we would find something."

I didn't know what to say. In fact, I was sick of talking about the past and all the damage done to the people I loved. I made one last attempt to defend Henry, even though his guilt was undeniable.

"Maybe you misjudged him," I said. "Maybe he wasn't what everyone said he was." But deep in my heart, I had to admit it was me who was wrong.

Returning home, I sat on my deck overlooking the back-yard and lit a cigarette. Pleased as I was to have seen Kenny, the afternoon left me with a deep sense of unease. The more I thought about Marley's unborn fetus, the more disturbed I grew. I stubbed out the half-smoked cigarette and went inside. Digging into my files, I found a copy of the witness report that Doris Keating kept for all those years. I flipped the page and used my finger to scan the attached insurance form. There, in box thirty-seven, I found what I was looking for. Report in hand, I picked up the phone and dialed the number on the card Kenny gave me before we parted.

"I need to speak with Inspector Bennett," I said.

"May I ask who's calling?"

"Cate Stokes. Tell him it's urgent."

Chapter 34

"God damn it to hell, where's that fucking report?"

Even with the door closed, Kenny's voice reached me where I stood in the reception area. The young man sitting at the front desk swiveled around in his chair and peered anxiously at the closed door. He grabbed a folder from his desk and disappeared into Kenny's office.

Left alone, I cast my gaze around the room. The last time I was there, I didn't know it was Kenny who ran the Computer Crimes department. I remembered the Child Protection Services poster and the collection box on the desk. It all made sense now. Kenny, a victim of the system, was doing what he could to give back.

The young man returned, stuffing a crumpled dollar bill in the box before asking me what I wanted.

"I'm here to see Investigator Bennett," I said.

"He's kind of busy right now." He glanced over his shoulder at the closed door then turned back to me. "Is there something I can do for you?"

"I'm Cate Stokes," I replied. "He's expecting me."

The young man hesitated, then opened Kenny's door a crack. I heard him mention my name in apologetic tones. He then stood aside and beckoned me to enter. Kenny rose to greet me, knocking a stack of papers off his desk in the process.

"What's with the dollar bill?" I asked.

Kenny blushed and a grin spread across his face. "Cost me a buck every time I swear."

I laughed at that, remembering Kenny's mayonnaise jar. Though I hadn't cured him of cursing then at least the Child Protection Agency was benefiting.

"Ready to go?"

"Give me a minute." Kenny bent down to sign the report that his receptionist had placed on the desk before him. "Does Leland know we're coming?"

"I called yesterday and put our names on the visitor list. We have to get there and sign in by 11:45. The doors open at 1:00 p.m. sharp. It should only take us an hour to get to Concord but I want to allow extra time to find the State Prison."

"What about lunch?"

"We'll grab something up there."

"Are you nervous?"

"Like a teenager on her first date."

"Well, you're hardly a teenager and this is no date." Kenny grabbed his jacket and followed me out.

As instructed by the man on the phone, I parked the car by the trailers and we entered the guard house. I presented my photo ID to the man on duty and handed over my jewelry, belt, and purse. He put the items in a clear plastic bag, handed me a receipt, and set the bag on a shelf behind him. Glancing down at my shoes, a growl escaped his throat.

"Didn't no one tell you you're supposed to wear sneakers?"

I followed his gaze, wondering how my leather shoes could possibly present a problem. For a moment I worried that he wouldn't let me in, but the guard just shrugged and signaled for me to pass. We walked outside and stood facing the Concord State Prison.

The building could have passed for an old, brick high

school if not for the barbed wire, sooty exterior, and soaring guard towers. I shuddered to think of the men and women imprisoned behind those walls, and the crimes they committed. Kenny put an arm around my shoulders and guided me through the door. We found ourselves in a holding area with other visitors. Mostly female, mostly young, mostly people of color. Children skipped behind their mothers like they were out for a day in the park. A large clock on the wall counted down the minutes. I sat rigid in my chair, waiting for someone to tell us where to go.

When the hands of the clock finally reached one, a pair of prison guards appeared and led us like a herd of sheep down a passageway. We passed through another set of doors and into a large, open room. After everyone was gathered, the guards stood with their backs against the closed doors to prevent anyone from leaving.

I blinked in the harsh fluorescent light. Nothing was what I expected. Chairs and tables, clean and free of graffiti, were bolted to the floor. Prisoners began to trickle in through a set of doors on the other side. They moved rapidly to join with their wives, girlfriends, children. No walls separated prisoners from visitors or each other. I took a step closer to Kenny, drawing comfort from his presence. In what seemed a rehearsed routine, a few visitors rounded up the children and led them to a corner where they played together. With the children thus occupied, several couples wasted no time engaging in frenzied sex while other adults took turns shielding them from view. I noticed the guards discretely turned a blind eye to the activity. I watched for a few minutes in shocked disbelief before turning away. My gaze dropped to my feet and I pressed against Kenny, murmuring my apologies for dragging him into this circus.

Leland stared at me from across the crowded room. I

wondered if he recognized me. After all, I wasn't the teenager he knew from forty-four years ago. Raising my hand in a half-hearted wave, I watched him approach.

"You came." He said it like he couldn't believe I was really there.

His million-dollar smile was no less radiant than I remembered, but nothing else about the man was the same. Leland was gaunt, stretched thin from his years behind bars. His gray hair would have lent a distinguished air to his appearance if it hadn't been for the stoop of his shoulders. Kenny extended his hand in greeting, and Leland shook it.

"Let's find a quiet place where we can talk." We followed him to an empty table near the guards and as far away from the rest of the people as possible.

"My lawyers tell me there's a good chance I'll be out of here soon. When I think about what that bastard, Burquest did to me, the years I've lost . . ." He cleared the thought with a shake of the head. "I can't thank you enough for everything you've done to get him to finally tell the truth."

"Did you hear about Henry?"

Leland spoke through clenched teeth. "I hope he rots in hell."

"The evidence against him is all circumstantial." I rubbed the nape of my neck. "Of course, there will never be a trial."

"Right. But at the end of the day, we all know he killed my wife and kids."

"Can you help me understand something?" I asked.

A wariness crept into Leland's eyes that I never saw there before. He nodded slowly. In that moment I realized his time behind bars had drained him of trust in all humanity. I weighed my next words carefully.

"You realize I've had access to your trial records. And

255

that I've seen the medical reports Dr. Keating sent to the insurance company?"

Another nod.

"I was sorry to learn Marley was pregnant at the time of her death."

"Yeah, me too." Leland didn't sound sorry. He sounded bitter.

"Forgive me for raising what must be a painful subject, but your medical record suggested that you couldn't be the baby's father."

Leland hesitated before responding, his face twisted with pain. It looked to me as if he were wrestling with an internal demon. I was about to apologize for trespassing on personal ground when he cleared his throat and spoke.

"You're right, I wasn't. After Robin was born, Marley and I decided we weren't going to have any more kids. She didn't want to take The Pill for the rest of her life, so I had a vasectomy a few months later."

The sounds in the room—moans, grunts, and children's laughter—seemed to rise up and swallow us in our silence. I stole a glance at Kenny who nodded encouragement for me to continue.

"Didn't it occur to you that whoever was the baby's father might have been her killer?"

"Do you think I'm some kind of idiot?" He balled his fists and I instinctively leaned back in my seat.

"Sorry," he said. "I didn't mean to snap like that. After all these years, you would think it shouldn't hurt so much."

"I guess you have every right to be mad, all things considered."

"Let me explain. I didn't learn Marley was pregnant until after she died. You can imagine how I . . . Anyway, of course I wanted to find Marley's lover. But my lawyer advised me against it. He felt the strategy could backfire. If the jury heard she was pregnant, it was only a short hop from there to learning I wasn't the father. Husbands have been known to kill their wives for less."

"Did you ever find out who the father was?"

"I ignored my lawyer's advice and hired a private investigator. He took every penny I owned. When the money ran out, I sold Marley's jewelry to keep the investigation going. At the end of the day, the investigator came up empty. I had no choice but to ask my lawyer to make a deal with the prosecutor. I guess neither side wanted to risk how the jury would react to knowing Marley had a lover. Could have gone either way."

Leland reached across the table and patted my arm. "It doesn't matter anymore. Henry killed my wife and kids, and there's no way he was her lover."

My eyes darted to Kenny who met my gaze. He shook his head in a gesture that told me he wanted to wait until we were back in the car to talk. I turned back to Leland.

"If I knew you were forced to sell Marley's jewelry, I never would have kept her diamond bracelet."

"What diamond bracelet?"

"Marley lent it to me for a party at the club and I . . ."

Leland banged his fist on the table. "I never gave my wife a diamond bracelet." One of the guards started walking toward us. Leland saw him out of the corner of is eye and lowered his voice. "Someone else must have given it to her."

Even as he said it, I knew what happened. Lying on a bed of silk, deep in her vanity drawer, Marley hid that bracelet from her husband. It was a gift she kept secret.

"I'm sorry," I said.

"Yeah, me too." The creases in his brow disappeared and Leland gave me a weak smile. The anger in his eyes vanished.

A warning bell sounded. I glanced up in surprise to

see most of our two hours had passed. Kenny and I stood. Reluctantly, Leland stood also.

"I'm going to sell that bracelet and send you the money," I said.

Leland pulled me into an embrace. "Thanks for the offer but I want you to keep the damn thing. Wear it the next time you come to see me."

"I hope the next time we meet you'll be free," Kenny said.

Leland grasped Kenny's hand and shook it vigorously.

"Thanks for coming," he said. "You don't know how much this meant to me."

———————————————

I puzzled over that bracelet all the way home. Kenny must have noticed I wasn't in a talkative mood for he didn't bring up the subject of Henry. When we reached Keene, Kenny asked me to drop him at the Court House so he could pick up his car. We parted with a hug, promising to stay in touch. Late into the night, as I lay awake listening to the crickets outside the open window, an idea came to me. Crystal clear, I wondered why I think of it before. My heart pounded with the realization that the murderer was still out there. By the time the first light of dawn brushed across my bedroom walls, I knew what I had to do.

Chapter 35

I chose the timing of my arrival carefully. The club was deserted in the hours between lunch and dinner. Serious golfers were out on the course, and social members had no reason to be there. I had asked Jack to meet me there as backup, but I wasn't sure he would come. Leo Bishop's office door was open so I decided not to wait. Leo looked up from his desk as I entered.

"To what do I owe this pleasure?" From the look on his face, I gave him no pleasure whatsoever. He scooped the loose papers before him into a neat pile and covered them with his arm. It was easy to see he didn't appreciate the intrusion.

"I need to speak with you."

The adrenaline in my veins was pumping overtime. My heart could have raced the Indy 500. All morning I vacillated between confronting Leo and ditching my plan as one of those crazy middle-of-the-night ideas. Now that I was here there was no going back. I took a deep breath and continued. "I believe you know I'm helping with the Booker investigation."

"I don't recall any mention of that."

"You were in the restaurant when I discussed the case with Jack Burquest. I assume your waitress filled you in on our conversation. I know my mother always did."

"Now that you mention it, perhaps I might have heard something." He scratched his neck with his index finger. "What is it you want, exactly? As you can see, I'm a busy man and—"

"Leland Booker may be released soon."

"Yes, I saw something about that in the *Sentinel*. The police are linking Henry Rusak with that horrible affair."

"Do you honestly believe Henry could have killed anyone?"

"I trust the authorities know what they're doing. I dare say this just goes to show you never really know a person."

"Henry was my friend."

"Of course. And mine too. I'm sorry he's gone, but if what they say is true, he was a murderer as well."

"Are you really sorry?"

"What are you suggesting?" Leo's face grew red with anger. "It's a tragedy, the man taking his own life like that. But let's face it, Henry had a certain . . . let's call it infatuation with Marley so quite possibly . . . that is, I never dreamed he would . . ."

"He didn't." I glanced over my shoulder. The conversation was not going well, and I was beginning to regret not waiting for Jack.

"Yes, well, the police don't necessarily care for your opinion, Cate. Now, if there is nothing more, I have work to do."

"I came to show you something."

I pulled the red box holding Marley's tennis bracelet out of my pocket. Opening the lid, I held it open for Leo to see. The panic in his eyes told me all I needed to know.

"You gave this bracelet to Marley."

"Nonsense. Whatever put that idea into your head?"

"It was obvious, really. I can't believe it took me so long to figure it out. I have to hand it to you, though. You did a pretty good job of covering the affair."

Leo's eyes remained riveted on the bracelet. "Where did you get that?"

"I imagine you must have lost a few nights' sleep, wondering when or where it might turn up."

Leo snatched at the jewelry box but I was too quick for him, snapping the lid closed as I backed toward the open door. I clutched the box behind me, out of Leo's reach.

"Who do you think you are?" Leo's face turned beet red. "Barging into my office, making these ridiculous accusations? I never saw that bracelet before in my life."

"I can prove you bought it," I replied softly.

"How?" Leo spat the word in my face.

I could never afford anything so expensive, but I recognized the brand and knew the jeweler marked each piece of jewelry with a registration number. Sure enough, when I put on my reading glasses and checked earlier, I saw the number etched into the gold. I explained to Leo how the bracelet could be traced to the original owner.

Leo's eyes narrowed. "I see. Now that I've had some time to think, I seem to remember. I might have bought a bracelet like that as a gift for my wife."

"And I'll thank you to return it to me."

Though Mildred Bishop's voice betrayed her age, the skin on her face was smooth and tan. Her eyebrows were lifted a fraction too high, creating a fixed expression of mild surprise, a telltale sign of plastic surgery. She closed the door behind her, then reached out and snatched the bracelet from my hand.

"Mrs. Bishop, you don't understand," I said. "Your husband gave that bracelet to Marley Booker."

"She's lying!" Leo's face flushed with rage.

"Shut up, you old fool. There's no sense denying your little distractions."

"You knew?" His jaw dropped in surprise.

"Of course. You had your spies at the club. I had mine."

An image of Henry standing outside Marley's window

leaped into my mind. "Henry told you," I said. "He saw them in bed together."

Mildred's mouth twisted into something that could only be called a grimace.

My mind raced. "I remember you cancelled your lesson that morning. You must have gone to the house to confront Marley and your husband."

"Confront them?" Mildred sniffed. "No, my dear. That would have been beneath me. I just wanted to confirm what Henry told me before I took steps to dismiss that man and rid this town of his family. But when I got there . . ." Mildred closed her eyes and took a deep breath before continuing. She turned to glare at her husband. "The windows of the house were wide open. You were arguing with that woman, yelling at her for the whole world to hear. It didn't take me long to realize what you were fighting about. You were trying to convince the whore to get an abortion."

A single word printed in red lipstick on the vanity mirror. WHORE.

"I would have handled it," Leo whined.

"It was abundantly clear that you couldn't. She told you she intended to keep the baby and there was nothing you could do to stop her." Mildred's voice sent a chill down my spine. "So I took matters into my own hands."

"What are you saying? You . . ." Realization dawned on Leo's face. He stared at his wife in horror. "What have you done?"

"She killed them," I said. "She killed Marley and the girls."

Mildred reached into her bag, withdrew a small pistol, and pointed it at me. "You should have minded your own business."

The sight of the gun should have shocked me, but for

some reason I wasn't surprised. Merely terrified and ludicrously angry at Jack for not being there when I needed him most. Gripped in a fist of fear, I fought for breath. A high-pitched ringing filled my ears. I took hold of the back of a chair to steady myself, fearful that I would faint.

Leo stared at his wife, his mouth working soundlessly as he struggled for words. "This is madness. Give me the gun, sweetheart."

"I'm afraid Cate has put us in a very awkward situation," Mildred replied. "You do realize we can't just let her walk out of here. She'll go right to the police. We have to take her someplace quiet and finish this. I need a minute to think. Maybe she's so distraught over Henry's death that she'll follow in his footsteps and poison herself. Or maybe another robbery. Yes, that's it. Everyone will assume she was shot by an intruder."

Leo held up his hand. "Mildred, I'm begging you. Stop this now before you go too far."

"Too far?" Mildred glared at her husband. "Don't you think it's a little late for that?"

"We'll get you the best lawyer money can buy," Leo begged. "Just put down the—"

A sharp rap on the door interrupted Leo's plea. Jack Burquest's voice reached me from the hallway. "Leo, are you in there?"

I looked up and the room began to spin.

"Jack, call the police!" I shouted, but the sound that came out of my mouth was little more than a whisper.

Out of the corner of my eye I saw Leo lunge for his wife. The blast of the pistol rang in my ears; gun smoke filled my nose. A bolt of pain ripped across my chest and down my arm. Letting go of the chair, I felt myself slide to the floor.

Then everything went black.

Chapter 36

The pain was unbearable. I opened my eyes, blinked a few times at Leo's office ceiling. Turning my head to the right, I met Jack's worried gaze. A man dressed in blue was strapping me to a gurney. Before I could say anything, another man placed a mask over my nose and slipped an elastic strap behind my head to hold it in place. I could feel the gurney rise. Jack dropped out of my view as the men wheeled me away. In the ambulance, one of them clamped a device on my finger, and within moments I heard an unseen machine beep rhythmically to the beat of my heart.

"Glad to see you're awake." The EMT barely glanced at me while he wrote something down on a clipboard. "Try to relax. We'll get you to the hospital in no time."

I was surrounded by equipment. Mounted on the wall were monitors, radios, and a plethora of medical devices. One of the men—the guy with the clipboard—rode in back with me, the other presumably behind the wheel. The siren blared an urgent note and though there were no windows in the back of the ambulance, I could feel the speed of the vehicle as we careened around the bends in the road. Imagining the inconvenience of other drivers pulling aside in deference to the flashing lights, an unexplainable feeling of embarrassment washed over me. I was glad to be tucked away anonymously in the back of the van.

Lying there, everything came back in a rush. Mildred. . . the gun . . . Jack. The beeping monitor picked up a pace. The attendant looked up from his paperwork and frowned.

"Take it easy, Mrs. Stokes. We're almost there."

I closed my eyes, trying to slow my heart. I'd heard Buddhist monks could do that through meditation, but I'd never gone in for that sort of thing. Would have come in handy now, though, I thought.

The ambulance came to an abrupt stop and white-clad orderlies reached in and pulled me out. Oxygen tank, heart monitor, and all, I was whisked through double doors.

My prior experience in the emergency room was not what I'd call positive. I once had fallen on a Friday afternoon and twisted my ankle. Not one to fuss, I let it go, using an ice pack in the hopes that the swelling would go down and the pain would subside on its own. Needless to say, by the end of the weekend I was virtually crippled. My husband insisted on taking me to the hospital. Hours later, after seeing the doctor for about ten minutes, I emerged with an ace bandage and a prescription for painkillers. The doctor sent me away with the brilliant advice to stay off the foot until the swelling went down. And for that, he billed my insurance company an amount equal to the price of a small car.

This time I was far more impressed. The orderlies moved me from the gurney to a bed in one of the examination bays. Before they left, a nurse appeared by my side, listened to my heart, and checked my blood pressure. She nodded, and checked a form pinned to her clipboard.

"How are you feeling, Mrs. Stokes?" The nametag pinned to her uniform said JENKINS.

I told her that I wasn't feeling too bad, considering I was just shot in the chest. She gave me a puzzled look and removed the oxygen mask from my face.

"I'm sorry, could you say that again?"

I repeated what I had said. She gave me a hesitant smile and shook her head.

"The EMT report states that you fainted, hit your head and couldn't be revived at the scene. When they took your vitals, they detected an irregular heartbeat. There is no mention of a gunshot wound in their report. And to be honest, I don't see any indication that you've been injured in that way. Perhaps the knock on your head caused you some confusion?"

I pushed myself up and glanced down at my chest. No blood anywhere. A sharp pain gripped me and I dropped back onto the bed with a gasp.

"Are you experiencing some pain?" Nurse Jenkins asked.

I nodded.

"The doctor will be with us in just a few minutes. In the meantime, I'll need to get enter your information into the system. Do you have your insurance card with you?"

If the pain in my chest didn't choke my breath away, I would have explained that I didn't exactly plan ahead. Fortunately, Jack appeared at that moment. He looked flushed and a bit foolish with my pocketbook slung over his shoulder. I was never happier to see him. He passed my wallet to the nurse so she could take down all the information she needed.

"You had me worried back there," Jack said. "What happened?"

"That's what we're going to find out," Nurse Jenkins replied. "You can stay with Mrs. Stokes until Dr. Lane arrives. Then I'm afraid you will have to leave."

Dr. Lane was a model of proficiency, asking me about my symptoms and medical history before ordering a chest x-ray, blood tests, and a CT scan. Before moving onto the next patient, she entered something on the computer that sat on a table next to my bed. When she was finished, she told me she was admitting me for the night, and that someone would be along soon to take me upstairs for testing. She said she would see me in my room after she received the test results and we'd "take it from there."

Later, Jack stood by my bed and held my hand with a look of concern on his face. I was exhausted from the regimen of tests, but comforted by his presence. He acted like nothing had changed between us. It was as if our recent falling-out never happened. I was relieved to finally have the chance to speak with him about what happened in Leo Bishop's office.

"You saved my life," I said.

"Yeah, sorry I was late. You didn't say why you wanted me to meet you there, but I heard voices coming from Leo's office so I knocked to ask if he knew where you were. Everything got quiet for a minute, then someone shouted and BAM! After the gun went off, Leo came running out of his office yelling something about you fainting. You really gave us a scare."

I thought about Jack being scared, and wondered how he would feel if he were staring down the barrel of Mildred Bishop's gun.

I gave his hand a squeeze. "Did the police arrest Mildred Bishop?"

"Why would they do that? The gun went off by accident. The cops only showed up because I called 9-1-1. You were out cold. When the EMT arrived, Leo explained you fainted dead away from the sound of the blast."

"Accident, my eye. She tried to kill me."

To my utter astonishment, Jack erupted in a fit of laughter. I let go of his hand and his amusement dissolved into a mere chuckle. "You think Mildred Bishop tried to kill you? I'm telling you, it was an accident." A final guffaw burst from his mouth before he regained control. "She said there have been some recent robberies in the neighborhood, so she went out and bought a gun, you know, for protection. She stopped by the club to show Leo, but when she pulled it out of her purse, the thing accidently went off. The bullet smashed into Leo's bookcase and hit a collector's edition of Tolstoy that I'm sure cost him a mint. Anyway, that's when you passed out and went down for the count. Mildred feels terrible about the whole thing. She'll be happy to hear you're okay."

"Where are they now?"

"Who?"

"The Bishops."

"I don't know. Home, I guess."

"I have to call Erika Tripp."

The beep of the monitor increased with my rising panic. What would the Bishops do when they heard I was awake and talking? Just then, Dr. Lane entered the room. She glanced at the monitor, caught sight of Jack, and gave him a disapproving stare.

"You have to leave now, Mr. Burquest. I want to go over Mrs. Stokes' test results with her."

Jack reached for my hand again. "I'll be right outside in the waiting area."

The heart monitor raced, matching my pounding heart. As Jack started to leave I clutched his sleeve to pull him back.

"I'm telling you, they're lying. Mildred tried to kill me."

The doctor took another look at the monitor. "Really, Mr. Burquest, I must insist."

"Why in the world would she do that?" Jack planted a kiss on the back of my hand before letting go. He looked into my eyes and must have read my level of desperation. "Okay, if it will make you feel better, I'll call your detective friend."

Without another word, he left.

I only half listened as Dr. Lane explained that I'd had an angina attack. She was telling me I needed something called an angioplasty. While she described the procedure—she was going to inflate a balloon in my vein to open a blockage—my mind was preoccupied with another danger facing me. Mildred tried to kill me once, and I had every reason to think she would try again. I nodded as Dr. Lane continued to talk about stents and recovery times, but only really paid attention when she said I would have to stay in the hospital for a week.

"But I have to get out of here."

"Not an option. Your condition is serious, Mrs. Stokes. I'm going to hold you for observation. One week. No compromise."

Nurse Jenkins entered the room with a tray bearing a syringe and paperwork. The doctor gave her a nod and stepped aside. With a swipe of an alcohol pad, the nurse jabbed my arm. Using the pen that hung on a chain around her neck, she made a note on a form.

"What was that?" I asked.

"A little something to help you relax," the doctor replied. "Now try to rest. I'll see you in the O.R. in about twenty minutes."

"But I . . ." The monitor slowed as the medication kicked in. A wave of dizziness washed over me and I closed my eyes, willing the sensation to pass. When I opened them again, Dr. Lane was gone.

Dressed in a membrane-thin hospital gown, I looked up at the face of a male nurse who wheeled me into the operating room. He helped me onto the padded table. Within minutes, the cold air leached all the warmth from my body. Dr. Lane asked me what kind of music I would like to listen to while she worked. I requested something classical, and as if by magic Vivaldi's "Four Seasons" filled the room. I shivered with cold, or maybe just nerves. Being draped from the neck down I couldn't see past my chin so I had to assume it was the nurse who placed a warm blanket over my feet. A prick, and my

groin went numb. Dr. Lane kept up a steady stream of reassuring comments, telling me that I was "doing fine." Since she
was doing all the work and I was doing absolutely nothing, I
considered shooting back a sarcastic retort. But truth be known,
I was grateful to hear everything was going well.

Back in my room, Nurse Jenkins gave me a yet another
injection. Whatever was in the syringe this time knocked me
out. Once again, I sank into darkness.

I woke to the sight of Erika Tripp standing next to my
bed. In my confused state, I wondered why she was there.

"You look like shit." She grinned at me. "Jack Burquest
said you wanted to see me. Caught me on the way home from
the store with my kids, so this better be good."

"You have kids?" I fought to clear the fog of my drug-in-
duced sleep.

"Two girls who are pretty pissed off with me right now. I
promised them we'd dye Easter eggs this afternoon."

I tried to picture Erika Tripp with children. Two girls.
The memory of Robin and her purple eggs sliced like a knife
through my mind.

"Seriously, you don't look too good," Erika said.

"I'm fine." In fact, I didn't feel well at all. I was overwhelmed by a desire to close my eyes and go back to sleep.
With determination, I attempted to push myself up into a sitting position. Dropping back onto the bed pillows, I struggled
to catch my breath.

"Hey, take it easy." She looked around in alarm. "Maybe
I should call a nurse or someone."

"No!" I gasped for breath. "Give me a minute."

"What the hell happened? What's all this about somebody taking a shot at you?"

"Mildred Bishop tried to kill me."

"Burquest says it was an accident."

"I'm telling you, she aimed the gun at me and pulled the trigger."

"Okay, calm down. But let me tell you, if that woman really did try to kill you, then she's a lousy shot. A chimpanzee could have hit you from that range."

"Her husband knocked the gun away. That's the only reason I'm laying here, talking to you. Otherwise I would be in the morgue."

Erika glanced up at the EKG monitor on the wall. I remained hooked to the machine, but since moving me into the room someone had muted the sound. The display was turned to prevent me from seeing the lines bumping across the screen. Judging by the frown on Erika's face, I could tell it wasn't good.

"If you don't take it easy, that ticker of yours will do the job for her. Tell me exactly what happened."

Erika pulled a visitor's chair to the side of the bed. She filled a cup with water from the pitcher on the nightstand and passed it to me. I accepted her offer and took a sip.

I began by telling her about the tennis bracelet. From there I went on to explain about Leo's affair with Marley. When I got to the part where I went to the club to confront Leo with my suspicions about Marley's unborn baby, the detective shook her head.

"Do you have some kind of death wish or something?" I could read the anger in her green eyes. "Why didn't you tell me all this sooner?"

"Because I wasn't sure. All I had was the bracelet. And an idea that maybe Leo killed Marley."

Erika held up her hand indicating she wanted me to take a break. She pulled her cell phone from her pocket and set it on the table.

"I want to get this on the record. Start over. Tell me why you went to see Leo Bishop."

I began again, pausing only when Erika stopped me to ask for clarification. By the time I reached the part about Mildred and the gun, I felt drained. I closed my eyes, exhaustion tugging at my brain.

"Cate?"

With a start my eyelids flew open. I realized I had drifted off for a moment.

"That's enough for now." Erika picked up her cell phone and returned it to her pocket. "I'm going to have a little chat with the Bishops. But before I go, there's one thing I need to ask. Off the record."

I nodded.

"How did you get the tennis bracelet?"

I counted the seconds before answering. Not long ago I would have lied about Jack, his involvement in the break-in, and the theft of Marley's bracelet. I would have lied to protect him. But now, knowing I had no choice, I told the truth.

"Jack Burquest sent it to me. I decided to keep it, even though I knew it was Marley's."

Erika's eyebrows shot up. I expected she wanted to know how Jack got the bracelet, but she didn't ask. "Well, by now Mrs. Bishop has probably ditched the thing. We may never find it. Too bad. I would have liked to trace that registration number."

"I wrote it down." I pointed to the cabinet next to my hospital bed. "You'll find the paper in my pocketbook."

The smile returned to Erika's face.

The room was dark, the hospital quiet. A sliver of light stole in from under the closed door, throwing shadows against the wall. I was hungry, a good sign I guessed, but my mouth was dry as sand. The pitcher of water was beyond my reach and rather than try my luck at sitting again, I closed my eyes and tried to go back to sleep. My brain was firing on all cylinders. I couldn't get the Booker case out of my head.

Mildred Bishop was a cold-blooded murderer. Whether or not she meant to harm the girls, I couldn't know. But clearly, she planned to kill Marley with the Aldicarb. Or at the very least, she wanted to cause a miscarriage and purge her husband's mistress of the unwanted baby. Before she left, Erika said something interesting. She said poison is a woman's tool, a weapon of passion. That made sense. I had seen for myself that Mildred wasn't satisfied with killing Marley quietly. She'd left a message. WHORE, written in Marley's red lipstick.

So how did the lipstick end up in Henry's house?

Even as the question formed in my head, my thoughts turned to Henry. If he didn't kill Marley and the girls, then . . . Just then the pulsing line on the heart monitor must have jumped off the screen as I realized something was horribly, desperately wrong.

Chapter 37

Kenny came bearing gifts. He set the potted tulips on the windowsill and handed me the egg carton that he held tucked under his arm. I opened the lid to see all twelve eggs dyed various shades of purple.

"Happy Easter," he said.

Tears filled my eyes, the pent-up grief for three lost lives spilling over at last. I looked up to see Kenny's eyes were brimming too.

He filled me in on what he knew about the case against Mildred Bishop. As he spoke I learned Erika had been busy in the twenty-four hours since I saw her.

"The good news is that she found a judge to sign a search warrant—not an easy thing to do on a holiday weekend. While her partner went to the club to look for the bracelet, she called around, looking for a Forensics tech to come in. Double pay on Sunday, so she didn't have to look too far to find one. The good news is, the technician checked Mildred's prints against those two sets of unidentified fingerprints on the container of Aldicarb from the Bookers' garage and the juice carton. One of them was a perfect match."

"What's the bad news?"

"No luck finding the bracelet. Probably gone for good. At the moment, Erika's holding Mildred in the county jail. If she doesn't find some tangible evidence soon, she'll have to let her go."

I smiled to think of Mildred's face when Erika arrested her on Easter morning. I would have loved seeing that.

"Aren't the fingerprints enough to keep her locked up?"

Kenny shook his head. "There were three different people who handled that pesticide and two who handled the juice carton. Nothing definitive about that." The crease between his eyebrows told me something bothered him.

"What's wrong?" I asked. "What aren't you telling me?"

"Here's how it works. Erika is holding Mildred because she has a suspicion that Mildred committed a crime. But the law states that the detention time also has to be reasonable. In this case, forty-eight hours. The clock is ticking. By Tuesday morning, Erika has to demonstrate probable cause or let her go."

"You know my knowledge of criminal law is rusty. What does she need, exactly?"

"Enough evidence to file charges against Mildred. And with a case this old, that's going to be next to impossible."

"You're telling me Mildred is going to get away with killing Marley and the girls?" I stared at him in disbelief.

Kenny sighed. "Here's the other problem. The District Attorney's office is against prosecuting Mildred for a crime that was tried and solved years ago. And even if Leland's lawyers could get past the DA, convincing a jury is going to be tough. They're working every angle, but don't get your hopes up."

I'd heard that before. Exactly the same thing Adam told me months ago. Thinking of Adam prompted me to mention the one bright spot in the whole terrible mess.

"There's still Adam's wrongful conviction case," I said.

"Officially on hold. Leland's lawyers are debating whether it's better to proceed or wait and see what the DA decides to do about Mildred Bishop."

"Why wait?"

"You should ask Adam for the legal explanation. He's decided to ignore the advice to stay out of touch. He'll be here tomorrow."

Kenny continued to talk about the race against the clock to gather evidence against Mildred. Erika sent an email to the jewelry manufacturer requesting information about the registration number etched on the bracelet. An auto-reply bounced back informing her that the company was closed through Easter Monday—too late to meet the forty-eight-hour deadline. Erika also went to her boss to see about exhuming Marley's body. She explained that it would help to prove Leo was the father by testing the baby's DNA, but unless she found enough evidence to convince the DA, there was little hope for approval. Kenny went on to describe the long process of exhuming bodies for forensic evidence. The more he spoke, the more desperate the situation sounded.

"Wait a minute." The words tumbled out of my mouth as my mind raced in a new direction. "We're looking at this the wrong way."

Kenny gave me a confused look.

"Don't you see? The police didn't find any Aldicarb."

"What are you talking about? Of course they did. It was in the garage."

He still didn't get what I was saying. I slowed down to explain.

"I'm talking about Henry's house. There was no Aldicarb on the search warrant return that officer Pisoni showed me. Now I know why. There wasn't any there. The EPA banned Aldicarb from general use a few years ago. You have to have a special license to buy the stuff."

"How the hell do you know that?"

"When I started working with Adam, I did some research on Aldicarb. It seemed like useless information at the time, but now I know Henry couldn't have bought the stuff, even if he wanted to."

"Then someone else—someone with access to that pesticide must have killed Henry." Kenny was catching on quickly.

"Guess who."

"But why would Mildred kill Henry? He's the one who told her about Leo's affair with Marley in the first place."

"Exactly. Which made him the only other person in the world who knew. He'd kept her secret for all these years, but when Adam and I started poking around, Mildred must have worried that he'd talk."

I reflected back on the day when Adam interviewed Henry, and how agitated my old friend became when Adam pressed to find out what he was hiding. I should have taken the time to ask Henry about it when we were alone. He might have told me. It would have saved his life.

"Mildred could have planted Marley's lipstick in Henry's house so we would think . . ." The words caught in my throat as the scene in Henry's bedroom took shape in my mind. My stomach lurched with the realization of all Mildred Bishop had done.

"I'll find out if KCC has one of those licenses from the EPA." Kenny stood to leave. "Then we're going to search that fucking place from top to bottom until we find it."

I leaned back on my pillow, my heart pumping blood through my veins like water through a fire hose.

"There's something else."

"Make it quick." Kenny bounced on the balls of his feet, rattling the keys in his pocket with his right hand.

"The thumbprint on the plate in Doris Keating's condo. Did anyone check to see if it was Mildred's?"

The expression on Kenny's face told me all I needed to know.

"I'll let you know what we find."

Kenny left me still holding the carton of eggs, wishing I could run out with him. Seeing him so charged up, so determined to get to the truth, I dared to believe that justice would finally be served. But I was also aware that Mildred Bishop took care to cover her tracks at every step of the way. I had no reason to think she had grown careless now. Perhaps, like Marley's bracelet, the Aldicarb she used to poison Henry would never be found. I set the eggs on the table next to my bed and glanced at the clock on the wall, counting the hours left until Erika's deadline.

With every hour that passed, my anxiety rose. The hospital staff encouraged me to venture out of bed for brief walks around the ward, and I felt my strength returning with each step I took. I had every intention of renegotiating an early release with Dr. Lane when she made her rounds later in the day. Nothing was going to keep me hanging around for a full week while so much was going on outside. When Adam entered my room, he held a pink and orange bag in one hand. With the other he passed me a mug of coffee from the donut shop.

"Did you miss me?" he asked.

"Not much," I replied, returning his grin. "I've been too busy to notice you were gone."

"So I heard."

I dipped my head and inhaled the steam rising from the coffee. Taking a sip, I closed my eyes, relishing the flavor.

"Thanks," I said. "I haven't had a decent cup since I got here."

"Dad told me what happened. Are you okay?"

"Better than ever," I replied.

Adam filled me in on the latest news. Now that the focus had turned to Henry, Kenny's team kicked into high gear and managed to get information from the airline regarding Henry's flight to Tampa. They confirmed that though Henry had a reservation, he never boarded the plane. In addition, Kenny spoke with the receptionist at the Veranda Inn who, after some persuasion, told him that Henry never registered as a guest in the motel. The conclusion was that Henry never stepped foot in Venice. But someone went to great pains to make it look as though he had.

"Any luck finding the Aldicarb that poisoned Henry?" I asked.

"Erika tried to get the warrant application signed by the same judge she saw on Sunday. He accused her of going on a fishing expedition and told her not to come back until she could give him more than a hunch to demonstrate cause. Erika went ballistic—not exactly a great career move. You would think by now she should know that pissing off a judge isn't the best way to get him to cooperate. Anyway, when she didn't get what she wanted from him, she found another judge who didn't even look at the application before signing. She and a uniformed cop are searching the club now."

Though I drained the mug of coffee, I hadn't touched the bag from the donut shop. Now Adam eyed the sack greedily and asked, "Are you going to eat that?"

I waved permission and watched as he unwrapped the sesame seed bagel and smeared it with cream cheese. I waited for him to swallow the first bite before prodding him for more information.

"We're running out of time. What happens if they don't find the Aldicarb?"

A few crumbs were trapped in Adam's two-day beard. I signaled to indicate where to wipe, and with one pass of a napkin he got them.

"I saved the best news for last," Adam said. That grin, so like his father's.

Incredibly, no one had checked with the Venice sheriff's department earlier, but when Erika placed the call she learned that the print left on the rim of the plate in Doris Keating's apartment was a perfect match with Mildred's right thumb. That, together with her prints on the necklace found in Henry's bedroom, was enough to hold her while the investigation moved to the front burner. Erika was getting full cooperation from all departments.

I let my head drop back on my pillow, overwhelmed with relief. Closing my eyes, I resurrected an image of Lissa and Robin from memory. I took a moment, reflecting on all that was lost.

"Cate, are you okay?" Adam asked. I detected the anxiety in his voice and met his gaze.

"More than okay, thanks."

"I owe you an apology," he said.

"What for?"

"For not listening to what you said about Henry Rusak. You were right about him all along."

"Don't worry about it," I said. "You're not the only one here who misjudged someone." Thinking about Jack, it seemed ridiculous that I ever thought he murdered Marley and the children. I made a silent vow to give him the apology he deserved as soon as I saw him. Jack and I had a lot to discuss, and I couldn't put it off much longer.

Chapter 38

Dr. Lane and I reached a compromise and Tuesday morning she released me from the hospital. She cautioned me that the stent in my artery should serve as a reminder to take better care of myself. I thanked her for everything and promised to heed her advice. As soon as I stepped out of the building and onto the sidewalk, I lit a cigarette.

"Are you supposed to be smoking those things?" Jack asked.

"Shut up and take me home."

The whole time I spent in the hospital, Jack had been wonderful. He came to visit every day, bearing flowers and chocolates. We sat for hours, allowing the silence to rest comfortably between us. He remained sober, and most days he appeared to be content to just hold my hand. On those occasions when he bent down to kiss my cheek, I caught the faint smell of his dandruff shampoo. My time in the hospital gave me plenty of time to think about us. Since Arnie died, I did my best to fend off feelings of dire loneliness by keeping busy. Now and then my sister invited me over for dinner, but with Ben away at college, I found those evenings with Nancy and her husband, Tim too tedious to bear. I buried myself in work, but after what I'd just gone through, I realized there was more to life. I needed to make a change.

"Do you have time for a cup of coffee?" I asked.

"That sounds great. We can stop at Gordon's if you need anything from the store."

I remembered Dr. Lane's warning to alter my diet. She wanted me to start drinking decaf coffee but I figured it wouldn't hurt to finish the rest of the hi-test in my pantry before making the switch.

"That won't be necessary. I've got some banana bread in the freezer that I can warm in the microwave. We'll have that with the coffee."

We made small talk while I ground the beans and made the coffee. Sitting across from him at my small kitchen table, I could read the affection in his eyes. Affection and hope.

"I've been thinking about what you said the other day."

"About us getting together again? You know how much I—"

I raised my hand, signaling for him to stop. "I know. And believe me, there was once a time when maybe we could have made it work. But recently I've been doing a lot of thinking about us." I reached over and covered his hand with mine. "It's too late, Jack"

"You always tell me it's never too late!" Jack's voice betrayed his rising panic. "Just give me a chance."

"I'm sorry, Jack."

He slumped in his chair, staring into his empty cup. I rose and grabbed the pot, refilling his cup in silence. Before I sat back down, I caught him wiping a tear from the corner of his eye.

"Nothing in my life turned out the way I expected it would," he said. "Back in school, I was on top of the world with my whole future ahead of me. Now look. I'm a drunk whose kids won't give me the time of day, I have two ex-wives who hate my guts, and the love of my life wants nothing to do with me. And if that weren't enough, I'm unemployed. Thirty-four years working for that firm and what do I have to show for it? Not a damn thing."

I took a deep breath and let it out slowly before responding.

"Your future is in your own hands, Jack. Make something of it. Spend more time with your kids. Stick with the AA meetings. You're going to be okay, especially after I tell you my news."

Jack looked up, eyebrows raised in question. His curiosity trumped his self-pity.

"I've decided to retire," I said quietly. "I'm going to contact my clients in the morning and tell them to seek new counsel. If you'd like, I'll give you their names and numbers. You can start making calls to see who you can sign up."

"But . . . what are you going to do?"

"I'll figure it out," I shrugged. "All I know for sure is that I'm finished with the law."

I was glad when Jack fabricated an excuse for leaving. After he left, I reflected on our conversation. I let him down as gently as I could but I knew him well enough to realize just how deeply hurt he was. Still, I knew I made the right decision. My life was about to change, and though I didn't know exactly what the future held, I knew Jack wouldn't be there with me.

Chapter 39

Three weeks later, I heard from Adam. His mother was organizing a large, elaborate affair in Durham to celebrate his graduation from law school. Adam called to tell me my invitation was in the mail. His father had something else in mind. Kenny planned to have a more private celebration and he wanted me there. He already made reservations for the following weekend at one of the area's better restaurants. I didn't relish the long drive up across state to socialize with a bunch of people I didn't know so it was an easy decision. I told Adam I would RSVP my regrets to his mother, and that I looked forward to the evening with his father.

"Great, thanks," Adam said. I knew I'd made the right decision.

The Chesterfield Inn was an historic landmark, one of those restaurants locals reserved for special occasions. The interior was luxurious, the menu pricy, and the service stellar in a town that worked hard to keep tourists happy. It was also a place Mildred and Leo Bishop frequented. With Mildred in custody, I didn't expect they would be back any time soon.

Days ahead, I started planning what to wear. After pulling several dresses out of my closet and spreading them across the bed, I realized none of them would do. I made an appointment to have my hair and nails done, then cast aside all resolve to be more careful with my budget and hit the shops on Main Street. Hours later, after spending an amount that would have made Marley proud, I was satisfied with my purchases.

Adam stood when I approached the table. He was dressed in the same suit he wore when I first met him but here it didn't seem out of place. He held out my chair and I took a seat, nodding thanks to the waiter who appeared from nowhere to place a linen napkin on my lap. I looked across the table and caught Kenny staring at me.

"You should wear your hair like that all the time."

I smiled and waved off his compliment with a comment about Marley teaching me how to put my hair in a French twist.

There was an empty chair to my right, a menu set on the plate. I was surprised Jennifer didn't arrive with Adam, so I asked if she was driving down from the city in her own car.

"Jennifer and I . . . well, we . . . we're kinda taking a break." Adam cracked his knuckles. "She landed a summer internship in a prosecutor's office in Boston. I guess she'll be back in the fall to finish her last two years at UNH."

He glanced down at his menu, and I took the hint. Jennifer was history.

The mystery of the empty place setting was solved when Erika appeared. "Hey." She snatched the napkin from the waiter's hand. "Sorry I'm late. Got tied up with something important. Have you ordered yet?"

"You're just in time," Kenny replied.

We gave the waiter our orders. I chose clam chowder to start while everyone else ordered raw oysters. Kenny asked for a bottle of champagne. The bubbles tickled my nose, reminding me of my first taste, sipped under my mother's disapproving glare so many years ago.

I turned to Adam. "Any idea what you'll be doing after graduation?"

"As a matter of fact," he paused for effect. I could tell

from the look on his face that he had good news. Adam picked up his champagne and took another sip.

"Tell her," Kenny said.

"I applied for a job at the Defender Project," Adam said.

"The organization that's helping Leland?" I asked.

"Right. My professor wrote an amazing recommendation, and of course my work on the Booker case helped. I guess everything went pretty well because they called back yesterday and offered me a job in their New York office."

I looked at Adam, feeling something like parental pride swell up in my chest. I was happy for him, of course, but I also experienced a deep sense of loss. Our uneasy alliance had turned into something special, and now we were going our separate ways. I would miss him.

The conversation shifted to Mildred Bishop. Kenny told us the Venice police had discovered the rest of Doris Keating's stolen jewelry in the Bishops' Florida condominium. Together with the thumbprint on the plate, and a few strands of Mildred's hair that were found on Doris' couch, the Sarasota County Sheriff's Department appeared to have built a solid case.

"They're trying to extradite Mildred Bishop to Florida so she can stand trial for murder there," Kenny said.

"Can they do that?"

"They can try," Erika chimed in. "We'd rather keep her here. But the thing is, Keating's murder predates Rusak's so technically, Florida gets the first shot."

"Is there any way she'll be brought to justice for killing Marley and the girls?" I asked.

Erika seemed to ignore my question as she stole a sideways glance at Kenny. I got the feeling he already knew what she was about to say. "Let's talk about Henry Rusak first. I guess you already know that we lifted a bunch of Mildred

Bishop's fresh prints from an old container of Aldicarb we found in a shed at the country club."

"How can you tell they were fresh?" Adam asked.

Erika explained that the lines and swirls on hands fade with time—the depth of Mildred's ridges eroded with age, so her prints lifted from the Aldicarb at the club were not as well defined as those found in the Booker's garage decades earlier.

"We also found another Veranda Inn pen in the Bishops' house," Erika continued. "Since they owned a condo in Venice, she had no reason to stay there, so she probably picked them up for the express purpose of leaving one in Rusak's house. I suspect the bitch used his credit cards to book his travel reservations. Unfortunately, we'll never be able to prove that. She tried to frame Rusak, and then staged his murder to look like a suicide to throw us off track. Almost worked too. Everyone— well, almost everyone—bought it." She gave me a big smile.

"What about Henry's suicide note? I asked.

"Doesn't mean a thing." Kenny asked me if I had a pen and paper in my purse. Fishing them out, I handed both to him. He took the pen in his left hand, wrote SORRY and passed the paper back to me. I looked down and sighed. Anyone could have done that, making a decent forgery of Henry's handwriting.

"The DA thinks we've got a pretty solid case against Bishop for killing Rusak," Erika said. "But you asked me about the Bookers. That's a different story."

I looked up and met her green eyes. I had a bad feeling about what she was about to say.

"For starters, all the evidence is circumstantial. The DA closed the Booker case years ago and he doesn't want to open a new can of worms. He's pressing me to work Rusak's murder and drop the Bookers."

Adam started protesting, using language I would have

expected from his father. After letting him rant for a few minutes, Erika waved her hands and shouted, "What the hell! Let me finish."

Heads at the surrounding tables turned. Erika glared at the people sitting across from us and growled, "What are you staring at? We're having a private conversation here." One by one, the patrons went back to their dinners, trying their best to ignore us.

"Do you people really think I would give in to a little political pressure?"

I shook my head, feeling a glimmer of hope.

"Damn right, I wouldn't. That's the reason I got here late. I just had a little coming-to-Jesus meeting with Mildred and her lawyer, during which I took the opportunity to explain a few facts of life to her. Took longer than I wanted it to, but when I walked out of that room, I had her signed confession for the Booker murders in my sweaty little paws."

"What?" The expression on Adam's face was one of disbelief.

"You heard me," Erika said. "I informed her that we're prepared to give her a one-way ticket to Florida—the land of lethal injections and electric chairs—where the DA's office is charging her with first-degree murder. You should have seen her face. I don't think she understood at first, but then her lawyer whispered something in her ear and she went all white. I mean Casper-the-ghost white. I thought she was going to pass out right there in front of me. Anyway, I suggested she might be better off taking her chances in New Hampshire. But the only way we could arrange for that was if we charged her with a crime that predated Keating. In other words, the Booker family murders. If you ask me, she made a good choice."

"You bluffed?" Adam was laughing. We were all laughing, Erika loudest of the bunch.

"Bluff? No, I'd say it was more like I opened the door for negotiation. Bishop claimed she didn't intend to kill Marley; she only wanted her to miscarry that baby. And she's adamant that she never meant to harm those little girls. The way she talked, I could almost believe her. Anyway, we met somewhere in the middle and I got the DA to agree to three counts of manslaughter in exchange for a full confession. Mildred will serve her life sentence at the women's prison in Concord without parole. She'll never set foot in a Florida courtroom."

"Then it's over." I couldn't hold back the tears.

Adam reached out and took my hand. We exchanged glances and I could read the triumph on his face.

"Word went out to Leland's lawyers yesterday," Erika said. "He's a free man."

Chapter 40

A few late-season tomatoes sat in a basket on the kitchen table. The last of the carrots from my garden were in the kitchen sink, waiting for me to wash them off. As I stood in the laundry room brushing the dirt off my jeans, I heard the doorbell ring. Opening the door, I looked up into Leland's dark brown eyes.

He looked good, better than the last time we met in the Concord State Prison. His gray hair was cut short, his face cleanly shaved. I detected a trace of his old aftershave, a musky scent that went out of fashion in the seventies. Wearing a button-down Lands' End shirt and Dockers that were still new enough to have a knife-edged crease down the front, he looked like he just stepped out of a Sears catalog. Which in a way, I guess he did. I was surprised to see him. Surprised and happy.

"How did you find . . .?" I answered my own question before I finished asking. "Of course, Adam gave you my address. Come in, I'll put on the coffee."

Boxes were stacked in all the rooms, waiting for the moving men to come and pick them up the next day. I had packed everything but the essentials. The pot and one mug remained on the kitchen counter. I pushed the basket of tomatoes to one side and moved a box from one of the chairs to the floor. Waving Leland to take a seat, I measured the beans into the machine and pushed the button.

"I remember you take it black." I had to raise my voice for him to hear me over the grinding noise. "Good thing, because the sugar and creamer are already packed."

"Where are you going?" Leland looked around the room as if noticing the boxes for the first time.

"I bought a little place on Florida's Gulf Coast. Flying out tomorrow."

Leland nodded. He pointed to the urn sitting on the window sill. "What's that?"

I explained that I was planning to go down to the park after sunset to scatter Henry's ashes when no one was looking. That way, I figured Henry could finally watch the children play without anyone complaining.

Leland nodded again. Nothing seemed to surprise him. Not Henry, not my decision to leave Keene. Nothing.

"What about you? Will you be staying here?"

"There's nothing here for me. I'm going back to Georgia. Somewhere I can spend my days in peace. Maybe take up golf again."

After I filled the solitary cup and set it down before him, a daddy longlegs started across the table. I picked it up by one leg and threw it out the open window.

"If she were here, Marley's skin would be crawling after seeing you do that." He picked up his coffee and took a sip. "She was terrified of spiders."

"I know."

"Tell me, what do you plan to do in Florida?"

"I haven't quite figured that out yet. The house I bought has a backyard big enough for me to start a vegetable garden. And I plan to take long walks on the beach every day. We'll see."

Leland tapped his empty shirt pocket and glanced down. I hesitated for a few seconds, taking the time to scan the boxes surrounding me. It wasn't my house anymore, so I decided why not. I got up and retrieved a pack of Marlboros from my purse. Passing them to him, he looked at me in surprise.

"I didn't know you smoked. And my brand too. Thanks."

I offered him my lighter and shook out another cigarette for myself. He lit mine first, then sucked greedily at his own. Coughing the smoke from his lungs, he shook his head.

"I'm trying to quit."

"Me too."

He laughed which sent him into another coughing fit. After he caught his breath he turned to me and smiled. "I stopped by to thank you before I leave. And to give you this." Leland handed me the small package that he set on the table when he first arrived. "I found it in a box of things they kept for me in storage while I was inside. I want you to have it."

Through the paper I felt the outline of a picture frame. When I removed the wrapping, I found myself staring at a photo of the five of us. Recognizing the clothes we wore—Marley's tennis bracelet on my wrist—I knew the shot was taken at the club on the 4th of July. Leland stood between Marley and me. Marley held a glass of champagne in one hand, her other lightly resting on Robin's head. I had both arms wrapped around Lissa, holding her close. Looking at the image now, I remembered the feel of Leland's warm hand on my bare shoulder.

I wiped away a tear. "Thanks. This means a lot to me."

Leland took the frame from my hand and studied the photo. His eyes rose to meet mine. "I never realized how much alike you looked. You could have been sisters."

I shook my head, embarrassed by the compliment. Leland's attention remained focused on the picture, a slow smile spreading across his face.

"She really sparkled, didn't she?"

"Yes," I agreed. "She really did."

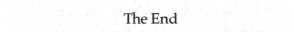

The End

Author's Notes

This book is a work of fiction. Names, characters, organizations and events are the product of the author's imagination. Any resemblance to actual persons, living or dead is entirely co-incidental.

Keene, New Hampshire is a real place as is Venice, Florida. To the best of my knowledge no murder was ever committed in either of these towns. Some locations cited in this book such as the Cheshire County Courthouse and several eating establishments are also real. And if you ever have the chance to sample Pompano at the Crow's Nest you won't be disappointed.

The Defender Project does not exist, however there are several worthy nonprofit organizations in the country that work diligently to assist innocent people who have been wrongly convicted. They depend largely on the heroic efforts of attorneys, law students and other volunteers who offer their services for free. Unfortunately, the need for their good work shows no sign of stopping.

I would like to express my gratitude for the help and encouragement of the following: To the talented writers of the Sarasota Literary Guild—Scott Amsbaugh, Michele Draper, Roger Hooverman, and Sheila Reed—without whom this book would never have been written. To my sister, Nancy Merel, who spent untold hours reading and rereading drafts of this novel, providing much needed encouragement all the way.

And to my husband, Pieter Heijens, who with his critical eye and forthright feedback kept me going in the right direction. His unwavering support means more to me than words can express.

Janet Heijens

Janet Heijens was born in Cocoa
Beach, Florida in 1954. After receiving her Bachelor of Science in Business at New Hampshire's Keene
State College, she pursued a career
in international business. Thirty
years later, she returned to Florida
and began her second career as a
mystery writer.

Janet is the Kirkus Review
starred author of the Wrongful
Conviction Series including *Kendall Road*, *Snook Wallow* and
Caspersen Beach.

A founding member of the Sarasota Literary Guild, she
is an active member of the Florida Gulf Coast Sisters in Crime.
Janet and her husband, Pieter, live in Sarasota, Florida.

She can be found on Facebook or contacted through her
website www.janetheijens.com

The Wrongful Conviction Series
By Janet Heijens

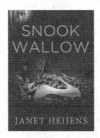

Snook Wallow
A decade ago Logan Murphy reported a murder and was ulitimately convicted for it. His only hope is Cate Stokes' relentless pursuit of the truth.

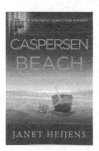

Caspersen Beach
A mother's worst nightmare occurs on a Florida beach and a man goes to prison for the kidnapping and murder of a child. Twenty years later, the deathbed confession of a confused homeless woman reopens the case.

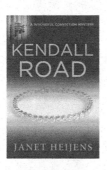

Kendall Road
How far will you go to help free an innocent man if your own secrets might be shielding the guilt of someone you love?

Calusa Shores
Coming Fall 2022!